Emma and the QUEEN of FEATHERSTONE

Emma and the QUEEN *of* FEATHERSTONE
LINDSAY FRYC

Maitland, Florida

Orange Blossom Publishing
Maitland, Florida
www.orangeblossombooks.com
info@orangeblossombooks.com

First Edition: January 2023

Library of Congress Control Number: 2022920526

Edited by: Arielle Haughee
Formatted by: Autumn Skye
Cover design: Sanja Mosic

Print ISBN: 978-1-949935-53-0
eBook ISBN: 978-1-949935-54-7

Printed in the U.S.A.

Dedication

For Emma and Jane

The Princess and The Hurricane

Table of Contents

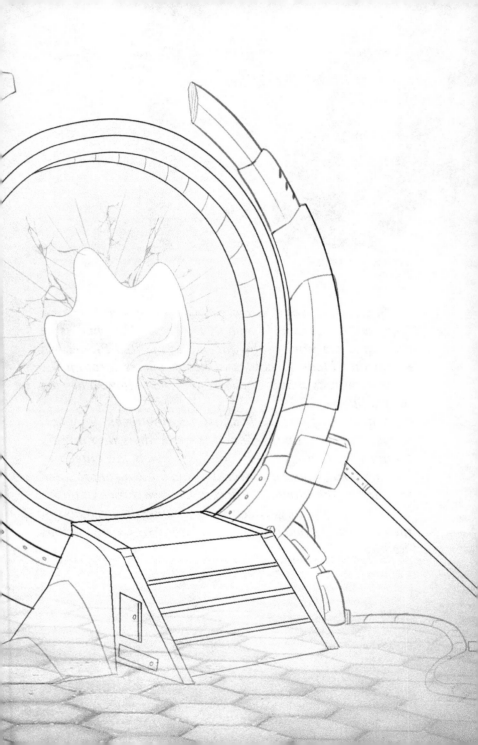

Secrets are what killed the Queen of Featherstone. "They are dangerous," Emma's Dad would tell her as he recounted the story of the queen and the Red Planet— a world that bled the colors of deep embers through the skies with trees that burned orange and yellow, and then turned black.

Whispers of this world's fast growing technology flew across the skies and wrapped their tendrils into any listening ear. Those secrets finally reached the Queen of Featherstone, whose own world would blind an unprepared traveler by the glimmer reflected from vast rock deposits. The formation of large, deep green, feather-like geodes created a world so beautiful its only rival was the mysterious "Red Planet."

The Red Planet, as her Dad would affectionately call it, was tucked away in its own hidden pocket dimension, kept there through technology not fully understood. Circular portal gates made of metal were sporadically placed as the only entrances to this world. Only those familiar with the deepest of its secrets knew how to reach them. The portals opened into this world of red and black with lakes of turquoise pooled in the deepest edges of forest. A particular lake of brilliant turquoise water sat at the center of a valley with dark black and orange arched trees. Large caves and mountains filled the countryside with etched silver circles as signposts leading the way.

A wanderer of the queen's galaxy claimed to know the location of an access portal to the Red Planet. Armed with that secret, she gathered her supplies, telling only her trusted advisor, and headed alone toward the deepest part of Featherstone to transport to the other world. The queen was never seen by her people again.

1

Emma

While Emma's thoughts lingered in space, her body sat in a cold cinderblock-encased classroom. *I wish I could discover the hidden planet, just like the queen.* She stared at the scribbled story file she wrote on her tablet. Her teacher droned on with the same faster-than-light, FTL, speech as year one class.

Mrs. Stapleton interrupted her thoughts, "Now, what is the best use of the FTL drive? Emma?"

After a quick glance from the teacher to the eyes of her classmates staring at her, she realized she must answer. She managed to blurt out, "Um, the FTL drives in the newer shuttles for the Mars runs have made travel for my parents a lot easier and faster than before." She held her breath and closed her eyes.

"That's correct, Emma."

She opened her eyes one lid at a time, and Mrs. Stapleton continued with her lesson. "From recent studies of the routes between Earth and Mars, we are expanding our knowledge of the physics of travel. We'll be able to calculate further jumps than Mars soon. Very astute observation." Ms. Stapleton smiled, ignorant of the several eye rolls in the room.

"Yeah, *nice observation*, trucker girl," came a snide whisper from a girl two work stations over. The nickname "trucker girl" followed her around everywhere. Most of the kids accepted into the program had parents who were scientists. They made "actual contributions" to the success of the Mars missions, while Emma's parents were nothing more than common transport shuttle pilots. The quieted snickers around her grew. She tried to ignore her device, but the screen filled with words.

trucker girl   *trucker girl*   *trucker girl*

trucker girl   *trucker girl*   *trucker girl*

trucker girl   *trucker girl*   *trucker girl*

No one else should have access to her tablet, but that didn't stop some of Veribo Industries' spoiled gifted kids from doing it anyway. Emma knew the culprit without even looking. She turned to the whisperer, and Sarah's face shined pure delight. Emma shook her head and faced forward again.

The screens of each student all pinged. Time for their class transfer. Emma shoved her tablet into her bag and tiptoed toward the door. As she tried to escape the room and tense air, Sarah pushed behind her and knocked her into the ground. Emma hit her head with such force, she saw stars. When she sat up, something trickled down her cheek. Her face burned, and she held back tears. She clambered for the first restroom she could find. She stumbled in and leaned into the mirror to check her wounds, wiping the blood streaming down. Her head pounded, and she blinked away the tears. Turning on the faucet, she used the cool water to sooth her reddened face.

A squeaking hum came from the stall behind her. The door opened to a kid in a wheelchair who wheeled himself out from behind the stall door. He quickly cleaned his hands, and rolled next to her. After a glance at her face, he whispered, "You okay?" with a furrowed brow and a nod toward her wound.

Emma bit her lip, let out a shaky exhale, and slumped to her knees on the floor. She released her breath in between large swallows. Her eyes were still wet when she finally opened them, and a soft hand tapped on her shoulder. Each tap felt methodic and deliberate. A melody. Emma looked up.

"What song is that?" she managed to squeak out.

"It was one of my grandma's favorites, Pacabel's Canon in D. Know it?" he replied in a whisper.

"Yes, I secretly love that ancient song. I should've known it."

"It's a classic that always calms me down when I'm too inside my head. But it is still in weddings so much, people primarily think of it as only a wedding song. I think its beauty extends further than the sole purpose of being used as a wedding march. Don't you?"

She smiled at him. Somewhere in her brain that thought had made its trek before. "I love to dance to Canon in D," she admitted.

"You dance… to Canon in D?" He lifted his eyebrows in surprise. "It doesn't feel like it would be a fun song to dance to."

"Well, if you were in ballet, like me, you'd absolutely dance to it." She dropped her bag on the ground and stood up. "Watch." She slid with a fluid motion across the bathroom tile from a pirouette into an arabesque. Her feet melted into their positions, and instinct took over. At that moment, all the thoughts of her confrontation with Sarah, the tablet hacking, and everything else bad fell away and she smiled.

Then a feeling of unease crept over her body. Her eyes met with a stranger's, his shocked gaze penetrating her and the boy. Her heart lurched into her throat and she stopped. Her motions triggered the sensor for the bathroom door and exposed her to the whole class in the hallway gaping at the "trucker girl" and the new kid… in the boy's bathroom. Emma's face flushed pink. *Run.*

She pushed past the crowd of whispers and giggles. "Excuse me," she mumbled. Behind her the boy called out, but she ignored him. She raced away from the school faster than she ever had before with her feet grazing the sidewalk in long strides. Her muscles burned. The voices and laughs of her classmates blurred into background noise. Her house sat in the distance, but trees just passed her sidewalk called to her. Their leaves waved her to safety, pulling her toward the center of the forest. She continued forward, completely forgetting about the bag she left on that cold, tiled bathroom floor. The bag that held secrets.

4

Lina

Location: Merah
1 month until E2 contamination

The sky burned its deep, dark red while its two suns were on the cusp of rising. Orange trees slow-danced in the breeze. All around her, creatures of every color with stripes and spots crawled in and around the branches. Mylinah flexed her purple legs back and forth, prepping to race across the forest. She pulled her thick raven-black hair up away from her face. Her cloak covered the length of her entire body but caught around her legs when she moved too fast. A bit inconvenient, but it was made from thick, warm boden hair. Those scurrying creatures had more than they needed anyway. Her sharp eyes searched and darted across the forest.

"Which site am I being sent to today?" she muttered to the small yellow-scaled dragon on her shoulder. She searched her map projection from her wristband. Her winged friend's green eyes flicked to a scampering fur-ball twenty feet away. His sharp black claws dug into her cloak. "Go get it, Maut," she whispered. He leapt from her shoulder and unfolded his wings which were twice the size of his body. He let out a screech before he snatched up his prey. Maut landed next to her and his black teeth tore into breakfast. Mylinah turned her attention to the message from her superiors on her holo map; the yellow projected lines of her location sprung from the metal band on her wrist along with a message. They always sent her on the most boring assignments with the same curt message.

Protector 42, Area Assigned: Site 65,
Target: Foreign Fungi Growth

She clicked her tongue in disgust. "ANOTHER gardening job. I wish I could finally get something more interesting than invasive fungi growth." She placed her small hand on the blaster at her side. "Maybe one day you'll be used for something bigger than cutting off invasive organisms from their home worlds." Lina had only been a Protector for a few months, but she was the youngest to ever be assigned as such. The job proved difficult for everyone given the task. The planet needed to be protected from anything that made it through a portal on its own. And there were more portals to guard than there were Protectors. She had to prove her worth.

Maut finished licking his breakfast off his claws and scuttled into flight back to rest on her shoulder. They walked along the winding pathways in the forest. "At least today I'm being sent somewhere fairly close to home. I'll be back to the village in time to get a decent meal, like you just got." She patted Maut's head, and he nuzzled into her neck.

Her village of Nira was the furthest from the Kabiren Headquarters, as well as the smallest. Headquarters was centered in the largest city on the planet, which consisted of glass and metal structures taller than any of the buildings in Nira. Her Protector training held at Headquarters showed her the benefits of being closer to the city—way more technology centered around the city than out here in the outskirt villages. Some of her more recent assignments had been closer to it. She preferred being sent to portals closer to the city, even if it resulted in a less-than-appetizing meal. She hated being assigned back home after her training.

When she arrived at the site, she analyzed the large silver cylinders that housed the mechanisms to hold open a triggered portal and the deep purple puffs of fungi growing around their sides. Their spores always flourished, but this was more advanced than Lina had ever seen before. "They must have been slow to get me this assignment." Maut jumped down from her shoulder to inspect the area around each cylinder. It looked burnt from all the life growing down the sides. "Back, Maut." Lina pointed her blaster at the purple fungi and squeezed the trigger. The purple exploded into nothingness. She reported back with a message to her superiors.

> *Protector 42, Site: 65. Observations: Numerous fungi found. Target: destroyed. *sent**

"Probably the most boring status report in the history of Protectors." She held out her arm, waved her fingers to Maut, and he scurried next to her. She started her long trek back through the narrow pathway in the forest. By the time she reached the outer rim of her village, the suns were high in the sky. The wind bent and swayed the soft orange trees, and shiny oils appeared on the leaves. Lina ignored the beautiful majesty around her. The suns' height meant she needed to quicken her pace to make it to the market. All the best deliciously roasted boden meat sold out within the first few hours after the market opened. She raced through the trees and stomped on the hard surface of the sidewalk heading into the village with Maut landing close at her heels. Fellow Amethites, short and nimble creatures with purple skin and small rounded faces just like hers, made their way slowly to the market's center. As she walked on by, thousands of smells from the food stations made her mouth water. The smoke wafted all around, filling her nose with scents like garlic butter mixed with a hint of rosemary. Stands lined the market in neat rows of wood and thatch displaying red, yellow, purple, and green piles of fruits and vegetables. She finally arrived at her favorite stand. The crispy, roasted-to-perfection meat laid right ahead of her. So did the line.

"How could there be so many people in this one line in this tiny town?" she said, scratching at Maut's head.

"You really need to work on your patience, Lina," a voice said from behind her.

Mylinah knew the voice before she even turned around. She grinned while still staring ahead. "Vargas, my Pinneat-born boy, you have no idea how hungry I am, and so help me, if you cut in line, I will make you and those big, round gray ears of yours pay for it." She laid her hand on her blaster ever so gently and patted it.

He peered down at her small purple hand laying gently on her blaster and then glanced up to her scrunched Amethite face. "How do you put up with her, Maut?" He patted the small dragon's head and snuck him a treat. "She thinks just because she is some big Protector now that she has the guts to use a blaster on me." Maut finished his snack and rubbed his rounded head into Vargas's hand.

"Remember, I still beat you in Primary with a scepter stream projector. I can most certainly do it again," she reminded him.

"We were kids." He crossed his arms in protest. "And you cheated."

Lina ignored his complete truthfulness and turned her attention to the line dwindling ahead. It moved slowly, but the company of her friend made her forget the ache in her stomach. She'd known Vargas all her life, and he knew everything about her. Except, of course, what she couldn't share with him from her Protector training at Headquarters.

He hated Protectors and called them elitist. He never understood why she reached out for the title or training. Sure, she had a sense of duty to protect her own planet, but in reality, she needed a way out of her boring home.

"Next!" The vendor shouted from behind the stand.

She paid for her feast. "Finally got my hands on some."

"If you weren't out traipsing around for your superiors, those old Kabiren Scouts, and doing their gardening for them, you would be able to eat a more balanced meal," Vargas snarked. The Kabiren organized everything on the planet. In a society built on the growth of technology, it didn't leave much time to eat.

"Mighty shame I have a job to do," Lina replied through gritted teeth. Her wristband beeped a new message.

Protector 42, Site: 72, Target: Monsuta

"I have to scarf this down so I can head back out. I'll see you around, Vargas. C'mon, Maut." She tossed up a small piece of her meat. Maut grabbed it in the air, and he munched on it while he followed behind her.

Vargas nodded, unphased, and Lina ran to her home to gather a pack for another assignment. The dome house stood smaller than the rest on her street. Curved wooden walls trellised with metal. The perfect combination of old village architecture held up by new world tech. She loved her home; it was perfect for her small Amethite frame. Inside, she hung her cloak on the wall over a hook she never had to stretch to reach. Perfect. Smells of polished metal and lacquer greeted her. Her hand grazed the empty walls inside her living room. No point in adding more to a place she always had to leave. Her feet carried her to her bedroom to gather things for her journey.

Lina read the orders on her wristband's holo screen while stuffing random clothes into her pack. "Site 72. I don't think I have ever traveled there. How many portals are there?" she wondered to Maut and expanded her map. The cylinders constructed to sustain the portals were rarely very close, maybe three together in the same area, tops. She glanced at her mapped out portals and the dots of Protectors. "Twenty! I wonder why they're sending me. They must have at least fifteen Protectors in the area already." Maut curled up next to the bag she packed. She paused to look up the purple trackers showing the locations of other Protectors.

On the map, sure enough over twenty purple dots condensed into one small area.

Getting to site 72 would take the entire day, even if she rented a roller. The personal vehicle could go way faster than her small feet and cut her arrival time in half but it would cost a hefty price. She needed to get back to the market. All she could do was hope that the rollers left were in working order, no sputtering wheel drives. "Gardener and mechanic, that would be a wonderful addition to my work history." She scrunched her nose. "Ready to go for a ride?" she held out her arm to Maut. He flew to his spot on her shoulder.

Only one roller was available by the time she reached the market, but she was assured by the mechanic of its working order. Maut hopped onto the seat next to her. " Here goes nothing." The energy igniter sputtered and choked. Then, the roller sprang to life, ready for long distance travel. "Why can't I be a fifth year Protector already? They at least get their own runner shuttle." Shuttles could travel to site 72 in less than an hour, on a roller it would take all night.

The road out of the village wasn't crowded when she started her journey. Being one of the oldest villages meant less tourism. Who had time to be interested in old relics when, under the guidance of the Kabiren, Merah's technology improved so quickly?

The Old Ones changed the perspective of her small village when they arrived. They called themselves the Kabiren, and they bestowed their knowledge upon the Amethites, her own native race, short in stature but tall on hope. Merah swiftly changed, and it seemed like every Amethite focused on Headquarters and the tech it produced. As the Kabiren introduced new and exciting technologies, the Amethite's understanding of their potential grew. They were able to expand their knowledge of other species, planets, systems, stars, and ultimately themselves. The schools, started only at Headquarters at first, taught every piece of technology and their use.

Protector training in particular felt more elite and covered a lot more tech. Lina determined that she would become a Protector and leave her small village. She learned a vital piece of information while studying to be one. Merah had an advantage that none of the other planets in the galaxy had—the unique, hidden location of Merah could help the Kabiren create more technology faster than ever before. The planet had a binary star system with the capability of being pulled out from the known universe with the right tech, a hidden secret, allowing the Kabiren to grow their technology undisturbed by other beings. The Kabiren requested full access to the planet, and in return they shared their tech. The Amethites, grateful for the Kabiren's help and the glimpse of possibilities that were now opened to them, quickly agreed.

Lina arrived at Sairon, the nearest village to site 72. She looked around at the village square with several Protectors standing outside the sleeping quarters building. Dust filled her lungs, kicked up from the commotion around her. The sharp angles of the constructs cut into the original village square—small sections of old world black wood buildings overlaid with glass and stone of new world tech. Stacks of rooms stretched above her in a glass structure built just for Protectors who were frequently assigned to these portal sites. One of them nodded toward her. There were not many younger protectors. The training courses were hard, and very few were granted the title. Forty were accepted into her course and only three had passed. Lina recognized her fellow coursemate and nodded back before she took her things to her room in the Protector building.

"Well Maut, this is our room for the day. Let's go see if we can find out anything about this job." She placed her pack on her bed, and Maut jumped down to follow her back out to the village square. Lina's eyes found a familiar face, and they walked over to her.

"Hey Harimanne, you've been given the orders for site 72 as well?" Lina briskly asked, winded from her rushed arrival.

"I was assigned *two* days ago. However, nothing has come through the portal yet. I am not sure why or how long we have to wait. How've you been since graduation? Any good assignments?"

She searched her memories for an exciting adventure. However, she could only think of forest fungi and plant growth. She looked down at the ground and replied, "Not especially. You were assigned to a village close to the Headquarters, right?"

"In the Dvaarapaal village. There've been so many orders, it's hard to keep them straight. Once I had an entire pack of lagartija come through my portal at one time. Figuring out how to contain all fifty of the scaly creatures with their long legs was a dizzying task. I had to set up an expander field around them. It was the only thing that would quickly contain them!"

"Quick thinking to use the expander. I may need to get one of those."

"Think you will actually need it for your gardening orders, Protector?" a deep voice from behind said.

Lina winced. Of course someone would expose her plant-based orders amongst all the other Protectors. Lina turned to look at the brute of a being. He stood taller than her, an easy task, given her genetics. But he was much younger than the other Kabiren Scouts—the old ones assigned off-world portal assignments—with a small scar on top of his light red wrist peeking out underneath his Protector suit. His face was made up of only hard angles and a fierce jaw.

"I'm sorry, but do I know you? Because someone must only *think* they know me to say that." Her steady glare locked on him.

He smiled and chuckled.

She blinked.

When he composed himself, he continued. "My name is August; I used to be stationed at Nira village, probably before your assignment there. Frequently orders came down for site 65, also known as the 'Fungi world.' I wondered which poor sucker started receiving my old orders."

"Well that sucker was me, apparently," she groaned.

"Chin up, you're not doomed to a life of *gardening*. There's actually a portal over there that has konig invasions. I'm surprised you haven't gotten orders for them yet. It's fairly frequent."

Harimanne gasped. "I remember reading about konigs in training! They're pretty fierce and large, right?"

"Four times as tall as me. And super heavy. It took me a while to figure out exactly how to take care of them without letting them get too far."

"Want to tell me your secret, in case I happen upon new orders for their portal?" Lina requested, trying to hide her curiosity.

"Do you visit those portals often?"

14

Lina nodded. "Most of my assignments are there, unfortunately."

"So you are familiar with the Cliffs of Stad?"

Lina looked up at him, her mouth rounded in an *O*. "Is that why I have seen so many marks at the edge of the precipice?"

"They never see it coming and always try to claw their way back up. It never w—"

"CAN WE HAVE YOUR ATTENTION PLEASE?" the loudspeaker boomed. An Old One, a Kabiren, stepped out of the corridor by the quarters and stood with a solemn face and a knowing glare.

"We are glad so many of you were able to accept your orders to be here. We believe there is a very real threat that will be arriving through site 72. The general has created a plan to stop an attack from a *very* dangerous contaminate. The portal is expected to open soon, and you all need to be ready to contain it. There are multiple monsuta, a new creature we haven't fully assessed, about to come through the portal. You will receive your specific orders from the General Proximate. Thank you again, and happy hunting."

The Old One turned and walked back into the corridor. Lina searched the many Protector faces to see who she should look to for her orders. She turned and mouthed to Harimanne asking for her new boss, but her friend only nodded to where the Old One had stood. There she saw her new friend, August.

3

Dexter

Earth
Morning of Emma's disappearance

The small room pressed in upon Dexter. Every moment in it stifled his creativity. Being the youngest of four, a tiny room, a small bed, and an even smaller desk were the only things available to him. He got used to the idea of always drawing the short stick when it came to furnishings and an even shorter stick when it came to general courtesy in his house. His three older brothers hardened him to insults, punches, and moosing matches. They were not allowed to call them wrestling matches. Mom and Dad never liked the idea of fighting. So the brothers renamed their shoves, punches, kicks, and rolls to "moosing," a delightful term which held the pretense for their parents while allowing the boys to dominate each other, or rather dominate Dexter. He loathed the phrase.

Light shined directly into the boy's eyes. He squinted trying to read his tablet through the glare. There were very important Mars terraforming facts he needed to memorize displayed on several open tabs. The processes for making Mars a livable ecosystem for humans was hard to understand. He moved outside of the glaring sun and dangled his legs off the edge of his bed. He tried to read the blurring words but turned distracted by some slight movement. It stopped, and he returned his gaze to his screen, then a quick blur slammed a pillow into his face.

"Gotcha, Dorkster. I can't believe you didn't even see me coming!" exclaimed Ryan, Dexter's closest brother, if you could call the one-year age gap between them what made them the closest. He shook his head and lifted the pillow off his face.

"Don't you have anything better to do? This is really getting old." Dexter clutched the pillow in his hand, and in one fluid motion, flung it with surprising accuracy, landing it squarely on his brother's chest. It knocked Ryan's body clear into the hallway.

Ryan quickly regained his balance. "Respect." He nodded. "You actually got me this time. Someone must be practicing his aim." He smiled then trailed off to the other side of the house.

At least Dexter avoided a full-on punching mode from his brother for now, but no guarantees for later. The bustle echoing from downstairs meant his other brothers were home and ready to torture. He didn't want to be their entertainment today. So, he did what he always did when he needed to get away — Dexter yanked his thick striped sweater over his head, slid out the window, and climbed down the side of the house.

Once his feet hit the sidewalk pavement, he ran. Fast. When the world of moosing and insults got too much for him, he knew who he had to find. Emma, being one whole year older than him, knew everything about how the world worked, or at least more about the universe than he did. Her stories about Featherstone and the Red Planet mesmerized him.

His parents worked for Veribo Industries, same as Emma's. Many pilots volunteered for their terraforming supply runs, and it seemed like it was the only work available for them with the current unemployment rate. His parents had been without jobs for over two years, and it had taken a toll on them. When the terraforming platforms were created on Mars, everyone clambered to fill the influx of jobs created. Veribo Industries took all who passed their tests, and luckily both his and Emma's parents did. Life returned to a sort of normalcy, and Dexter entered into their Mars Specialized Training program, MST. After consistently seeing his jobless parents, now they were rarely around. They took on more shuttle runs than they physically could handle, and with every trip, it showed. Yet, the need for pilots quietly overlooked the strain on his parents.

Usually, every company-required activity he was dragged to spewed endless speeches of how great it was to be a part of Veribo Industries and how their terraforming plans would benefit all of mankind. He had no idea the first Mars Celebration Day would be the best day of his life— the day he met Emma last year.

It was the first of many ridiculous company picnics to energize its employees. Emma stood across the lawn watching his brothers inflict their usual torture. Dexter sat in a pitiful state after a square punch knocked him breathless on the trimmed lawn. His oldest brother had landed that fist to keep him last in the food line. With the wind knocked out of him, he sat on the ground not causing a stir. As he caught his breath, he saw the blades of grass wave in the direction of a tall girl walking over to him. She plopped down next to him. A few moments of silence passed, and they sat together watching the crowds of people walk by, unphased by their presence in the middle of the lawn.

"Sometimes kids can be jerks. At least you landed with some style." Emma held out her hand. "I'm Emma. What's your name?"

He grabbed her hand, and she stood up to lean back and help him up. His muscles loosened, and he let out a long breath. He stared at her light blue eyes, and whispered "Dexter." He pressed his palm to hers. She responded with a fairly aggressive handshake and raised eyebrows, not hearing him clearly. "Ummmm, it's Dexter. My, my name is Dexter."

"Okay, Dex. Nice to meet you. Where is the rest of your family?"

"They are over getting food. I should probably get over there, too." He dragged his feet toward the group of people he called family. Not wanting this calm to pass quickly, he paused, looked over at Emma, and stammered, "Want to come with me?" He gulped.

"Well, I did already go through the line." She brought her hand to her chin. "Meh, I can ALWAYS eat. Sure." She strolled right up next to him, and they walked to the line together. "Are you in Veribo Industries' MST program at school?" she asked with a mouth half-full of food she only just put on her plate.

"Yeah. I'm in the terraforming fast track program currently studying the particle enhancers for the terraforming stations. The vent-like tunnels are large but effective at carbon dioxide collection and dispersion. Not sure how I feel about Mr. Fastverd's teaching methods," he openly admitted.

Emma continued to layer food onto her plate in the buffet line. She looked down at her plate, blushed, and then shrugged. "I told you I can always eat..." She nodded beyond him. "Oh, that's my dad. I should be heading back. See you around, kid!"

Dexter's head came back to the present once he reached the forest to the south of his house. Now, they frequently met up in the woods, Emma always trying to find some adventure, and him ready to join her. He knew she loved it there, and he hoped he would find her sitting by her favorite tree.

4

Emma

Earth
Day of portal activation

The birds chirped in the trees overhead. Emma sat slumped at the foot of her favorite tree, her arms wrapped around her knees. Maybe if she squeezed hard enough her body would disappear. Flashes of kids laughing at her as she ran from the bathroom at school replayed in her mind. *Trucker Girl.* Always and forever.

"Let me be sad for a moment!" she screamed at the happily chirping birds. Footsteps approached her hiding place. She looked up to see who approached, and her body tensed.

"Hey, Emma. I knew you'd be here. Even during school hours, I knew it."

Her muscles relaxed at the sight of Dexter. The only one in the entire world she trusted as much as her dad... almost.

"You knew I wouldn't be able to stand being in those walls today, eh?" She wiped the tears from her face.

He looked down at her, likely eyeing the small line of dried blood. He frowned. "Who do I have to kill?"

"It's nothing, really. I'm trying to *stop* thinking about it. You can divert my attention though. How's your day going?" She smiled at him.

"Oh, it's going swell. Ryan only punched me once today so that's three times less than normal." He held his thumbs up.

Emma hid her pity well. Dexter hated it. She felt sad for the family he had, and she loathed his brothers for the torture they put him through. They had been brutal ever since the first time she met Dexter. There had been some altercation between him and his brother at a Mars Day celebration, one of many. He looked so small and defeated on the ground, and she knew how that felt. She walked over to him to offer some friendly support and little did she know they would become best friends. Dexter interrupted her reminiscing with a snap of his fingers.

"Uhhh, that's supposed to be funny... Guess I gotta work on that, not even a smirk." He examined her face.

"Yup, not even an infamous upside-down Emma smile."

"I do *not* have an upside-down smile." She said while the corners of her mouth turned down.

"Ahhh, *there* it is! I got one. Bam!"

"Okay, okay, maybe I do have a weird smile."

"No, I didn't call it weird. It's perfect." He beamed.

"So, kid. You have your classes this afternoon?"

He winced at the word "kid." She pretended not to notice. He had recently turned eleven, and she had already completed one full MST year ahead of him. She knew he looked up to her, so she couldn't resist calling him kid.

He nodded. "I have three of them this afternoon. I probably should get going. Mind if we hang tomorrow? I may need some help with my classwork."

"I should be free. See you tomorrow," she replied without hesitation. She watched him stand up and withdraw into the forest path, smiling at his thoughtfulness. Now this was the least she could do, to help him with a few equations, after he had helped her so many times since they first met.

The sun scarcely moved, so Emma got up and turned to the north to start some sort of diverting adventure. Stepping off her worn pathway, she continued deeper and deeper into the thick of the woods. Trees slowly separated further and further apart, no longer connected by ground but by rocky masses. The piles of rock naturally stacked taller and taller as she approached. A large rock wall loomed before her, and she stared at a small section of it ahead. A faint trickling of water revealed a crack in the wall next to her. She examined it to see where the water came from—it hadn't rained in the last forty eight hours. The expansive rock mass had several lines eaten away by each water drip about two feet from each other. She walked further, noticing the cracks growing larger and larger.

"This must be limestone here." She arrived at a small opening to a cavern. The opening in the rock measured just large enough for her body to squeeze through. Her ballet-trained feet carried her carefully through the opening, but her shin caught the edge of a sharp piece of rock. She winced while the blood streamed down. She ripped off the bottom hem of her shirt, wrapped the wound tight and continued down the small passageway. The air around her thickened with particles that interfered with her breathing. She slowed her pace and scooted toward an opening just up ahead.

The stone passageway widened, and she stepped out into a large room. Emma surveyed the height of the cavern all around her. How could she see in the dark? There were no cracks above to let the sunshine through, yet the room seemed illuminated by soft candlelight. Her eyes searched for a source. It seemed brighter toward the back. She continued further into the cavernous room. She felt movement in the air, like a shifting of the wind. *But where is the wind coming from?* she thought. A small clicking sound surrounded her.

"Hello?" She spoke softly at first. "HELLO?"

A whirlwind of black rushed past her. The clicking grew louder. Her heart raced as her eyes searched through the cavern to discern what rushed past her. Then she saw them. Small black creatures hanging above.

"Bats!" She stared at the sheer number of them. There were over a hundred. One of the small creatures flitted nearby and landed on her outstretched arm. Emma studied it. "Look at those beautiful tiny wings of yours," she whispered. She gently lowered her arm so as not to startle it. It flew off. Her heartbeat slowed after the burst of adrenaline, and the bats returned to the top of the cavern.

Above her, two beams of light shone through the cave. Her eyes followed their source to gray cylinders mounted on the ceiling emitting two beams of bluish-green light on the floor. A circular pattern showed on the ground, a metal plate. She examined the layers of dust over and brushed off the dust to reveal two precise gaps. She leaned down and grazed her hands over them. Her hand blocked the beams of light from the ceiling from reaching the metal plate underneath.

All at once, Emma felt tiny vibrations underneath her body. A pulse of red light replaced the blue-green candlelit haze. A rushing sound pulsated around her, forcing her to stand. Emma's eyes darted around the room to find an escape, but her body was trapped, immoveable. She felt an immense weight, like her body lifted toward a magnet attracted to some outside force. She cupped her hands over her ears as the pulses grew louder and louder.

A flash of bright red light filled the cavern. A hole opened in front of her. As it spun and fractured, it tugged at her stationary body. Her atoms were ripped from where she was standing and yanked through the opening.

Everything went black.

5

Lina

Merah
Day of E2 contamination

Protector 42, Site: E2, Target: Pfoteros

Lina flicked her message away on her holo screen. The days blurred together since the Monsuta job one month ago. Every job assigned taught a new skill, and Lina reveled in it. It was everything she wanted. Purpose. A life. The Kabiren had her running to all different types of assignments. Lina had proved her worth that day on the Monsuta assignment, and the Kabiren knew she could be trusted. The Old Ones, as they were referred to by the Amethites, were Scouts that handled larger jobs, including off-world assignments. Maybe someday she would find herself among their ranks, but for now she handled every Protector job better than anyone else.

"Oh those creatures are making their way through the portal again. I might need your help to get all of them." She nodded at Maut sitting next to her in the roller. "Good thing we still have the roller. We'll get there much faster."

She plotted her route back to her home village. She could make it there in less than three hours, but she had to leave now. She travelled between Nira and Porta four times in the last month, but this last assignment took about two weeks to contain. At least she knew she was closer to her old village than before. She called for the map on her wrist-band indicating Protector locations, her indicator dot being the closest to the job. "Probably why I got this assignment," she said to Maut still sleeping on his seat next to her. She scratched his head. "Let's go get us some pfoteros." The small, brown leather-winged creatures were making their way through the portal again. Maut screeched in compliance, and Lina drove them toward the next portal site.

She neared the site of the portal and knew exactly what she would find there. Merah needed protection from the pfoteros. That protection was *her* commission granted by the Kabiren. She hopped out of the roller and pushed through the trees to the site location. A rushing sound began almost as soon as her feet hit the ground. Her body stiffened, and she took aim.

6

Emma

Merah
Arrival Day

The ground beneath Emma turned into deep-black ash. The heaviness around her body faded. She could breathe again. Her body was no longer forced into a stationary position. She wiggled each arm and leg. *All present and accounted for.* She squinted up at the crimson sky. Distracted by the expansive deep red hues, she did not see the figure hidden in the trees. Two quick shots were fired in her direction. Emma stiffened. She slowly lifted her hands up.

"I'm not armed!" she yelled into the forest.

"Oh, sorry about that." A voice escaped from behind an orange tree. "I am assigned to get rid of those tiny brown rats with wings that usually come from that portal, not, well, you. They wreak havoc on our ecosystem here. Annoying little things. I have to make sure they don't escape into the forest, but seeing as there are none around you I guess my assignment here is done." She held up her wrist with a small band of metal wrapped around it projecting a 3D holo screen above. The creature pressed buttons vigorously.

Emma looked toward the purple creature and back at the cylinder below her feet.

"This is a portal?" she asked.

The creature cocked her head as if she didn't understand the question. "You didn't know it was a portal? Why did you use it then?"

Emma pondered the question. "I didn't *mean* to use it. I was adventuring and accidentally triggered it. What do you do with unfamiliar things you see? Examine them or walk on by leaving them undiscovered?"

The creature peered at Emma. Her lips were deep brown and curved slightly upward, indicating her approval of the response. "What is your name, creature, and what world did you come from?"

Emma stepped off the cylindrical platform to approach the purple creature. "I'm Emma. I come from a planet called Earth." She turned her attention to the sky above her. "And from looking at those red skies, am I correct in assuming I'm no longer on that planet?"

"So *that* must be what the *E* in 'E2' stands for! *Earth— eeeeaaaarrrrrtttthhhh*. Hmmm, not sure I like the sound of that, I think I'll stick to calling it E2. You are definitely not on Earth. I'm not even sure it's nearby. I've heard of many planets, and this is the first time I've heard of Earth!"

Emma thought how strange to be in this world — skies she had never seen and lives she didn't know existed.

Everything was odd. She pushed away that thought. How self-centered we are when we view the worlds we know as the only representation of the universe and the rest of them *odd*. This was their normal, and she the strange one. She looked up with eyes that yearned to understand. "You asked for my name, but did not mention yours. What do you call yourself, and where am I?"

"Mylinah is the name I was given. But to most I am known as Lina. And the name of this planet is Merah."

"Well, it is very nice to meet you Lina, as well as nice to meet this planet. And thank you for not shooting me." She smiled and met Lina's eyes. In the rush of her arrival, she failed to notice them. The creature could not have been more than a couple years older than her, but those eyes, with slight wrinkles around them, seemed much older. *Beautiful, not odd,* she thought to herself with a small nod. Her eyes widened. "But wait, I can understand you! How can that be? If you have never heard of Earth, and I have never heard of Merah, how can we understand each other?"

"Do you not have translation beams on E2? A planet-wide field that triggers your brain to reprocess words as you understand them? Mighty irresponsible of your species, eh?" Lina quipped.

Emma laughed. "I guess so, but...." A whirring sound interrupted her.

The soft vibration came from across their path near a second gray portal about twenty feet from where they stood. Black trees with orange leaves and needles surrounded them. The dark grass squished below her feet like blades of thin, soft plastic. She was in the middle of a forest with only a small worn-down path leading to and away from four tall cylinders.

A beam of red light descended onto a platform between two of the cylinders. A piercing screech escaped a figure's large shadow. Suddenly, there stood a towering creature. Emma's eyes widened as she saw brown scales and thick legs. Its many sharp teeth were held in a squared mouth. The yellow eyes glared straight ahead, stuck in a stationary position. The creature appeared to be a mix between a dinosaur and a cheetah. The disk beneath the creature cracked slightly under the weight. Frozen in place, she tried to process what she saw and almost missed Lina's urgent command.

"E2….. RUN!" Lina pushed Emma forward, pointing her body in the direction she should go. She raced straight toward the creature. Emma sped off through the trees. Their shapes blurred, and she heard screeching and crashing through the forest. In her peripheral vision, Lina slid passed the immense creature and fired two distraction shots. The creature's face sharpened toward their direction. It let out a bellowing roar and jumped off the portal disk. Orange-colored trees bent and twisted as the ground vibrated with movement. The creature shook its head in a confused rage while it jumped over the fallen trees. Lina ran harder and harder with her head fixed forward. Emma paused as the danger ran in the opposite direction.

Her small purple friend was quick and succinct in her movements. She darted between the fallen trees and escaped into the thickness with the creature crashing forward not far behind her. Emma searched through the orange waves of trees and tried to locate Lina. The ground shook under Emma's feet, followed by a tumbling roar in the distance.

Lina appeared through the thick trees, searching around her. Emma slid out from behind a fallen tree to meet her.

"What happened?" Emma asked.

"The upside of being here is that we are near a fairly large precipice called the Cliffs of Stad." She looked distracted by a thought and chuckled. "They really do never see it coming." She let out a loud cackle that reverberated through the forest.

Emma giggled with nervous laughter. Her stomach still knotted from the excitement, but the rush of relief released every single one of them. She wondered how she would have handled the creature had she not met Lina. She shuddered. *Let's try not to think about that.*

Now that the rush of her arrival and danger had passed, she took in the full beauty of her surroundings. The orange trees and their black roots reached through the ground of black ash dirt. Emma saw tiny flecks of white and amber when she looked into it. The plants coming up were leaves with shades of deep purple and yellow blooms. She never saw such striking colors against a dark backdrop. The colors were deep, deeper than any shade she recalled seeing on Earth.

Earth. How would she get back there?

She walked slowly toward the gray platform. Emma looked back at Lina and pointed. "Can I use this to get back to Earth?" she asked.

"These are arrival portals. They will not get you back to your planet." She flicked the band on her wrist. Blue holographic lines surrounded tiny red dots. There were about ten dots indicating where they were. One purple dot and one green dot displayed their location. "We have to travel… hmm. I can't see the E1 departure portal on this map. That's funny. I wonder if my system needs an update. I think we need to make a pitstop before getting you to the E1 exit portal, if you don't mind."

"Not at all. I have no idea how to get home, and I would appreciate any help you could give me," she replied, relieved that someone would help her.

"C'mon E2, guess you are with me!" She smiled and nodded her head toward the small pathway in the forest. "I have to go see if I can get an update."

Emma looked toward her new friend. Her only hope to find the portal was to follow Lina. She dragged her feet over the foreign ground. Lina called this area entry portal grounds. Emma's curiosity abounded. "Lina, who enters these portals?"

"They haven't been used by sentient beings in years. Mostly just plant life and fungi come through now."

"Why is there an entry portal from Earth though?"

"I am actually not sure about that one, there is not much information on E2 in my records. Maybe my update will show different information. Hop in the roller," Lina responded.

Emma followed Lina's directions to a small three-wheeled vehicle. Lina jumped in on one side and motioned for her to sit next to her. In the distance, the trees opened wide to a clearing. Large bright flowers as tall as mammoth sunflowers popped up here and there. Emma, distracted by their immensity, suddenly felt her butt on something hard while climbing into the vehicle. A sharp screech escaped from next to her and nudged her off her seat. A small yellow dragon bared black teeth, and she eased her body back.

"Ignore Maut," Lina said. "He was lazy and didn't even get out to help." Lina tossed some kind of treat into the back seat, and he jumped back to gobble them up.

They sputtered off in the vehicle down the road. Small square pods of a village lay ahead of them bustling with life. Creatures of similar shapes and sizes to Lina travelled to their own destinations.

Lina pulled the roller up to a small building in the village and the three of them hopped out. Soon all the creatures were slowing their pace to stare at her. Each one looked away immediately upon catching her notice. Lina's eyes, however, were fixed ahead. Emma wondered if she really didn't notice all the attention, or if she was just hyper-focused on her destination. Lina hadn't explained where they were going, and Emma hadn't asked. The creatures' faces were either filled with amazement or concern. She didn't know which was worse.

They arrived at a large market at the center of the village containing many stands and a main corridor that teemed with life. The thatched roofs of black wood tied together with metal lined the main market path. Swaths of dark crimson-colored fabrics were displayed behind one stand, while another encasement held tungsten-colored metal spheres and cubes all bouncing with power in the display case. Scores of small creatures just like Lina were bustling in and out of it. Their faces—each peculiar with their purple skin, small noses, and high cheekbones with scrunched features—still noticed her every move. The unnerving situation forced her to question Lina with eyes darting back and forth between them all. "What exactly is this place?" She tried to hide the slight crack in her voice.

"It's, uhh, a general gathering place and market for the village. You can buy anything from holo screens from the Spragel galaxy to the ale of the Vermonthian death planet."

"And what exactly are we doing here?"

"We're here to see a friend, and I sincerely hope he can help with updating my portal chart," Lina said. She walked through the corridor with amazing confidence and surety. The crowds parted automatically at her presence. Emma clung to the small impressions Lina's feet made, not veering from her lifeline and her only way home.

The market carts and booths grabbed Emma's attention. Shades of red and deep burgundy set in what Emma could only think was glorious and ornate circuit boarding and parts. Such beauty in technology she rarely saw on Earth. Sparkles of light danced as each of the pieces displayed their glory. "Wow!" Emma muttered. Lina walked on without notice of Emma's gawking. They stopped squarely in front of a booth with a dark paneled curtain around it. A sign hung around the enclosure with words Emma couldn't understand.

"Vargas! Vargas, get out here you lying piece of flout monger!" Lina yelled. The curtain moved slightly. Two large feet slowly splayed out from underneath the back of the booth. A creature with light gray skin and larger ears than a human's showed himself from behind the curtain. He had deep brown eyes and an uneven divot created by a small scar on his chin. He stood taller than Emma, maybe the same age as Lina, an age she wasn't even sure of exactly.

"I knew you were back there. How dare you make me wait." Lina's lip curled. The words were curt, but that curl expressed admiration. "Let us back there, or so help me I will come back there on my own!"

Vargas smiled, and he pressed the red panel next to the curtain. The curtain opened to display a large slew of electronics of all shapes and sizes, one of which looked like the wristband Lina wore, and Emma wondered if they had maybe come to the wrong place. Baseball-sized metallic spheres with broken electronic screens were piled up on one side of her. On the other side, crates of handheld blaster grips and loose bolts lined the shop. Toward the back, there were computers and keyboards with letters she couldn't read. Her toe caught on the tip of a jutted-out metal frame for a circuit board. She caught herself by gripping the crate next to her.

"Of course you can come in, Lina. You know you're always welcome." Vargas motioned them into his shop. "What do you need this time? A short-range receiver, or maybe another blaster?" He snickered.

"Shove it, Vargas. You know it wasn't my fault the blaster was incinerated by the Barian soldier. How was I to know he had his finger on the trigger? He was only supposed to have four."

Emma interrupted them. "So how is it you two know each other?" She nodded between them.

"Lina and I grew up together on the same block of this village. She pretends she doesn't really belong here since she became a big Protector, and hates that I remind her of it constantly," Vargas explained with such an open and soft manner, Emma instantly loved him and felt the warmest calm since she arrived.

"Shut up, Vargas," Lina snipped. "I need to find the most recent portal upload. Do you have it available here in the shop?"

"Sorry, Lina, the most recent one was difficult to get. I only just got it downloaded at home. You weren't able to download it from your, ahem, employers?" Vargas asked.

"No, I tried. But the location of the portal I need to find wasn't shown. I thought maybe I had a corrupted file and wanted to check if you had the most recent one."

"I have some things to finish up here at the shop, but if you meet me at my house in an hour, we can see what happened with your file and compare it to mine."

"Shall I bring my new friend?" Lina pointed to Emma.

He smiled. "Please do."

7

Dexter

Earth
1 day after Emma's disappearance

Dexter sat on his bed with several screens splayed out before him. The carbon-bearing minerals for Martian soil were displayed and something did not seem to add up. "How can we possibly be creating enough CO_2 up there?" Dexter worked through the spreadsheet that calculated the numbers for him. His head fell back, contemplating the complexity of the problems.

Maybe Emma can help me to make heads or tails of this, he thought. *I should head out to meet her soon anyway.* He tucked the main tablet into his jacket pocket while he slipped out of his window.

He passed the identical neighborhood houses with his eye on the thick line of forest trees. The location of this particular neighborhood was strange. A small community plopped in a thick forest. The trees were carved out in a rushed manner in order to complete the community. The launch sites were placed further out. The lightly worn path, which led to Emma's favorite tree, wore flecks of dewy trickles. The sun had not yet burned them off on the green blades of grass.

As he arrived at his favorite spot, or rather, Emma's favorite spot, he saw no evidence of her. The base of the knotty tree had been worn away with shoe prints pressed into the ground. She always wore those shoes, always tied and ready for an adventure. Dexter stretched his arms around the trunk in a big hug. He kept his eyes and ears open for any hint of his friend. She was always early, and it seemed odd that she wasn't already here to meet him. *I did ask for her to help in the afternoon, right?* he wondered. *I'll just check around, maybe she's still exploring*. He walked around the forest. He doubled back in his trek several times to her tree, but she never appeared. His small legs ached after he searched in the woods. He didn't know how long he had been looking, but the sun was now low in the sky. His heart began to race, and he quickened his pace.

"I should try her house; maybe she forgot. She did have a bad day yesterday, and I think she had a head wound." He headed back up the path in the direction of her home. She always adventured close enough to be able to run home for food, but far enough away to have her own corner of space. He reached the sidewalk, and his feet took to a run faster and faster.

He reached her home and stood staring at her doors, then shook his head to turn back "Why am I here?" he muttered to himself. *Maybe she stayed home today, or maybe she had to go to school to finish classwork. Or worse, maybe she didn't want to see me at all, and I'm here to make it all awkward.* The crickets started chirping, and Dexter turned back toward her door.

It suddenly slid open with Emma's father racing through. Without looking down, the father's long arms flung into him, and knocked him off kilter. Dexter quickly recovered and replanted his feet. No going back now.

"Oh, so sorry, little man. I did not see you there. Are you okay?" Emma's father hurriedly asked while glancing at his car.

"I'm fine. Is Emma here?"

"No, she isn't home right now. I thought she was at school, but it's kinda late for her to be there still. Why don't you go inside with Emma's mom and wait for her here. She should be home any time now."

"You sure that's okay?"

"Of course, head right in. I'm sorry I can't stay and wait with you. I have to get to a shuttle launch. See you later, little man."

Emma's father got into his car and drove off toward the launch site. Looking back at the door, Dexter summoned the courage to go inside. He'd met Mr. Riley before, but never Mrs. Riley. Emma described her as distant and a little bit cold, something he didn't want to encounter at this particular moment, but he pushed back his hesitance with a gulp. After all, he had been given permission to enter. The door sensed his presence and slid open. "Hello?" He entered the foyer. No one came. "Hellooo," he said, louder now.

"Ahh!" came a battle cry. A small girl of barely five slid down the stairs at lightning speed. She ran up to Dexter with a stick. She thrusted it at him once, twice, three times before it landed square on his jaw.

"OW!" Dexter exclaimed. "Man, for such a little person, you sure know how to wield that thing."

A woman with bright golden hair appeared at the top of the stairs. She gasped, then raced down and snatched up the violent little girl. "No, Janie. You cannot keep hitting people. We play nice, and we play over here." She placed the little girl in a soft area with plenty of teddy bears and other stuffed animal targets. The little girl exclaimed with pure delight, bashing every single one of them. The woman scrunched her face apologetically at Dexter. "I'm sorry you were attacked by my tiny monster. You're Emma's little friend, right?" she said while side-eyeing Janie.

He winced a bit at being called "little." The average size of boys his age was exactly *his* size. He didn't know why everyone decided to call him that. He was a normal-sized kid for his age.

"Yes, I'm Emma's friend. We were supposed to meet up today, but she never showed.

She was going to help me with school stuff."

"Hmm, I don't remember where she said she was going earlier today. I figured that she went to school to finish up some things there." Her mother went to the wall nearest the door to display the calendar screen. Flicking through the days, she came upon today's date. "Nope, nothing here. Emma is normally so organized. She always notes where she will be. When were you supposed to be meeting her?"

"Earlier today, in the afternoon. I was there most of the day, but she never came."

"Well, you are so sweet to be so concerned about her," she replied. The words *sweet* and *concerned* dripped out of

41

her mouth like a slow-leaking faucet. They gnawed at his skin, and he scratched at his arm. The worry on his face must have shown. "Oh, you don't have to worry dear. I'm sure everything is fine. Look, I'll message her instructor right now." Emma's mother opened her email screen and quickly hit send. "I'm sure we'll hear something very shortly."

They sat in an awkward silence. He scanned her face. She was an older version of Emma exactly, only a few wrinkles to show her age. The same dip in her chin. The same golden hair, minus the curls that Emma naturally sported. Very pretty for an older lady, but she looked tired with dark circles around her eyes. Those were the same bloodshot eyes that his parents always had after a longer-than-normal shuttle run.

A crashing of glass spurred them both from their trances and with it a scream from the living room.

"OW-EE. I hurt my arm." Out came small Janie with blood trickling down her hand.

"Oh dear, what happened to you?" On the floor lay a broken glass screen with blood around it. Mrs. Riley rushed over to the incident and cradled Janie in her lap. "Let me see it. This will need some special care. Let's go upstairs. Okay, sweetie? I'll get you fixed up." The mother grasped her little girl with all the softness in the world. The two rushed upstairs to handle the injury. She didn't seem as distant or callous as Emma made her out to be.

Sounds of Emma's mom attending to the wound escaped the room upstairs. He wondered if he should leave since he wasn't exactly told to stay. He would wait in that seat until morning if he had to. But there was this incredibly personal moment of a mother caring for her young he had witnessed, and it deserved a moment alone. He started on his way out toward the door when an incoming message displayed across the house screen. He looked up the stairs to see if Emma's mother came for it. When she didn't come back, he peered at the screen and opened the message.

> *Mrs. Riley, Emma was not in attendance at her courses today. Please note that our program only makes allowances for six absences before we consider termination from the program. We hope this will not become a habit as there are many applicants for this course. Please inquire at Veribo Industries' office if you have any further questions.*
>
> *Sincerely,*
> *Administrative Assistant for Veribo Industries and the Offices of Mars Special Training Program*

Dexter assessed what he just read. His heart pounded, and he couldn't breathe. He knew Emma too well. Even for all the adventuring in the world, she would *never* skip school completely. She loved the MST program and her classwork. What could have happened to her? He already searched all around the woods. She was nowhere to be seen. Worry grew larger in the pit of his stomach, and he couldn't take the stillness and discomfort of this knowledge. The confines of Emma's house choked his ability to process this news.

"I have to find her."

And he made his way out the door again toward her favorite woods.

8

Lina

Merah
Day 1 of E2 contamination

L ina and Emma stared silently at each other in the
sparsely furnished room. She never really took the time
to ensure her place had everything she needed. She didn't
plan to stay there for long periods. It was just a pit stop in
between assignments. Lina, not quite sure what to discuss,
sat silently looking at the creature she found at site E2.
Emma definitely was not part of the *pfoteros* species. Those
small winged creatures that were *so easy* to get rid of paled
in comparison to the young girl who sat before her. And
yet, the girl looked oddly familiar. Nothing in her training
prepared her for this sort of unspecified intruder. The girl
did not look menacing at all. She had light pink skin with
yellow hair. There were the scrawniest of legs below her

waist but she sat taller than possible for any Amethite. The girl, Emma, nodded her head in short bursts up and down and up and down. Maut sat next to her staring and bobbing his head in a curious unison.

"What exactly are you doing?" She imitated the motion with her head.

"Was I doing something?"

"Yes, this with your head." Lina nodded her head up and down in very un-rhythmic beats.

"Oh wow, if that is what I looked like, then I'm sorry you had to see it. Whenever I can't think of anything to say, I start playing music in my mind. I guess my head tends to bob a bit when that happens."

"Why would this *music* make you bob your head?" Lina tilted her head and patted Maut next to her.

"You don't know what music is? Devices that play sounds and sometimes words together, for fun and enjoyment?" Lina stared at her blankly. Emma held up her finger. "It might sound like this." She hummed soft melodic tones.

"I believe we used to have something called a viresitor that was played in the same manner. Not sure if words were included with it. I don't think one has been made in *at least* a generation."

"Why hasn't one been made in such a long time?"

"We don't need them anymore," she said flatly.

Emma blinked at her response; she was a puzzle to be figured out. Lina became suddenly aware that her exchange was something out of the ordinary, but she had no idea how to continue.

"If you don't have musical devices anymore," Emma said, "does that mean you don't have music?"

"I haven't really thought about it, but I guess not. We don't exactly have the resources for it. Since the Kabiren came, they have distributed resources pretty tight."

"What exactly does that mean? *No one* has the resources?"

"Maybe 'resources' is a bad translation of the word. But many of us have very specific jobs that take all of our time, but with good reason. The Kabiren specify what resources are needed, and we work with them to accomplish that. We have been able to create a vast array of technological advances working this way." That was the best way to describe it. Those were the exact words used in many of the Protector training sessions, and in so many course sessions. Her parents even uttered them in mockery. Childhood memories seeped to the forefront but she readily pushed them back. No need to think about a past that failed to supply her with any real skills.

Emma pointed to the sky. "I never imagined a planet with two suns before."

"Well, it's necessary," Lina replied.

"Necessary?"

"Some time ago our data showed that a black hole was heading for Merah. The second sun was the solution."

"How so?"

"It pulled Merah out of its position in the known universe, creating a safe pocket dimension for us. That's why we have the portals to travel off-world," Lina said.

Emma stared off, lost in thought.

All of her instructions for her assignments were for the destruction of intruders and invasive life that escaped into Merah. But for this, she had no assignment, no instructions, and no guidebook. All she could think to do was move forward with the intent of returning this creature to her home world.

"If only my map had the portal on it. This would have been finished already," she whispered to Maut, slightly irritated with the extra work that lay ahead.

The girl sat quietly. Lina glimpsed a small trickle that fell down Emma's face the girl quickly tried to wipe away. The motion of the creature unnerved her, and she needed a change of scenery. She held out her arm to Maut, and he scuttled to her shoulder.

"Come on, it's almost time to meet Vargas." Lina gathered up her things and rushed the girl from E2 toward the door.

9

Emma

Merah
Day 1 of E2 contamination

There was no music here. Emma tried to fathom a world devoid of it. She kept pace easily with her new small friend through the village alleys. *Why didn't I notice it before? We were in a large market place, and there was nothing more than the echoing of voices around us.* Here was a world with so many creatures and people and technology but an absence of a necessary part of life and living. This new world needed more study.

She slowly followed her friend's gait, trying not to outpace her. A small happiness crept over her in this walk for it allowed more time to explore and take in the wonder of this village. She needed the distraction. The world was all at once strange and new and lovely. She thought about the woods she arrived in, with their bright trees and darkened ground. The way the trees dripped their orange and black seemed so familiar to Emma, and she wondered why she wasn't more scared. She knew her emotions got the better of her at the least convenient times. In many moments, she lacked the ability to control herself from spiraling, but here, in a village surrounded by the most foreign of colors, she was calm and comforted.

Lina interrupted her thoughts. "Here we are. Hopefully Vargas has made it back here quickly after market hours." The small building was darkened by some kind of hammered sheet metal. The door slid open to greet them, and Lina made a face at the cam. A dark shadow in the background moved between the corridor.

"Vargas! You should have already checked your camscreen. You have visitors," Lina blurted loudly, while she glanced toward the back of the flat. The figure in the back startled and dropped a bowl filled with food. A yellow piece rolled towards the front door.

Vargas sheepishly requested, "Umm, can you both please turn around? I need to run to my room for a quick second."

Lina's eyes widened in either disgust or shock, Emma couldn't tell which. "Are you seriously cooking while naked? Please don't tell me you were planning on offering us this food..." She picked up the yellow spiked, turnip-looking fruit from the floor and held it out to him as she turned her head.

"Listen, I *raced* home from market day, because I *knew* you would be early. I rushed around, and noticed my stench was less than desirable. Took a quick evap. But needed to throw the food in for it to be done in time. *Please*, for all of our sakes, let me get to my room so I can put on my pants in peace." Lina snickered while turning her back to Vargas. Emma's back had already been turned, eagerly peering out the window pretending to notice something very interesting outside.

Vargas quickly returned fully clothed. "Okay, I'm back. Can I finish making the food for us all, or will you both be entirely disgusted now?" The girls turned forward and made their way closer to Vargas.

"It is safe, I believe." Lina darted her eyes between the food generator and Vargas.

Emma was a bit overly cautious now, but curious. "What is an evap exactly?"

Vargas analyzed the young girl with a tilt of his head. "You don't know what an evap is?" he asked   .

Lina laughed, "It's how we get clean on this planet, E2. Go ahead, you are welcome to try it. I'm sure you feel dirty from all of your adventures." She looked at Vargas. "You don't mind, Vargas, do you?"

"Not at all." He pointed Emma to a small room down the hallway.

Emma pulled her shirt to her nose and took a quick whiff. "Ugh, I would love that, please and thank you." She also had a sudden need for a toilet, and she hoped there was one in there. She quickly asked, "Is there also a method of waste disposal in there, or do you have another room for that?"

Lina and Vargas laughed. "Go in there," Vargas replied. "Take all the time you need. You'll figure it out. Enjoy!"

Emma walked into the evap room, and there stood a tall, mounted, glass encasement like a step-in shower and a smaller in-ground hole with a glass lid. "At least it looks to maintain the same principles as a shower and toilet. Here goes nothing." She opened the glass lid and squatted over the waste disposal. She had been holding in her pee since she got to Merah, and she was grateful for relieving herself. Her body relaxed after eliminating her waste, and she headed toward what must be the evap. Her clothes dropped to the floor, and she kicked them off to the side. The motion of her leg strained a bit, and she remembered the cut on her shin. The rocks from the cavern dug only slightly into the skin, she would heal quickly. She removed her bandage, and part of the glass of the encasement slid open as she approached it. She hopped into the evap.

"Okay, I got this," she muttered to herself. She pressed a triangular blue button with lines on it hoping it was the "on" switch. The evap hummed while it pulled the bacteria from her skin. "Ahhhhhh," she whispered, feeling the sweat melt from her body. She decided to take all the time she needed in here.

Lina

Merah
Day 1 of E2 contamination

Lina and Vargas stayed by the kitchen in a forced silence. Vargas gathered a small bowl of food and placed it on the floor for Maut. As the hum of Emma's evap started, Vargas's curiosity stirred, and he could not hold back any further.

"Okay, spill it. Where's she from?"

Lina looked off to the side, not sure what information to give him and what to withhold. But this was Vargas. She had known him since they were small, and she could at least *partially* trust him. "The girl came off a portal nearby. E2 to be exact. I did not have orders for her species specifically, and I'm at a loss as to what I should do with her. My only hope is to find the primary portal, E1, and get her on her way home. The portal is not showing up on my scans though. That's why I came to you. You have different resources than I do, and I was hoping your download had it on there." She raised her brow and clasped her hands tightly together.

"Here, let me show you my most recent back ups." He called up his home screen. "So this is the most recent download I have." He dragged his download to the wall. "It looks like if we do a direct search query it's not there either. We could do a randomized search for all the potential E zones, but I'm not hopeful. If it's not here, it's not on any known map." Lina's face dropped a bit. "I'm sorry, but you may *have* to contact your employers directly for this one."

"I was hoping to be able to take care of this myself. I'm not sure how they'll react to me letting a contaminate through." The disappointment seeped through her face and worry escaped her voice. Vargas opened his mouth to say something but paused slightly before mentioning his thought. With him, curiosity always won.

"Doesn't she look a bit like the Nerezza to you?"

"Too soon," she replied. She didn't mean to be harsh and immediately regretted it. She should have known she wasn't the only one who noticed the similarity; there were several quizzical looks when she first brought the E2 girl around the market. A whisper at the back of her mind urged her not to drag her oldest friend further into this mess. She pushed it aside. "She may be the same species as the Nerezza, but it's not her. This girl is too young... I think." Lina tried to reassure herself, but she still wondered.

"What do you think the Kabiren will *really* do? Once they find out, I mean."

"I'm not sure. Maybe that's why I'm hesitant to bring this up to them. I wanted to handle it on my own. It's not as easy as I thought it was going to be."

"But you still would need approval to use an outgoing portal from the Kabiren anyway, right? They will find out whether or not you tell them. There are so few portals that are actually working at optimal levels. And even more restrictions have been put into place since the Nerezza. How did you think you were going to get her passed their notice?"

Lina held her hands up. "Whoa, one step at a time. I haven't been thinking that far ahead. I feel like there's no way for me to come out of this without losing my post. But I'm trying to figure it out. I will figure it out."

"Well, you know, without a doubt, you have me. I'll try to help in whatever way I can."

Lina held out her arm and clicked her tongue, and Maut quickly flew to his place next to her head. "Mind watching Maut for me for a bit?" She patted his back, and he nuzzled into her hair.

Vargas shook his head "Of course. C'mon, you tiny beast." He poured more food into the bowl, and Maut jumped down to devour it.

The hum of the evap stopped, and soon after Emma joined them fully clothed and fresh. "I feel so much better. Thank you, Vargas, for letting me use your evap. So, what did I miss?

Where are we at with the portal?"

"It looks like we have more work to do to find it, E2." Lina responded with a waver in her voice. "We searched Vargas's map for it, but it was nowhere to be found. It looks like I will have to make a visit to headquarters for verification of its existence."

"Are you saying there is a possibility it doesn't exist?" Emma focused on them.

"Yes." Lina said plainly. She wasn't sure if Emma processed the information she just heard, figuring out a solution, or was about to let another drop of water fall from her eye. She hoped it wasn't the latter. This creature unnerved her, but she wanted to understand her, to anticipate what she was capable of. She had a kind face. Indeed, a smaller copy of the Nerezza. It scared her, one who looked so much like the thief and destroyer, but it also baffled her. *How could this one look so similar to her?* The three of them stared in an awkward silence.

"Well, Maut can attest to my cooking skills." Vargas nodded at the bowl on the floor licked clean. "If you both are still hungry, would you like to finally eat? I promise it's safe." Lina smiled. He never could handle silence for too long. It wasn't in his nature to be quiet, brooding, or pensive. He always tried to maintain his jovial nature, even in the worst of circumstances, and she loved that about him.

Emma quickly replied, "Yes, please! I'm seriously going to die if I don't get something to eat soon." She laughed.

Vargas and Lina stood and looked at each other, eyebrows raised in confusion at the outburst of laughter.

"Oh, never mind. Can we please eat now?" Emma stopped laughing and analyzed the foods of varying shapes, colors, and sizes arrayed on the table. It was not possible for Vargas to disappoint when it came to a feast. He programmed the food generator better than Lina, but he also had more access to the grown foods. He worked in the market, always saw the best deals, and then grabbed the foods he could throughout the day before they disappeared.

Lina chose the closest food to her. Of course Vargas would make sure the sliced meat was right between her and Emma. She quickly grabbed her slice and dug in. The sooner she began, the sooner she could finish. The process was necessary for their bodily functions, but the time spent seemed to last forever. The Amethites had spent so much time feeding their refueling function that, after they arrived, the Kabiren set up a time limit for all food consumption activity. She learned to eat quickly and efficiently, and she appreciated the Old Ones' foresight to adjust their productivity. There was only one kind of food she savored with every bite.

A loud noise came from the young girl at the table. "Oh my ██, this is amazing! What is this?" Emma held out the small slice of boden meat. Lina smiled with a new connection to the girl, for how amazing it was to share a small joy with a stranger from another world.

"It is meat from a creature here called a boden. It's the best, isn't it?" Lina replied, while she thought that maybe, just maybe, it would be nice to spend more time enjoying these small moments. But she pushed back that thought and replaced it with her training. *Time is a commodity and shouldn't be wasted on pointless nonessentials like eating.* Her last bite slid down her throat, and she tapped her fingers on the table waiting for Vargas and Emma to finish.

11

August

Merah
2 days after E2 contamination

August sat in the center of the courtyard of his building. The light streamed into his chair while he studied his holo screen. What he noticed, more than the specs of the new gate plans he was supposed to be studying, was the number of people in their races to their next assignment. They buzzed around him, always moving. This courtyard, built for collection of the suns' light to disperse throughout the building, made it functional, but to August, it was beautiful. The suns beamed cascades of rainbow light off the reflectors. He sat in the only place where he could have solace in the crowds of people. They wouldn't notice him here. He grew up in headquarters. It was all he ever knew, until he went to a village on his first assignment. He loved to visit the villages and the history associated with them—the growth of the foliage of the black forests and the drops of glistening dew in the morning light. He wished for distant assignments, anywhere but here. His thoughts were interrupted by a familiar voice, invoking feelings of love and fear all at once.

"How are those new specs for the theorized gate plans coming?" a woman said abruptly, demanding the news only he could provide.

"The specs look good, Mother," he said without flinching.

"Ah, ah." She wagged her finger at him. "You know it's 'general' in public, Proximate August."

"Fine." He clenched his jaw before continuing. "The specs look good, *general*. We should be able to apply them to the new portal platforms. Not sure how the technology will merge though. It seems to be missing a component I can't quite figure out."

"No matter. We need to test out these plans. They are already in the building process. The Scouts will be able to take care of that quickly."

"Yes, I know. But it would be so much easier if I had the original plans for the portals. I wouldn't be working blind."

"Yes, it would be nice to have the origination plans. But as you well know, we haven't been able to find them since *she* took them."

"The Nerezza really did some damage when she deleted them from our systems, didn't she?" August glanced back at the plans he was working on and expanded his new addition. He wouldn't have had to work so hard if the Nerezza hadn't stolen all the original portal plans. Thief. The Kabiren couldn't even find a portion of the last portals completed because of how much information she took with her. She left before August was even born, but he always knew her as a destroyer and thief.

"More than you know." His mother nodded and turned her attention to two approaching men. "Have these plans done. We test them in two days."

The men were from the Scout division. He knew by the graying hair and the stern looks they gave his mother. They always meant business and demanded the attention of her way too often than he felt necessary. She became quickly absorbed in whatever they had to say.

"We need you, general, in the missions room. We have a…"— they looked at him with unsure faces—"situation." They flicked their file over to her screen.

When she opened the file, her eyes widened. "When did we receive this information?"

"Just now."

"Why did the planet sensors not pick this up sooner?"

"We are still working on that. But it looks like that portal vidcam may have a transference delay."

"Get on this now! I need more information." His mother turned her attention to August briefly. "I may not be home tonight. Continue to work on those plans. We need you up to speed on all of this information."

"Yes, general," he replied, and nodded in the same sullen fashion as he usually did.

Time was of the essence. The portals were breaking down. There was no concrete explanation for why they were malfunctioning. They needed a solution fast for the only avenues off world. This new gate was the answer to all of their problems, and he needed to know the ins and outs of it, but mostly, he needed it to work. He reached his quarters and plopped down at his desk. These plans were going to take him all night.

12

Lina

Merah
Day 3 of E2 contamination

They made it to the Dvaarapaal village sooner than expected. The Protector quarters housed their tired heads while Lina could figure out what to do with the E2 girl. She watched her young ward splayed out sleeping and wondered if there was any point in going through all this effort to return some girl, some foreign contaminate, to Earth. Her previous assignments were not as much effort as this. This created more work than she wanted. All this worry about returning a young creature like Emma to her home planet with absolutely none of the reward or prestige. This wasn't an official assignment, not even something she could log. She could have left the girl in the forest, and there would have been no repercussions. Why she felt a strange duty to protect this girl, potentially more than her own planet, escaped her understanding. A familiarity surrounding the E2 girl pinched her gut, and she didn't know how to sit with it. She needed some friendly advice, and she knew just who to talk to.

She took extra care not to stir the sleeping girl and quietly got ready to leave. Her blaster and cloak in hand, she ensured the control pad for the door was set to locked. When approaching the clerk at the exit doors, she glimpsed two Kabiren stationed in the back of the alley outside, but dismissed their presence quickly. "Hey, if the girl in quarter twelve calls down an inquiry, can you let her know I've gone out for a bit? Charge any meals processed for her on my Protector ID. I'll take care of them." With her instructions, she ensured Emma was cared for while she left for Harimanne's. Emma had little reason to leave the resting facility, and Lina wanted to make sure the girl didn't cause any upset in the village. A mini Nerezza walking around openly all alone was not the attention she needed. The entrance doors slid open effortlessly, and she followed the pings on her wristband which led to the purple dot—Harimanne. Thankfully, the pings led right to her door.

Lina checked the vidcam. "Hello there, my friend. Do you have a moment to speak?" She waited a few minutes, and the entry doors slid open to reveal a tattered and tired creature. "Harimanne, are you okay? You definitely don't look like it."

"Long assignment, late night. What are you doing here, Lina? And so, so, so *early*. The suns have barely risen and you are at my door. Did you message me you were coming?" She brushed the silver frays of hair away from her face and glared at Lina.

"No, my apologies. I didn't send a message. Something has come up. I need to speak with you. Can I come in?"

Harimanne groaned and waved her into her flat. They sat around the kitchen counter, and she poured herself a neon pink drink and gestured toward it. "Want some erythro?"

Lina wrinkled her nose. "No, I'm good. Let me get right to the point; I need some advice. I think I'm in trouble. Not sure what exactly is the right course of action. Will you, my fellow Protector and friend, hear out my quandary?"

Harimanne stopped at her formality. She replied with a nod. "I will."

Lina divulged the events surrounding her secret travel companion. "I was sent on assignment near my village to one of the portals there."

"Pfoteros or konigs?"

"Pfoteros, of course, the nuisances, but then also ran into a konig that same day!" She shrugged and continued, "When I was there to dispose of the vile creatures, what came through the portal was not any pfoteros, but a creature, a girl. Younger than me, but not by much."

"What did the foreign categorical list state about her species?"

"I checked. It isn't on it. Maybe the species hasn't been categorized yet? But she looks like she shares the same biological sequencing as.... um...," Lina couldn't look at her friend as she whispered, "the Nerezza."

Harimanne's eyes widened. "No! Are you positive they're the same species?" Lina sensed a bit of uncertainty in the question.

Lina shook her head. "No, of course not! She would need to be categorized before I could be *absolutely* sure. But like I said, she is not."

"Well, you need to be sure. If I were you, I would take her into headquarters and get her DNA sequenced quick. So what if she looks like the Nerezza? You don't know for sure, and it's not like it's your fault she came through. Maybe the general will like that you have brought in a new species!" She raised her brow in earnest excitement.

"But you don't think I would be removed from my post for letting a potential foreign contaminate live past the portal grounds? Do you know of any Protector who allowed such a contaminate into Merah and maintained their title?"

Harimanne shook her head slowly, in an unnerving way. Lina knew the sequencing of a new species could be good. The Kabiren feasted generously on any new information they could glean. Hopefully, she obtained a prize to be praised, and not a mistake to blacken her Protector title. She could satisfy her own curiosity if she categorized Emma's species at headquarters, too. She knew what she had to do. The metropolis headquarters was where they were heading, and they did indeed need to finish their trek.

"Thank you, my friend. I needed another voice to steady my resolve." Lina stood up to make her way back toward the door. She turned to say goodbye, but her friend interrupted her attempt at farewell.

"Maybe take your concern up with the General Proximate. He likes you. Maybe there will be mercy. Goodbye, my friend." Harimanne bowed, still in her disheveled state.

With that advice, Lina left the quarters. They needed to get on their way to make it to the city before nightfall, and they needed to leave now. The less the other villagers saw of the E2 girl before her species could be categorized, the better. She had no idea what would happen to the girl the longer they stayed in one place, and it was that lack of knowledge that unsettled her stomach. Only forward motion kept her fears at bay and so forward to headquarters they needed to go.

13

Emma

Merah
Day 3 of E2 contamination

E mma got into the habit of fidgeting, mostly when frustrated or unsure. Not because of a nervous energy that needed to escape her body, but more of an endless need for her body to *do something*. It helped her focus. Even when she studied in her home, her fidgets always included dance. She would stare at her screen, balanced precariously on a table, and weave through and around her furniture reciting information she needed to burn into her brain. That is why she loved adventuring. It was endless motion and movement. But now on Merah and in an adventure of her dreams, she felt insignificant and small. The world beyond her quarters' door contained a much larger expanse of knowledge. So she began to fidget.

Emma twirled and leapt in the small space. Two inset gray bunk beds overtook one wall. Her bed contained a crumpled blanket, but Lina's was freshly made and neat. Her hip bumped into a flat, silver table as she inched closer to the door. With every leap toward the door, she convinced herself of the reasons why she shouldn't leave her room. *I am unfamiliar with the area and should not explore an unknown.* Which of course quickly led to the exact reason why she should leave the quarters. *Of course I am. I'm on another planet in an unknown galaxy...but every true scientist is curious about the unfamiliar.* She leapt in a twirl and paused. All she needed to do was reach out and trigger the door open. Adventure waited just outside that door. She swallowed. Her arm reached for the triangular purple button with the dots and lines she couldn't understand on it. It was the one Lina pressed when she left. Her fingertip barely grazed it before the doors shot open. Emma creeped out. She walked toward the bustling noises, not knowing what she would find, but exhilarated by the possibilities.

Just beyond the hallway of lights that housed their quarters, was a small glass stairwell glimmering a rainbow of color with each step. Emma stared down as each of her feet tiptoed on it. The clerk behind a rectangular desk made of a copper-colored metal with holographic projections above it notified her before her exit that Lina had left her alone to handle some of her own business. That meant she had time to explore a little. Her feet itched to escape the small building. Her trek began at the alley outside of their quarter house, as Lina called it when they arrived. Rows and rows of flat metal structures that were simple square houses stretched out before her. She peered into the glass windows of each as she passed by. They were very similar to Vargas's place. The consistency impressed her. Like they were all perfect replications of themselves. She examined two adjacent buildings as if they were in a spot-the-differences picture. Here are two shots of the same exact things, analyze them to death before realizing there is no difference. The process in order to accomplish this baffled her.

Suddenly, a small creature with puce skin, a small tail, and the largest eyes a small head could contain, approached her. Emma stayed still but jumped slightly when the little being addressed her. "Where are you from? You have *such* small eyes. I don't believe I've met any of your species before! This is exciting." The small voice had a high-pitched tone. Emma couldn't help but be swept up in the all-encompassing sweetness and abruptness of the child. It looked like a girl, with large eyes and a dainty, yet bright-green oval face. Her cheeks jutted out, more rounded than the other child across the path. She reminded her of herself when she was very young, about six maybe. She always asked the most direct questions, no matter how embarrassing her mother felt they were. Probably why her mother rarely talked with her now. But before she could answer, another bigger creature of the same characteristics, tugged the little girl to come along while whispering "Not *her*! Not *her*, little one. Keep your distance." The parent/caregiver clutched and dragged the child's arm away so quickly, Emma barely saw which direction they headed.

As she searched around the alley, she realized all the creatures passing by were glancing at her.

"Not again."

"Can that be *her?*" One tall red creature said to another.

"Shhhh, no. She's too small. And her nose is different." The other plumper being responded.

These looks were not the casual glances of people in your way as you walked, but rather, in a way that was purposefully unnoticing. Like someone caught a glimpse of a big smear of dirt on your face and tried really hard not to show you they saw it. She tried to shake off the discomfort, but her heart quickened its pace with each gawker. She continued a little faster. Her palms and underarms started to drip. They watched, and she felt like a puzzle piece held in a hand just waiting to be placed exactly where she fit.

The road opened up before her to reveal a common area buzzing with noise. She couldn't tell where the hum came from, but it made her stop and hum along. "Hmmm, hmmmm, hmmmmm." Before she knew it, she hummed a familiar song with her eyes closed. It loosened her stomach and her sweat dried, and she began to dance.

"First position. Second position. Plié. Turn. Plié. Turn. Developpe...spin," she whispered and moved gracefully to the hum. "Plie. Arabesque. Turn en pointe. En pointe. Pirouette. En pointe. Pirouette," until she finally was out of breath and stopped. The rush of release of her worries pushed through her appendages. She bent her head to stretch her neck and as she opened her eyes, everyone had stopped in their tracks.

The stares were all in her direction. She waited to hear "Trucker girl!" with the usual snickers, but there was only silence and gaping mouths. The entire street stood motionless around her.

Two small creatures who stopped mid-play, shouted in exclamation, and waved their hands. The alley exploded in cheers of joy. A little boy spun in a circle, imitating her motions. She heard several comments, and the crowd pressed in on her.

Someone next to her said: "That was the most beautiful thing I've seen in all my life."

Another agreed, "Yes, amazing. What's that called?"

She did not expect the compliments and her face turned pink. "Oh. Um. Thank you. It's just dancing."

The creatures' voices turned to gibberish as they spoke too quickly for the translator. Emma turned her focus away from all the beings talking around her. Two tall red creatures were not full of glee or impressed with the display of Emma's dancing. Out of the corner of her eye, she spotted their unmovable faces. They had deep red skin, burly chests, and silvered hair.

Lina appeared, grasped at her firmly with a tense glare, and said "Follow me NOW. We need to be getting to headquarters. Hurry." Lina yanked her away from the crowd. Emma looked back and saw those two older men, motionless and calculating while they stared directly at her.

"Did you see the two aged creatures in the back? They did not look happy." Emma questioned her own sanity.

Lina replied, "Yes, they were Kabiren Scouts. I'm not sure what they are doing in this village. There are enough Protectors in the vicinity to negate a need for their presence."

"What's a Kabiren?"

Lina looked straight ahead, walking toward the quarter house. "The Kabiren is the race we refer to as 'the Old Ones' sometimes. According to our history records, my race, the Amethites, warred with a dangerous race called the Mentiren. They arrived on our young planet under a pretense of friendliness, offering to help us with the black hole. But their true intentions were revealed not long after— they wanted to control us—and we faced great hardship for years. In the early days, the Amethites worked hard and long days while still maintaining this Mentiren friendship. But it soon was clear that the Mentiren had other intentions for our hard work. They didn't care about the wear in our bones, and they pushed us too hard. Then by a miracle, one day the Kabiren arrived on our planet. They helped us fight off the Mentiren and rebuild our broken villages. We learned their technology, and the only thing they asked from us was to be able to stay on our planet. They help us maintain order and shared their technological wealth. We had to learn a lot very quickly, and the only way to do that was to do things the Kabiren way."

Emma thought about her own time in the Mars Specialized Training program. Good thing she learned quickly and thoroughly enjoyed the process of terraforming Mars. Every inch of mining led the human race closer and closer to releasing the amount of CO_2 needed to make Mars's atmosphere inhabitable. She had hope, and that is why she wanted to learn. Her growth and eventual work in the program meant more and more colonies could be sustained. Through all of this, Emma continued her dance classes. In fact, they were encouraged by Veribo Industries. "Humanity will never expand without art or creative thought. Feed your creations," was their motto.

But here the Amethites had accomplished learning an entirely new set of technology in such a short period of time. She wondered if the Kabiren and Amethites were on to something. On Earth, Emma could be distracted by her extracurricular activities. This distraction limited the speed with which she grew in the MST program. But was that truly an advantage? Maybe Lina was right, and they didn't need creative thought. But what gave Lina, or any Amethite, the drive to continue to work for a race at the expense of creativity? Residual gratitude? Or something else entirely?

They made it back to their quarter house. Lina quietly gathered her things, shoving her extra dingey clothes and some square knobs of tech back into the pack she brought in. The small bag held a lot surprisingly, even more when Lina took her blaster out and secured it to her waistbelt. Emma couldn't help but feel maybe she pried a bit too much in asking for the little history lesson from her friend. So she stayed quiet. They would need to make it to the city soon, and they packed in silence.

"Let's go," Lina said.

And they left the familiar home, ready to make their way to headquarters.

14

Dexter

Earth
7 days since Emma's disappearance

Six days, one hundred and sixty-eight hours, and fifteen billion minutes. Dexter counted them over and over. He shook his leg at his workstation in the Mars Specialized Training program. This week marked his advancing years, his birthday. He didn't feel any older and certainly none the wiser. The police had given up their rigorous searches for Emma; they couldn't find any trace of her, and this paused the investigation. His anger ballooned deep in his stomach. It burned through him and forged a brick wall. He retreated behind that wall whenever anyone tried to talk to him. He hated them. Everyone else carried on with their lives as if Emma never existed, while his life ended the moment she was gone. He couldn't focus on his classwork at his workstation. He sat there staring at all the people who gave up. His teacher, Veribo Industries, everyone he came into contact with, all quitters. He scowled.

"Dexter, can you please stay a bit later today to go over some of your test results?" Mr. Stretcher asked.

Dexter rolled his eyes in full view of the instructor. He knew it was a mistake, but the action was involuntary. How could he be expected to care about this classwork? When one human life didn't matter to the rest of the world, why should the lives on the colonies on Mars matter to him? After the ping for the next course pushed his classmates out the door, he waited in a determined sulk.

"Dexter, I need to talk to you about your test scores. I know you've been having a rough time since the disappearance of your friend, but you're a smart kid. You could be an amazing addition to this program."

"Why should I care about my test scores?" he asked.

"Well, Dexter, I wasn't supposed to disclose this information yet, but here in the MST program, we have multiple new science studies that can expand your current class work. This program is a stepping stone to those avenues. If you work hard, you could go into advanced programs." Dexter's eyes widened. "For example, gene detection fields and indirect topographical mapping. These are fields where I think you'd be amazing."

Dexter looked up at his instructor with a small glimmer in his eye. "Veribo Industries is studying gene recognition fields? I thought those were theoretical."

"Dexter, there is so much you don't know, but could, if you applied yourself. Some of our best scientists are working in fields funded by Veribo Industries because of the possibility of their use on Mars. But you don't have to be that short sighted, you know... They could be used for more."

The future of those technologies was vast, but Dexter saw only one use for them—to find Emma. If they could be advanced enough for field testing, he could hit the ground running in his search. The gene recognition field alone would cut down his search time, and enable him to have a broader search. That sort of tech could be programmed to sort through data and hone in on traces of specific DNA, Emma's DNA. He needed to be a part of this and would do whatever it took to get there. "What do I have to do?"

"Get your grades back up, work hard, study constantly. You need to pass the final exam with 2000 or higher, but with my help, you can make it. You can do great things, Dexter, but you need to try harder."

He made the calculations in his head. He did allow himself to get behind in his classwork; his last practice tests were in the 1000 range. How could he catch up in order to score that high? He needed to study nonstop and practice at his work station every single day. But he could do it, he needed to do it. For Emma.

Lina

Merah
4 days since E2 contamination

The city's buildings kissed the sky above them. The glass and metal stretched high, and the shuttle paths gleamed with indicator holograms between buildings. The streets bustled with people. The sheer expanse of the city indicated the hard work of its citizens. The Mentiren had burned the city to ashes before the Kabiren expelled them, and much work had been done to encourage growth and expansion since then. The city around headquarters had blossomed just within Lina's lifetime. As she grew, so did it. It was a reflection of what the Amethites could do under the guidance of the Kabiren—a reflection of what she could do in her lifetime. She reveled in the possibility. She held the title of Protector today, but the idea of becoming a Scout swirled through her mind. Off-world assignments intrigued her. While the Scouts were traditionally Kabiren, she occasionally saw a straggler species in their ranks, which gave her hope. She was young, much younger than all of the Scouts, but she hoped her actions with the Monsuta job had proven to the general that her skills and youth were not wasted on a small Amethite girl.

Emma looked up at the skyscrapers and the traveling shuttles overhead. "Wow, laws on our planet have limited our use of shuttles. They are mostly for interplanetary runs, and only to our closest planet. But looking at this! It really is amazing. How long did it take?"

"Oh, it was not long at all. Once the Kabiren took over, they were able to organize everything and implement the current shuttle structure. When we worked together, things were accomplished quickly. This entire city itself was built within my lifetime, and I have lived just under fifteen years."

As they passed the buildings and arrived at the Protector headquarters, Lina couldn't help but notice the two same Scouts, from the last village, hidden in the shadows. "This is the central building for the city. It is where some of the most important work of the Kabiren is accomplished. It is also where I received my Protector training."

Emma's eyes followed a line of invisible connect-the-dots. "You are responsible for protecting the planet from things that come through your portals, right? That makes sense now."

"Yes, but I wouldn't call them 'our portals.' The Kabiren are the brains behind them, but we maintain them." Lina hated to admit the portals were not designed by her species. The most powerful structures on her planet were engineered and maintained by the Kabiren.

They were forever upkeeping a technology they never completely understood. Sure, the Kabiren expanded on the technology, but not enough to refurbish or safely destroy the portals. The Kabiren needed them for their off-world traveling. The planet's position made it impossible to reach with any other method of transportation. The Amethites needed the portals for resources, and the Kabiren Scouts needed them to negotiate trades with other worlds. A symbiosis the Amethites knew they needed, and therefore, they cherished it.

The headquarters building had columns on the entryway. As the girls entered through the gliding doors, people rushed around in the foyer. High-vaulted ceilings of frosted glass and metal surrounded them. Kabiren and Amethites alike dressed in black rushed all around entering and exiting the building. Green holograph beams of light moved up and down every which way, constantly scanning everyone entering. Lina searched for August in the sea of people. Her eyes searched the building, and she casually mentioned to Emma, "I don't see the person we're going to meet. I need to send a quick message."

She displayed her wristband screen.

Outgoing: General Proximate August

We are here to discuss that issue I messaged about earlier. Please respond.

As she sent the message, August approached them with a smile. "Hey, I'm so sorry I'm late. I was up last night studying the new designs for the portal integrations. It was…well, it was a lot." He greeted them with a yawn but quickly shook himself to attention when he saw Emma.

"You really weren't kidding in your message." He inspected Emma, as if searching for something in particular, but couldn't quite find it. He grabbed for her face and arms. "She looks so similar." He continued his inquisitive search without a thought.

"Please do not touch me." Emma yanked herself back and switched her attention to Lina. "Similar to what exactly?"

"Don't worry about it," she assured Emma. Lina realized she had forgotten introductions. She rarely met new people and always forgot the customs. "Emma, meet my inappropriately invasive friend, General Proximate August. I apologize for his actions. He forgets himself. You just look similar to someone this planet knew well once." She searched around the building. "August, is there some place we can go that is a bit quieter?"

"Yes, of course. Let's go to my lab. We shouldn't be disturbed there." He led them both across the foyer and up to the elevation pad, a circle of carpet-like fabric with sharp lines cut into the floor surrounding it. They approached the pad, and Lina and August stepped onto it then turned toward a reluctant Emma. Lina gently guided her. "It's okay. This will take us to where we need to go. Completely safe." The girl cautiously followed onto the pad and braced herself to ascend.

August shot them a quick smile. He entered their requested level on his wristband. Lina looked up to see through a skylight above. A clear dome rose from the lines surrounding the pad and enclosed them in clear plexiglass. She wanted to visit August's lab after hearing all the whispers of important work he'd been assigned. She maintained her curiosity. The plexiglass and metal casing enveloped them and the pad hummed to life. The floor below them fell away to reveal a dark passage to the lower levels. Lina dropped her head in disappointment.

"August, is your lab in the *basement*?" Lina cringed. She figured that the general's son would have some big fancy upper level lab, but to her dismay, they continued down and down.

August chuckled. "I may be the general's son but that doesn't mean I automatically have access to the best lab… That is on the top level, and I *wish* I had access there. But my lab isn't too bad. Don't let your hopes drop too quickly, Lina."

They continued their downward motion and arrived at the lab doors on lower level fifteen. The doors opened to a brightened room containing several holoscreens, multiple lab stations, and a massive computing system. There were fully automated holographic display systems completely redefining the room's space. She almost couldn't tell what part of the room was real, and which was projected. Rows of bots worked on holo bands and blasters with several different grips. Lina's jaw dropped, and her eyes darted between all the toys in the room. "See? I told you not to drop your hopes!" He said in a self-satisfied tone as he proudly peered at his domain. "Look at this." He ushered their attention to the center of the lab. A huge interactive holo of the entire planet displayed in front of them. Lina traced her finger over their position and spun it around.

"This is amazing. Is it a live representation of Merah?" Lina asked.

"Of course," August replied, "Nothing less would suffice to show 'the red planet.'" He smiled proudly at his creation.

A small voice in the background finally let out an audible response. "Did you say, 'the red planet'?" Emma furrowed her brow examining the entire planet.

"Yes, girl, for those who live here, our planet is affectionately called 'the red planet,'" August quickly and proudly responded.

"Well, really, should you say 'our' planet? We were here first, and you lot merely rent it out," Lina replied defensively and continued about the room turning over everything of interest she could find.

Emma examined the live feed of the entire planet. "I knew the forests I arrived in looked familiar! I have heard stories of a red planet. A planet with secrets and technological advances that were coveted by all in the galaxy. I thought they were just stories my father told me. But how can the red planet be real?"

Lina and August glanced at Emma with piqued interest. "Merah is spoken of in whispers far and wide because of its secret location. It is not known intimately by many other than the Kabiren and Amethites. How could your father know about this planet? We have not yet catalogued your species for our archives and therefore have not had any..." August cocked his head and looked at Lina, "What portal did you say she came through?"

"E2 portal near Nira village" she replied.

"Very interesting, indeed." He turned his attention back to Emma. "And you say you recognized this planet from stories?"

Emma nodded slowly as if working on a puzzle in her head. "Yes, my father is a wonderful storyteller. Any story he speaks of immediately captures my attention. He paints vivid detail and glorious beauty with his words. The way the trees grew fiery orange as if majestically burning. He speaks of cliffs and mountains surrounding a thick lake of turquoise that almost glowed. A planet where its placement made it not too hot and not too cold for all who live there. I always fall in love with the Red Planet, and Featherstone, of course, when I hear my father talk about them."

August's jaw tightened when he heard Emma mention "Featherstone," but Lina brushed off his response. He quickly replied, "Well, I never heard of this Featherstone. But this is *our*," he looked at Lina, "Red Planet, and while we do specialize in technological advancement, we are far from where we should be. There is much room for growth. Emma, would you submit to a quick cataloguing of your DNA? Since we haven't come across any of your species yet."

"Cataloguing my DNA is *not* what I came here for. I came here to find a way home." Emma's exasperation was voiced in her brash tone.

Lina quickly interjected, "I couldn't locate the outgoing portal to E2 on my map." She called up the map on her wristband to show August.

"You downloaded the most recent update?" August asked.

"Yes, I have all the newest information, but the portal isn't there," Lina admitted.

August entered the information into the data sprawl on his holo screen. Several dots appeared on the planet's surface. "Hmm, I don't see it either." He looked at Emma and Lina back and forth. "It is quite likely there is no outgoing portal for E2."

August's words held no hope for Emma. She fell down to the ground and a loud moan escaped from her lips. Her shoulders shuddered and tears ran down her cheeks at an alarming rate.

Lina walked over to the young girl and stood awkwardly next to her. She didn't know what else to do. Emotion, while felt, should *never* be fully expressed. And here was a girl who gave her feelings a full and rounded expression. *Well, this is why I never get attached to anything, I guess.* Lina waited impatiently for the young girl to compose herself. This was agony she hadn't felt before—an expression of loss and loneliness, meant only for one's mind and not others. The original excitement of what her discovery would bring to her and her career faded. Saving the girl was pointless.

An older Kabiren entered the lab. Lina stood tall at the presence of the general.

"What are you doing here instead of studying, General Proximate?" The general raised her head to see where the awful noise came from. "Who is this young creature making that horrible noise?"

August stepped closer to his mother with a bow and an explanation. "General, Protector 42 has brought us this young creature from the *E2* portal. They were looking for the outgoing portal to return her to her home, but it is not in any of our records."

The general sneered at the whimpering girl and without diverting her pointed stare she said, "It doesn't exist. That is why you cannot find it. What is your name, girl?" the general asked.

Emma battled through the gasps for air. "Em. Em..... Emma of E2," she muttered.

"Well, Emma of E2, you must stop this outburst immediately. We will figure something out for you, and you will be at ease here in the city. General Proximate August will see to it that you receive quarters and instructions while we address your current issue." She switched her gaze to Lina. "I appreciate your hard work, Protector 42, as well as your discretion with this matter in bringing the girl directly here. Please continue on with your assignments. We will take it from here. You are dismissed."

Lina nodded, moved toward the doors of the lab, whispered a small and trivial goodbye to Emma, and stepped out of the doors. She hesitated slightly, but received a new message for assignment.

Protector 42, Area Assigned: Site 65,
Target: Foreign Fungi Growth

And with her new gardening orders, she exited the lab.

16

August

Merah
5 days since E2 contamination

Anxiousness showed through his mother's eyes. She tried to hide it, but there was more to this girl than she led on. He offered his hand to help raise the girl up from her pitiful state on the floor and placed her in a chair. Wide streaks of dried tears smeared on her face. The girl sat utterly helpless.

"What can we do with this one?" he finally asked his mother. "If she is lost to her home world, that is?"

"Well, there are several options. We need to categorize her species and test to see where she ranks for usefulness." She turned her attention to Emma. "What was your academic status on your home planet, E2?"

The girl wiped her cheeks with her hands and steadied her head upright. She inhaled a deep breath and replied, "I was part of an accelerated training program for our planet's expansion to another planet in our solar system. I specialized in the terraforming of the planet, while my parents were trained pilots for supply shuttle runs between our two planets."

His Mother smiled, intrigued at her response. "What method of travel does your species use in your solar system?"

"Our species recently developed the means to travel faster than light, which accelerated our planet's terraforming plans on a nearby planet. The warp travel was made possible by some very dedicated scientists, and it was a wonder to experience."

"Hmm." Mother's head perked up at that, and she raised her brows. "Are you well-versed in these 'faster than light' methods, or do you only have basic knowledge?"

"I have been in the Mars terraforming accelerated program for one year. My training has been specific and in depth, and I am the first in my class. So I would say it's not solely a basic knowledge."

Mother allowed a large smile to stretch across her face and nodded. It unnerved him. There were only a handful of times he recalled seeing his mother smile. Once, when he figured out his first uni puzzle, a 3D model of a hexagon that looked like a Rubik's cube, at age four. Another time, when the Scouts had made an alliance with a race that worked on gravitational fields. And lastly, when he graduated his Protector training faster than any other trainee. He couldn't remember any other times in which she smiled as big as she did now.

"Well, my dear, I think we may have a place for you after all. If you feel up to it, I would like to invite you to accept a training program, specialized just for you. Of course, in application of your current knowledge, as well as our Protector training program, you will be well equipped to be a Protector Emulate, someone shadowing another more experienced Protector preparing to step into the role when deemed ready." She finished her offer with a grand gesture. There was never a Protector Emulate position before. "If you pass the appropriate tests required for this training, you will be provided with food and shelter, along with a tailored knowledge of this planet and its resources."

August guessed his mother needed something in particular from the girl.

She looked at him, "General Proximate August, I am putting Emma in your charge. Please make sure she is adequately prepared for her tests by creating a specified training program, based on your Protector program. I imagine she will need lots of special care and attention. You can forgo the installation of the new specs for the new gate portal; I have others already prepped to take care of that. This is to be your first and foremost concern." Without waiting for a response, Mother turned and exited the lab.

Another official request from Mother he needed to comply with. This certainly would be challenging. Being completely ignorant of the differences in their two worlds, he needed to gather additional information from the creature before him. But with some time, he hoped he would be able to create the appropriate program to train her. She had youth, which meant she might be adaptable, but the Protector training was intensive, exclusive, and expansive.

The girl still sat silently staring directly through him. She needed a happy distraction to make her more talkative.

"Please get up, E2," he softly pleaded with her. "If you'll follow me, I can get you set up with your new quarters. I know they'll pale in comparison to your previous home. But I have something I think you'd love to see—a surprise." A large smile creased his cheeks. He motioned her to follow him.

She raised her head ever so slightly and slid off the chair. He could hear her feet drag behind him with every movement she made. But she followed him with her first step—this transition from one world to the next. He only needed to figure out how to lead her.

17

Emma

Merah
6 months since E2 contamination

The Red Planet of her dreams, her new home, consumed her days and nights. There had been so many she might have lost count of how long she had been here, if the large holo screen in her quarters didn't calculate the exact amount of time she spent studying. Her quarters in the city were in the same building as August's. She woke up every day eager to learn about all of this new technology. She felt closer to home nose deep in some sort of technology manual—which was all the time. When she spoke of her classwork back home, August already had an expansive knowledge of warp drives and the terraforming bubbles she worked on, and he didn't feel a need to continue her education there.

When Lina first introduced him to her, his larger stature created an intimidating presence. A tall biped creature with features eerily close to humans. This was a sharp contrast from Lina and the Amethites she towered over. Emma, at thirteen, had a good head length on most Amethites. But August was broader and taller, with squared shoulders and light red skin, and three long scars that dragged along his arms. She wondered where he had gotten them. The General Proximate title was intimidating, but soon she learned he wasn't. His voice soothed her when he asked about her life on Earth. He knew so much more about other planets than her, but he maintained a curiosity about Earth and the MST program. It was this curiosity that softened his towering presence.

Before her arrival on Merah, she had a plan for her life — now her life consisted of uncertainty. Six months ago almost to the day, in the lab where she learned she would never return home, it started to feel like a dream. Her thoughts drifted away from that day, and she tried to focus on the lesson August planned. Her holo screen spewed information about the history of the Amethite and Kabiren treaty and about them kicking the Mentiren out.

The cultural aspect of this society intrigued her. Six months on this planet didn't allow for much societal instruction. She needed to know more. August assured her that she could ask him any questions, but that meant frequently going back to his lab to find him. Every time she stepped in there, it felt too soon. The place where her hopes and dreams were abruptly altered was somewhere she didn't want to return. What could she do now, other than roll with the instruction prepared for her and stay put in her quarters?

She had asked him a question that had been bothering her. "What is the Kabiren home planet?" she inquired one day during her lesson.

August looked right at her, a deep sadness in his eyes, and she knew then the answer wasn't pretty. But she decided not to press him any more about it. She just put her head back down to her tablet.

Today's lesson made her antsy. It was a review of the previous days' work. She stood up from her chair in her quarters and cracked her neck. Then she spun around and hopped in her own fluid movement while her problems melted away. The rigidity of an entire planet without music, dance, or free expression was still difficult for her to believe, let alone live in. As she moved, the audio from her lesson increased and announced all the fantastic discoveries the Kabiren had made. This wasn't instruction, it was propaganda, facts presented in a very specific way to tell a specific story, the Kabiren's story. One she wasn't sure she believed. She shrugged, and the lesson continued to the physics behind the portals which brought her here. The technology felt so different from what she learned in all her other lessons, and she questioned their origin. The portal designs were more complex. The plans for them seemed incomplete too. Comparing the portals to all the other tech designs was like comparing apples and oranges. But for now, she needed to memorize this information for her next exam. She slid into an arabesque in between tapping her notes into her holo screen.

At that moment, August buzzed at her quarters and quickly entered. Without looking up from his holo screen he said, "I have your next lesson plan. The file was too large to submit in a message to you, but now my proximity should be good to push it to your holo… I wanted to explain a bit before you study it." He typed a few commands into his holo screen, paused and cocked his head as he noted her peculiar position. "What are you doing?" His brows furrowed. "I thought you were studying up here this morning."

"I *am* studying! This *is* how I process information. I need an outlet, an exterior distraction. It helps me focus." She shrugged off the simple explanation as a necessary aspect of her learning, when she really knew that dancing, while a wonderful focusing tool, also filled a need she had to create something. It gave her complete control of herself, her emotions, her surroundings, everything. Her creativity was being stunted while stuck in a ten by ten room receiving the Kabiren lesson plans and committing them to memory. She slid out of the arabesque and stood straight on her two feet.

August raised his head with a fascinated interest. "What's it called?" He paused. "This distraction you speak of. It looks…. interesting."

Emma smiled at his curiosity. For the first time, she held some information which August clearly wanted. It intrigued him instead of making him indifferent, which had been his general demeanor during her lessons. "This is ballet. It's a dance that's normally done to music. An expression and creative outlet. Wanna see?" She raised her brow in expectation of an answer she already knew.

"Yes, please." He spoke hesitantly.

Emma's heart lurched at a chance to share a piece of herself. She stood in the corner of the room and recalled her last recital on earth, and instinct from the exhaustive practice took over. It was her favorite one. She started from the intro and worked her way through the first act. She had to make a few changes to the performance, as space allowed. But she would give it the best performance she could. After all, August had never seen dancing, and she needed to do it justice.

Emma threw her whole body in one direction. She glided and danced around the quarters with a fluid motion. Thoughts of her lost home, of being marooned on an alien planet, her parents, her sister, Dexter....gone, they all exploded out of her body in an anger she didn't know she possessed. She raged through her routine and moved faster and more powerfully with every turn and glide, finally ending with a leap and a dangerous glare at her observer.

August's eyes widened, and he slowly rose with clasped hands. "That was... amazing. I... I had no idea something could be so powerful." He patted at his chest as if he clutched at his heart and bowed his head. She had conveyed her feelings in a way that was distinct, and he understood exactly how she felt.

Guilt filled her heart at her outward expression of hopelessness. Emma's glare softened at his response. His was deep and personal. She wouldn't wish losing her home upon anyone else, but as she expressed it with such clarity, it bled into his heart, and she knew it.

"I'm sorry about the loneliness you have here," August muttered when she finally met his gaze. "And I understand the need to express yourself in such a drastic way." He glanced nervously at the door to her quarters. "But please keep this creativity to yourself. It's not something we encourage on Merah. In fact, anything like this is strongly discouraged. There's no telling what the Scouts would do if they caught you during such a display."

Emma furrowed her brow. Maybe she misread his interest. "Why is it not allowed exactly?"

"That's just how it is." His lips tightened. "I do wish there was a way for you to get home, though. I really do, but there isn't." He shrugged his shoulders. "There isn't even a portal that can get you close."

Emma sensed the hopelessness in his response.

"Why can't the Kabiren *build* another portal to my home world?" The question slipped out of her mouth and begged for an answer.

August looked down at her with unsure eyes and traced his finger and thumb across his brow before he finally admitted, "Because we don't know *how*."

"The Kabiren didn't create the portals, did they?" She recalled the inconsistencies she noted during her lesson on portal technology. The portals felt like a different art form than the blasters, or the food processors. They were beautiful and detailed in their creation, and it was the beauty in its details that no other technology had.

August hung his head and breathed in deeply. "No. We… borrowed the technology, from the Mentiren," he confessed while looking out of the window pod. "Very few Amethites know—please keep this to yourself. Merah would not be able to handle the fact that we can only maintain the portals and nothing more. We have tried to retrofit many of them with new technologies we have found. The Scouts have worked hard to maintain treaties with other races in order to gain new information that will hopefully fix the problem. But for now we keep working and maintaining. We promised the Amethites safety and security with our presence here, and we must deliver. This requires sole focus on the current portals and the goods and services we obtain from them. Not creating new ones, unfortunately."

"Are you telling me that most of the Amethites don't know the origin of the portals? Why not tell them? They can help!"

August scoffed at the idea. "They do not have the ability to work on the portals; they are still learning about them. So we have assigned them to jobs at their skill level in order to help with technological growth. They need to focus on their own jobs, and let us focus on the portals."

Emma clenched her jaw, and she tried to withhold her shock and anger at his words. She didn't understand a lot, but one thing she did understand was the mistake of under-estimating people. She travelled further than any human ever travelled, and all she found was an age-old problem. Humans, and alien races alike, will dominate, if there is an opportunity. Her mind raced. When dealing with an entire society built on such a fragile idea, she needed to be cau-tious. She felt her anger burning through her, ready to over-flow, but she couldn't risk an outburst. So she gritted her teeth determined not to share her thoughts. But she did let some words slip out. "Lina would disagree."

August raised his head nonchalantly. "Yes, she is dif-ferent and a very capable Protector, I'll give you that. About as capable as you, which you have proven by your exams. But I could learn so much more if you let me categorize your species' DNA. Will today be the day you finally let me, for the good of Merah?" he said in a hopeful, cheery tone.

"No, I will not. But, I would like to learn more about the process." She hoped the excuse appeased him. It was only a matter of time before they would know everything they needed to know about her. She couldn't risk giving them all the information they needed from her. She was the only one training as a Protector Emulate. It was a position that could be dissolved as easily as it was created. She could only dangle the hope of her eventual consent, but she needed to figure out why they wanted it so badly first. Until then, she would melt into their society as much as possible and do what she needed to do in order to survive. Six months down, forever on Merah to go.

18

Dexter

Earth
1 year since Emma's disappearance

The screen displayed fifteen different formulas slowly calculating the requirements for Dexter's plans. He was close to finishing the mock-ups for a prototype of this new design. He needed his teacher to double check his numbers, but he thought he would finish sooner than he originally anticipated. The carbon-sequencing scanner became his life and his redemption. It was the only device that would be able to find traces of DNA after scanning an entire area of land, if he programmed it the right way.

Every day he worked on it meant a day closer to finding Emma. He lived in the lab at school and barely left to take care of his basic needs at home. Even now, he didn't know if it was night or day. He was in the lab again, but that was okay. No one missed him. He sat on the lab chair with bloodshot eyes and waited for the computers to finish his calculations. His fingers tapped anxiously on the desk as he waited for the completion of his work, which hung on these formulas working.

"Dexter, have you been here all night again?" Mr. Stretcher looked concerned holding his piping hot morning coffee.

"Is it morning already?" He quickly glanced at the time in the corner of his screen and returned his attention to the calculations. "I didn't realize."

His teacher adjusted his glasses on the bridge of his nose and sat down next to him. "Dexter, boy, you have to get some rest. I'll finish running the calculations. Go home, wash up, and get some sleep."

Dexter ripped his attention from his work to look Mr. Stretcher square in the eye. "I'm not going anywhere. This needs to work. I have to make it work…" He held back the words choked in his throat but muttered, "Tomorrow will be one year. She will have been gone for one whole year tomorrow." His eyes pleaded with Mr. Stretcher. "Please let me finish this…Every calculation for the sequencer brings me closer and closer to finding her. I need to finish this."

Over the course of the year, Mr. Stretcher tried to reason with him. "Please go home and get some rest, Dexter." "Please eat your lunch, Dexter." "Please make sure you are finishing your other course work, Dexter." The requests were never-ending, and they *always* failed. Dexter knew that Mr. Stretcher used the hope of finding Emma as an incentive to get him to work harder, but in doing so he now developed an unreasonable hope.

A screaming beep came from his screen. Dexter jerked his attention to the blinking dialogue box of results and scanned them with a penetrating look. When he reached the end of the report, he jumped out of his chair. "Yessssss!" He pumped his fist in the air. "It works!"

Mr. Stretcher slapped his back in congratulations. "Well done, boy. We can finally get the mock-ups off for approval for 3D printing. I'll try to fast track the paperwork, but with these numbers, there should be no problem getting it approved for field testing."

"When do you think it could be ready?"

"Not sure exactly. The fastest it could possibly get into the lab would be six months to maybe a year. Be patient. You did a good thing, and are one step closer to being able to use it in the field. I'm sure you'll get plenty of chances to test the scanner."

"Six months is too long. One more day is too long. Please tell me there is another way to fast track it. I need it."

"Sorry, boy. This is where company nonsense enters into your classwork. All you can do is wait. Go home, shower, get some rest. You will need it before starting the beta testing. You are worthless to the girl in this state of self-neglect. Please, Dexter." Mr. Stretcher's nose turned up at Dexter's stench.

He mulled over the request he had heard a million times before. At this point, there wasn't anything else to do. He worked and studied hard to get into this class. The calculations for the mock-ups were accurate, and now they were completed. He felt a rush of relief and nervousness. Utter exhaustion took over, and he slumped. "Maybe you're right. Maybe I should head home. But I will be back every day until the prototype is ready for beta testing." He grabbed his pack and stuffed his tablet into it.

Mr. Stretcher raised his shoulders and smiled at the tiny win. "I would expect nothing less. Now go." He shook his head toward the lab doors. "Just be ready for the field testing when we need you."

Dexter nodded. He would be ready at a moment's notice. He left the lab and started to make his way toward home. When the doors opened, the fresh air smelled foreign. He got used to the smell of must in the school and the labs—he started to equate that smell with home. Now the smell of the trees and the forest filled his nostrils with their freshness. Emma loved those smells of adventure, and now it felt like a betrayal to enjoy them by himself. No level of appreciation he could give those smells would compare to hers. She was the reason he loved it, and without her, there was no adventure in him anymore.

He made his way down the street toward his house. He really hoped his family wouldn't be there. With the amount of Mars runs his parents had to do, they most likely weren't home, but his brothers may be there. Their torments had mostly ended, but only because they never saw him. Whenever they got a chance, they still tried to moose him, but their attacks were hampered after the last summer. Dexter shot up in height and muscle after one big growth spurt, and he was at their level now. His brothers lost interest when they realized he bested them at every moosing match.

Dexter arrived home and slid through the door as quietly as he could. The house remained silent with only his footsteps creaking the floorboards on the stairs.

"Hey, Dorkster."

Dexter jumped.

"Where are you coming from?" shouted a voice from a room down the hall.

Dexter's eyes narrowed. "None of your business!" His "closest" brother Ryan's interest annoyed him to no end.

Ryan appeared in the doorway of the room. "You know there are better ways to spend your day than in a stuffy lab, right?" He folded up his arms and leaned up against the wall.

Dexter shook his head. "Just because you were too dumb to pass the entrance exams for the fast track program doesn't mean they are 'stuffy.'" He grabbed what he assumed were clean clothes from a stack on the floor.

Ryan cleared his throat. "I didn't get into the program because of my sweet piloting skills, and *you know that*." He sneered. Dexter knew he wasn't wrong. His brother did score impossibly high on the pilot program entrance exam. He had no idea how though. From what he could tell, his brother wasn't even interested in the shuttle program. In fact, his brother didn't care about anything in particular at all, other than always being around to annoy him. His presence always shadowed Dexter, whenever he was home, which was a good reason for Dexter to sleep at the lab so often. His older brother somehow turned into a stereotypical annoying little brother and appeared at the most inconvenient times.

"Get lost, Ryan. I need to shower." He waved his fingers like shooing at a fly.

Ryan shrugged and moved out of the way. "Fiiiiiine. You do need to shower. You smell horrible." He held his hand to his nose and waved away the stench from another late night at the lab. Dexter locked eyes with his brother and sauntered past him toward the bathroom. As he dropped his brother's gaze, a small smirk appeared on Ryan's face before he turned away. The little-brotherly jabs had finished for today, but they were a reminder, if anything, they were still brothers, and family.

19

August

Merah
6 months after E2 contamination

To: General Proximate August

Please give an update regarding the progress of your student. I expect a full report for my analysis before our meeting tomorrow. See you then. - General Sotora

H is mother messaged him right in the middle of a lesson with Emma. He hoped she wouldn't notice the shared screen notification on his holo. His weekly reports between him and his mother about this student's sessions were to be kept secret. She peered at the holo screen with widened eyes and roared in laughter. "You have a fungi problem here on Merah? That is hilarious," she said, and went back to studying. He exhaled, glad that she didn't notice the message on his screen.

Such a curious creature she was, not scared of her new surroundings, but racing through the storehouses of knowledge her holo provided. She ate up each of the lessons he gave her over the last few months. He trained her in many of their Protector ways, from the extent of the problems they managed through their portal assignments, to the technology they used to combat the testy weather patterns in the city sector. He had three goals, as his mother explained: First, to gather any and all information regarding her solar system; second, to critique Emma's capabilities; and after a full assessment, third, to assign her a small but very specific place in their society.

It had been six months of him training Emma. He hoped to gain more information from her for his next report to his mother, but he had to do so with limited interruption. His last report contained more information than he gathered today. The uniqueness of some of the arts described by Emma sucked him in, more than her planet's faster-than-light plans. The music, the dances, the art and paintings she spoke of intrigued him to no end. He asked so many questions about her society that sometimes he forgot to ask her about their technology and advancements in what she called their "MST program." It sounded like there were more aspects of their shuttle run supply services that might be useful. The science seemed fairly simple from how she explained it. The warp bubble created faster-than-light travel, and the gravity generator ensured their safety. The mode of transportation couldn't necessarily breach Merah's current safety measures, but, with some key updates, the planet's defense system could potentially be penetrated. Thankfully, he was fairly sure her solar system was too far away by this mode of travel, but only the Scouts really knew the capability of other planets outside his scope of reference.

August had been born on Merah. He lived the entirety of his life with an innate fear of an impending attack on their society. They had long banished the horrible Mentiren from ruling over the Amethites, but his mother constantly impressed upon him the possibility of an upcoming invasion. They needed to be prepared. They constantly needed to create the best tech and weapons in order to fight the impending doom they all knew awaited them. His whole life, none had made their appearance, but like the dutiful son he was, he worked harder to maintain the technology so it could save all of their lives.

For now, she hadn't assigned him any further portal work. His work on the portal had been slow, but steady. The capsule needed to attach to the T5 portal was to be installed earlier that week. He hoped that after a successful sync, they would be able to create a portal to a new world. The news couldn't easily travel to him while he was with his student, but he hoped he would get further information from his mother at their meeting tomorrow. For now, he had a report to write.

"Okay, I think that's enough for today. It's getting late. I'll message the food processing center to stay open a tad bit longer, if you think you can make it there fast." He offered this to her as an incentive to pry her away from studying in the lab.

"I guess I could eat." She couldn't resist the temptation of a late night snack at the cafeteria. She loved eating all the food she could on Merah. There was a time, probably two rotations into her Protector lessons, when she had stood in line, looking dejected. When he asked her what was wrong, she replied urgently, "I… I can't decide what I want. There are so many good things. They all look amazing. And seeing as I haven't had *any* of them before—no wait, what was that thing I had at Vargas' place?—oh, I can't remember. But it tasted amazing, and I can't believe I have so many unfamiliar choices. What should I start with? The green thing with the snotty tendrils? Or the purple crushed velvet apple?"

He softly eased her with his plain descriptions of the foods: which ones were sweet and which were savory, which helped each part of the body, for the Kabiren only ate foods that were beneficial for their body systems. He smiled at the thought of their exchange and in the revelation that she could be so motivated.

He started to send a form report, but lingered on his holo screen, and wondered exactly what he would tell his mother. But then, he started with the truth.

General Sotora,

The child from E2 is increasingly eager to be used in some capacity. She struggles with very little regarding comprehension, and we are closely coming to an end of her normal scheduled lessons. There are additional Protector field missions and outdoor training she could easily join. She excels physically for her small stature. I think she would make a great addition to the Protector team. Yes, she is young and very inexperienced in our world, but she has time for that, and she has proven to be an adept learner.

As far as additional information regarding Earth, the warp drives seem incredibly advanced for their species. I wonder at their intelligence if (in the short time that Emma has described) they have advanced their growth to their "Mars" planet and how much they could grow if they were allowed to continue at the current rate. The faster-than-light drives seem like they could be used to reach Merah, but the distance is still too great for them to be able to excel in a manner that would be noteworthy to us. I do not see any use for their knowledge, as we have shown in our trials that the FTL model for warp does not allow for arrival on this planet. The only method for arrival, as well as departure, is still the portals, and I strongly suggest we continue our studies and use my talents there. Please reference Emma's attached exam scores. I respectfully request her assignment to the Protector

*field, under the supervision of Protector
42 for the next year.*

He sent off the report to his mother with the hopes that he would finally be done with the lessons for the E2 girl, and life could return to normal for him. He learned a lot about her culture, music, the arts. He would remember every detail of her hums and her dancing. But he had grown weary of them now, for all his interest in these humans' capacity for beauty, it wouldn't advance their technology, and he felt it pointless to continue learning about them. The E2 portal had not shown any additional entries by the humans, and therefore they could rightly assess that no one would follow Emma or find the portal.

The Mentiren were smart. They had found the perfect hiding place to build the portal on Earth, but he wondered why they had not built the corresponding portal for arrivals on Earth. Something had to have happened in order for their work to be halted. Emma was so young to have been thrown off her world, but he wondered at the chances of her finding that portal. The odds were incredibly low, but find it she did. But he had fed his curiosity enough, and he needed to move on. The possibility of attack and portal work needed his attention, and he felt he had found a suitable position on this planet for Emma. Now he just hoped his mother would agree.

20

Emma

Merah
9 months since E2 contamination

Emma exited the lab and jogged down to the food processing center. Her lessons had proven useful. She spent nine months under August's mentorship. She squeezed enough information from him to prove that the Kabiren were hiding something. What exactly was hidden, other than the true creators of the portals, she wasn't sure. The logs on her holo screen showed further oddness in Kabiren tech. There were strange spikes in the advancement of technology in their history. Every single piece, whether a blaster, or her holo screen, seemed to be awkwardly combined like a piece of pottery barely held together by a clay mixed with a metal that wouldn't mesh. She pretended to be ignorant of Earth's technology enough, it seems, to ensure

August wouldn't question even more. From what she could tell, Merah developed a well-organized system when the Kabiren arrived. She dreaded thinking about what it was like with the Mentiren here if this is what the Kabiren-Amethite relationship was like. August asked unending questions about Earth. He hid his purpose very well, with his questions about her dancing and music, all a distraction to show a well-rounded interest in Earth, she assumed. Probably to mask his apparent need to know every detail about the FTL shuttles.

Why did he need to know so much? The entire city had a craving she couldn't quite describe when she first arrived. She also hadn't noticed it right away. Only after being in headquarters and only after her consistent interactions with August did she see it. All of these lessons ultimately led to the same conversations. This advancement here, that advancement there. The Kabiren had a snobbish pride in their seemingly helpful approach to the Amethites. They owed their survival to the Kabiren, and were grateful to do their part in protecting their planet from outsiders. She was the newest arrival, and the most curiosity-inducing. They hadn't had a new intelligent visitor in a long time it seemed. But her random conversations with the Kabiren got off track easily. They always discussed further and further about the stupidity of other races. The inventiveness of the Kabiren was praised as if they were the only ones in possession of technology, and the only ones capable of understanding it.

Emma enjoyed her science classes back home. The base for carbon life had always interested her, as well as the studies of Alcubierre. Miguel Alcubierre developed the mathematical equation that made warp travel possible.

Referred to most often as the Alcubierre or White drive, faster-than-light travel made vast-distanced travel possible. Now on Merah, she got to learn about how *she* was able to travel so far. Complexity in life showed in physics; she loved to entertain the possibilities of their compatibility. This allowed her to understand the process behind her transport through the E2 portal. It fascinated her, but the process seemed disjointed. August let it slip when she first began her lessons with him. The Kabiren *didn't create the portals,* and therefore were stuck in continual maintenance they didn't fully understand. She couldn't pry anything further during her lessons after that. It was a momentary lowering of his guard, she assumed, a small weakness he had shown her, but he didn't make that mistake again.

A blip of a message appeared on his screen before he hid it just now. She was sure of it—he kept detailed tabs on her. His mother was General Sotora, so it made sense for him to send her information regarding their lessons. Emma feared the woman, even her presence in passing made Emma's stomach drop. She could never let music or dancing slip out in the presence of the general or her Scouts. The Kabiren had rules. No extracurricular activities. They kept a firm hold on the population in this respect. A sense of urgency surrounded all assignments given which ultimately led everyone to believe they didn't have time to apply themselves to any of the arts. Each task and assignment had a veiled threat attached to it. The orders always ended with a "to stop an impending threat" or "to be prepared in the event of a threat." To be sure, this made for a very productive planet, but the lack of beauty showed through with choppy, meshed together, broken tech, all developed with a rushed hand.

The portals were different—created by the Mentiren—if what August admitted was true. All the information she was allowed to find on them only referenced a vague suggestion of "evil." They were known for placing the Amethites at a disadvantage, that part proven true by Lina's account. Emma wasn't so sure of the accuracy of the Mentiren stories. For how could a race that created tech as beautifully artistic and intricate as the portals lack the complete sense of goodness described in these accounts? It didn't add up.

August dismissed her from her lesson a bit early today. He used food as an excuse to get her to leave, probably so he could write his report, but she welcomed the much needed early release from being a prisoner of her tutor. She finally arrived at the food processing center. The smell wafted through the air from the food before her. "It smells like Boden meat! I thought you hadn't received the order with the last shipment!" she exclaimed to the cafeteria staff. They smiled and handed her the fresh food. The meat hit her mouth and immediately travelled to her growling stomach.

Satisfied with her quick dinner, she got up and headed for the main doors, but paused. August released her early. Finally, she had time to herself, alone. The complex wasn't bustling at its usual pace, and she could easily slip out through the cafeteria doors. She glanced around at the staff who disappeared into the food processing center. She tiptoed toward the back doors and slid outside. Time for her to explore.

The hill outside the headquarters was layered with fire-orange trees. She found this hill on one of her jobs where she shadowed August and knew it would be one of the first places she would visit on her free day. She wasn't given much down time, and though she had studied so much about this planet, she rarely fully enjoyed it. She inhaled a deep breath as she sat in the breeze. The scent was grass-like with a hint of honey. The sweetness in the air filled her lungs. Since her arrival over nine months ago, she accepted the terms of this new life and would take what she could get. Her own field training would start tomorrow and she was ready. The prospect held an excitement she hadn't felt since her adventuring days on Earth.

Earth...

She held in a choked breath and let it out slowly. Thoughts of Mom, Dad, and little Jane flashed before her. A gasping breath filled her lungs again, and she counted each of them. 1, 2, 3: The tall tree to her right beckoned her to sit so she could focus on evading the oncoming panic, and she crawled to sit under its boughs. Finally, her brain had a small break. She wasn't in a lesson with August, or studying her holo in her quarters. Normally, there wasn't much time for her to think beyond self-preservation. But at this moment, she could sit with the impossibility of her situation and the thought of never going home again. Trapped in a completely new world she needed to learn quickly, she didn't know who she could trust. Lina was helpful, but was only available by message, never in person. The only other person around was August, and he definitely hadn't given her enough of himself for her to trust. He evaded her endless questions. "What happened to the Mentiren?" she would ask, only to be met with some remark about how the monsters were gone for good.

Emma stood up slowly and refocused. She reassured herself of the good: She was on *Merah–the Merah*. That same planet in the stories her father told her every single night before she went to bed. He spun the story so that no detail was lost on her. She knew the feel of it and now stood solidly on it. Merah with its deep screaming colors, right down to the burning orange of the trees was *exactly* as he described. With her father having lived only on Earth, she wondered at the sheer impossibility of his detail.

"How could he have known the details of this planet?" Emma whispered to herself. She loved the tales she heard of Featherstone, but the Red Planet fascinated her. She always managed to pry more of the story out of her father after he ended with the normal "and the queen was never heard from again" phrase. The story he continued with was that the Queen of Featherstone reached her destination of the enigmatic red planet. With great advances and amazing cultures, it bled with knowledge and understanding of the galaxies around it. The queen found a hub with tech resources she planned to take back to Featherstone, but something went wrong. She fled, not back to her beloved planet Featherstone, but rather to an unknown blue planet.

Lost to her world, the queen eventually found love and family and resigned herself to a quiet life. Now, standing on that planet, one that she wanted so desperately to find, Emma wondered why so many would want to find their way *here*. The Red Planet fabled to have immeasurable and unending levels of technology, but the way August asked her about their warp capability made it seem like they lacked some knowledge of basic physics. Some of their technology *was* truly amazing—the holo screens, the universal translator beam, and lastly those beautiful portals. But even those felt like a hodgepodge held together by a weak piece of scotch tape.

August deliberately withheld information about their technology. Her lessons were filled with his dodges. But the high level of interest in a planet like this didn't make sense. Merah being the most technologically advanced planet in *all the galaxies;* it was a story that was too good to be true. This would be an amazing feat if the general population of galaxies outside of Merah all told the same exaggerated story. There were other species that lived on this planet, and she saw visitors come *in* through the portals by headquarters, but she never saw them *leave*. How could that same story get out if nobody ever left? She wished she could explore Merah without the uneasy feeling in her gut.

If the stories her father told were real, that meant the queen was real, too. How did he know her? Such a great loss for the queen, to have lived and visited such wondrous planets as Featherstone and Merah, only to be stuck on a random blue planet with no way home. Emma had lost so much, too. She closed her eyes as if to sear into her memory what she had lost, and she wondered if the queen had done the same. The colors of the outdoors swirled around her. She felt the wind pass around her body, thicker than the wind on Earth. Nine months had passed since she came here, and Emma forced herself to remember the details of her adventures in her small forest, in her small corner of her old world.

Emma stood up on the hillside and continued her adventure on the Red Planet, now *her* red planet. She was stuck here with no way home and had to navigate a veiled system she didn't understand. The suns began their descent into the night. The deep reds turned to dark blue with grayish-purple hues, and she watched the first sun, Miata, settle for a moment on the horizon. It was the first time in her busy schedule she allowed herself to watch the radiant suns set. The second sun, Cal—short for something she couldn't remember—made its trip toward the horizon. It seemed slower than Miata, but still as graceful, and for a quick moment before it fell beyond the horizon, Cal disappeared. Emma rubbed her eyes and shook her head, and by the time she adjusted, Cal sat in its place again still falling beyond the horizon. Emma looked around to see if there was anyone around who noticed as well, but she spotted no one in sight. Maybe she caught a glimpse of something she hadn't studied yet. She opened up a search on the older model holo screen that August gave her for her studies.

Search term: "Cal anomalies"

Returned results: "none"

"Huh, that's weird," she whispered.

Search term: "Cal is short for"

Returned results: "Cal, short for Calypso, the second sun of Merah, with an…"

"Calypso! That's what it is short for…Now why does that sound familiar? Let me try to narrow this search."

Search term: "Calypso disappearance"

Returned Results: "NULL"

"NOTHING!" She screamed at her screen. "How are there absolutely no results for that?" It must have been her imagination. She groaned and flumped her body to the ground. "I may be a little insane," she whispered and rubbed her temples. The confusion crept into her body, and she fought an urge to move out in the open—too much exposure here to spin and arabesque through it all. Someone from Headquarters could see.

A shadow crept nearby and raised a hand in a 'hush' motion. Emma dipped her body lower into the surrounding leaves. A second shadow met it with low tones of a greeting.

"Were you followed?" the first shadow asked.

"No one knows I'm here," the second replied.

"That's not what I asked," the first shadow said in an irritated whisper.

"There's no one out here. Not from here, to headquarters, to the village of Dvaarapaal. I *know* our people are scared to be out here this close to Kabiren headquarters, but we are normal beings, taking a normal everyday stroll. It is not that big of a deal."

Emma froze during the tension, and she could picture the first shadow's gritted teeth. "*It is a big deal, when you are meeting up with a labelled Mentiren sympathizer.* What if another Scout sees you meeting up with me? That would put you under great suspicion, and we *need* you to stay in your position."

"Fine, I'll check to see if there are any other Scouts in the area." The shadow returned a negative beep on his holo for the surrounding area. "Are you happy now? No Scouts are here."

"Yes. Now can you please give me a briefing of your last mission?"

"It was indeed a dud. The lead on the technology the Kabiren were hoping to get was a failure. Partly due to the false information we patched into the system, and partly due to the constant redirecting of the Scout groups. I swear the Scouts switching positions is turning out to be incredibly confusing. I assume that's what the general is wanting so we aren't all being sent to the same areas, and she doesn't want any of us getting too friendly with the locals we steal from."

"Were you able to obtain any new information since our last meeting?"

"Nothing conclusive, but there is some weird chatter resurfacing about the Nerezza.

Not sure what it means, but there are more searches about her logged among the Scouts. I also see a few more secret meetings with the general than normal. There is some sort of problem, but I haven't made out exactly what it is."

"Good, the more problems the general has, the less likely she will see us coming. Keep on that. I'd like to know if they're getting anywhere in the search for the queen."

"Great, I'll ping you the next time we need to meet."

"Until then."

"Until then."

The two figures parted ways and left, each in their own direction. Emma exhaled a long release of air bottled up in her lungs. Who were those people? This added an additional layer of confusion surrounding the Kabiren. Secret meetings, a Mentiren sympathizer, and a hidden queen was a lot to take in. Emma's tired brain could only process so much information in one sitting. What exactly are the Kabiren up to on those Scout missions? All of the reports she saw in her training with August stated they were working *with* the local people for technology. But those guys said *steal*. What exactly are they stealing, and why?

21

August

Merah
9 months since E2 contamination.

Uncertainty filled the air as August passed through the blindingly white corridor to meet his mother. Normally, his briefings were held in the main meeting room. But today, she demanded his presence in her private offices. He wasn't sure why, but he knew it didn't bode well for him. His last update regarding Emma didn't contain any astounding or brilliant information. The report contained his recommendation to complete Emma's mentorship. He couldn't gather any more from her, so his lessons were unnecessary.

As he walked down the hall, he hid his concern and nodded to the Scouts rushing past him through the hallways on the top floor. The guard by his mother's office stood silent, and he didn't flinch until August spoke.

"I am here to see my mother. Please note our meeting is in her personal calendar, not the official one."

The guard glanced at the holo screen on his helmet and tilted his body to display the entryway for August to enter. The connecting corridor to his mother's office was a maze. If you didn't know it by heart, you would easily get lost. He loved them. Of course he would, since he designed them. There was beauty in a job well done. He glanced at the fake hallway, trickery evaded and smiled. He came upon his mother's actual office and heard lowered voices. He waited outside of the entry door and listened.

"...with these instances?" a Scout questioned.

His mother responded matter-of-factly, "No, I don't think that will help. We need to keep the girl from finding the portal she seeks. You have done well in deleting the references of its disappearance from the official records, but we still may have to consider resorting to its destruction."

"But we have no idea where to look for it. The Nerezza ensured that would be the case when she stole the locations of the final portals. If we don't even know where it is, how can she, a girl who doesn't know anything about this planet?"

"I cannot risk her leaving this planet, or finding the portal, no matter how implausible it may be. I am not sure if she believed that it didn't exist. She will be kept busy by my son. Hopefully after she has been shown the wonders of this planet, she will give up any pursuit of going home. If she is truly who I think she is, we have to be on guard."

"Didn't your son report she has no idea about the Nerezza?"

"Yes, and I would like to *keep* it that way. Please continue in your search for the portal, discreetly, of course."

This lull gave August a good opportunity to appear. He didn't know why he felt the need to conceal his presence at first, but something impressed upon him that this information was a secret. He walked in mid stride trying to hide the fact that he listened at the door.

"General, I'm here for the meeting you requested," he announced loudly. The Scouts next to his mother gave a slight bow and left the room immediately. His mother barely glanced at him.

"You're late," she noted.

"To be fair, this meeting was scheduled for later today," he retorted.

She glared at him. "The meeting was adjusted to *my needs*, not to your whimsy. I needed to speak with you regarding your last report on the E2 girl. Your recommendation for her to enter the Protector field is approved, however, she will not be under Protector 42. She will be under your care."

"What? Mother, do you really feel this is where my skills are being fully utilized? I haven't worked on the upgrades to the portals in over nine months."

His mother's face hardened at his words. "You *will* do as I ask. How dare you question your general? Know that I have given every person the *exact* job for their skillset, and you are no different."

He lowered his head. "Forgive me, general. I will do as you instruct. Would you like me to set her up for field training immediately?"

"Yes. Make sure you continue to send me weekly reports on her progress. I would specifically like to know her reactions to her experiences here."

"Anything in particular you would like me to be on the lookout for?"

"Not really. We will make sure you get the *right* assignments. Help her as you would help any other trainee, but give her progress reports directly to me, not another supervising Protector."

"As you wish." He sensed that pressing the issue further would result in an even further tightening of his mother's lips. She still withheld her conversation with the Scouts from him.

He didn't understand it. He was, after all, the one solely responsible for the girl on Merah, and he doubted she was any threat to them whatsoever.

"You are dismissed."

He narrowed his eyes and hesitantly bowed to his mother while backing away through her office doors. He always knew the Nerezza did something devastating. But stealing the locations of the last phase of portals? There were other portals on the planet they didn't know about? How could that be? He always thought he mapped the planet in its entirety, and not knowing of a portal location made him uneasy. He would maintain a close eye on Emma, and see what assignments were the "right assignments" for them to complete.

22

Lina

Merah
10 months since E2 contamination

Another day, another job. Lina balanced herself on one foot outside the rickety portal, and she took aim at the contaminate surrounding it. The fresh ground had only a few burn marks from her blaster when she finished.

"That job was quicker than I thought," Lina said to Maut while she surveyed the portal. Noticeable cracks and fissures fragmented it, evidence of long-term disrepair. She would have to log it in. They may be able to patch it, but it didn't look good. The cylinders started to buckle. Apparently, this one hadn't been used in a while. Lina was surprised that any foreign element could make it through the portal under the circumstances.

Message: Headquarters Portal Repair Unit

Portal 48 contains multiple disruptions to the metal. Repair team requested.

The message sent with a riveting ping. "Oh, my life is soooo interesting," Lina muttered aloud. "At least I have you." She held out her arm and flicked her fingers, and Maut flew to her shoulder and screeched. "Yeah, yeah." She pulled out a treat from her pocket, and Maut licked it from her hand.

Since her portal assignment was by Nira, she didn't need a transport, but this meant a further trek on her own two legs, and they were already tired. She promised Vargas she would meet him at the markets the moment she finished this job, but it was getting darker earlier than normal, and she didn't know if she had the energy to make conversation, even with a long-time friend like Vargas.

The streets in her hometown teemed with life. She furrowed her brow at her former coursemates from primary, throwing up an expander field, just to run into it, being reckless just to feel more alive. The Kabiren would never approve of this behavior. She glanced at old familiar faces but names she couldn't place. Like a dream with blank faces that are recognizable only by a gut feeling. They nodded at her presence as a Protector but not an equal. She shrugged. They didn't pay attention to her when she was little, so how could she assume they would now? Maybe deep down she thought her "Protector" title would earn their recognition. Even her parents ignored her and disapproved of her title. Their veiled hatred for the Kabiren bled through all their actions. Deep down, she knew they would become betrayers. An invisible chill creeped over her entire body.

Her life had become a busy rush of assignment after assignment. She accepted so many in a row that she didn't allow herself an opportunity to dwell on thoughts of her parents. Her inconsistent upbringing made her cringe. The memories meshed with each other melting away in a blur. She shook them away, arriving at the bliss of her empty home — a place just the right size for her and Maut. He scurried over to a small pillow on the floor and tugged it into place with his black teeth.

Her Protector quarters were a few blocks away from the house she grew up in. The quarters were small and colorless. The beige walls and precise furniture were exactly what Lina needed. Her oasis from life became those empty walls. She was glad her kitchen was prepped with artificial nutrients ready for her arrival. If she fed the pit in her stomach, it would calm the disquieting thoughts and memories. Her instructor would be proud of her productivity for finishing her meal quickly.

After she cleaned up and placed her utensils in their precise storage spot, she retreated to her bedroom. She flopped on her bed. The softness of the cushion enveloped her. Her eyes slid closed and were on the verge of a peaceful sleep when she was interrupted by a nonstop ding from her front door. She turned on her holo screen for a view of the monster who dared to interrupt her rest.

There stood Vargas with his outrageous beaming smile. Lina hung her head in exhausted aggravation. She slid off her bed and trudged her heavy feet to the front door. She barely raised her head to unlock the doors before Vargas rushed in.

"You have such an annoyingly chipper presence when I'm tired."

"Yeah, but you still love me." He winked. "Were you sleeping? It is BARELY after nightfall. How old are you?" He pranced around with a disapproving click in his tongue. "I asked you to come to the shop when you were done for the day. Why didn't you answer my messages?"

"Yes, my whole existence is to be at your beck and call, wherever you command, my lord." She made a sarcastic bow but lost her balance.

"You *know* that's not how I meant it."

She shrugged. "I had a long day. What do you need?"

"Do you think you have it in you to make the looong walk to my shop? I have a surprise for you."

"Ugh," she said in disgust at the thought of having to leave the comfort of her home. On the one hand, she was exhausted. On the other hand, she was still a young Amethite who wanted to maintain at least the *perception* of her youth. "I guess I can come. Give me a minute to change." She walked back to her sleeping quarters and returned quickly with fresh fabric against her skin. Its crisp feeling renewed her vigor, and she was now capable of handling the world, or at least handling Vargas. "Bye, Maut. I'll be back soon." She bent down to pat his head while he slept curled up and joined Vargas. They left her home, and the fresh warm air pressed against her face with each step.

Her quarters were a relatively short distance from the market and Vargas's shop. The status of Protector came with many perks, one of them being the location of her quarters. Very few received housing so close to the markets, and she knew why she needed the proximity after her long days on assignment. They quickly arrived at the small electronics shop and Lina huffed at the noticeable disrepair. Vargas dabbled with used, old parts. His customers frequently needed replacement parts, which is why he maintained the shop's license from headquarters to operate. The Old Ones knew they needed these smaller shops in the outskirt villages to keep up with their—some of the time, or rather most of the time—failing parts.

Lina followed her friend to the back of his little shop and passed by the same slew of mismatched electronic parts. The twisted metal and wood walls hung bots, blasters, holo bands, and every other piece of tech she knew of. Everything showed a little bit of wear, a little rough edges with rusted metal. The smells of hot metal and glass were like home to her. She spent many days after courses here with Vargas and his family to escape the ever distant nature of her own family. How Vargas could maintain his chipper attitude after the fire was beyond her understanding. She was still angry about the accident, and they weren't even her parents.

He kept up the shop well enough to keep living on his own, and when they died he had something to delve into to replace the gaping hole they left. She loved the way he handled his loss, in a stride and an ability impossible for her. He, being the complete opposite of her in every way, had personality, grace, and even physical attributes. Maybe that is why she always loved him. He was loyal beyond all measure, and happy, and it made her want to be that kind of friend as well. He made her a better person, a more loyal friend, and she held onto the moments she felt like a good person.

They arrived at the back of the shop, and Lina noticed a large drape over some mystery item. It took up the entire back end of the shop. "What monstrosity have you acquired?" She asked him as they approached it. He smiled his gaping smile and raised his eyebrows twice with an excited nod.

"Ready?" he said, grasping at the edges of the drape.

"Will I ever be?" She held her breath in an exaggerated motion.

"You joke… but you won't be joking after you see it." Vargas tugged at the drape, and the fabric slowly fell to the floor. Lina's eyes widened at the reveal of a beautiful roller. Clearly, it was cobbled together by him; the meshing being a signature of his work. "How long did this take you?"

"Well, it would have taken me a lot less time had you not constantly popped by my shop. I had to frantically hide my starter pieces the first time you brought the E2 girl over here."

"How was I to know you were working on some master project? You never mentioned anything. Besides, why would you *need* to hide it?"

"Because… it's for you."

Her mouth dropped. Sure, it was a second-hand mess of a roller, but Vargas had made it for *her*, specifically. She couldn't think of a better gift she ever received. No blaster, no housing, could ever compare to this thing of beauty. And it was all hers. The process of expressing gratitude had always been difficult for Lina. It was always either too over the top or completely underwhelming. "I… I don't know what to say."

"Meh, you don't have to say anything. Do you like it?" He asked in earnest.

"I love it. I can't believe you did this for me." She shook her head.

"You always seem exhausted from walking out to all the mission grounds, and you still frequently get assignments everywhere. I wanted to help a tiny bit. When I saw the base of this beast being offloaded, I snagged it and turned it into my pet project. No big deal." He waved off her praise in that one quick sentence. She hopped in and leaned into the curves of the roller. She felt the controls and the circuits come to life with the flick of the switch. Its light hum energized her while the holo displays synced with her personal tech, and the blaster and her wristband options displayed on her screen. Lost in her excitement, she knew deep down she would never be able to repay her friend's kindness.

"I have no idea where I'm going to store this baby, but I really appreciate it. You do not know the level of my gratitude, Vargas." She reached for the drape that was tossed aside onto random tools and electronics strewn about. "Hey, can I take this too?" she asked yanking at the drape.

"Wait!" Vargas motioned her to stop pulling at the fabric, but it was too late. Her motion jerked the shop's inventory, and it spilled over the entire floor.

"I'm so sorry." She fell to the floor reaching to clean the mess. The fallen items revealed a backdrop of colors and stretched paper. She was enthralled by the swirls and texture of paintings—multiple squares with images of cliffs, trees, and vast planets depicted on them. There were so many different paintings she couldn't even count them if she wanted to. Vibrant reds and oranges depicted a landscape so familiar, yet so distant she couldn't place it. She marveled at their beauty. "What are these?" She examined the sheer volume of creations lined up against the wall.

"Umm, okay... so... please don't tell the Kabiren. But I have been working on these for a while now. Ever since the fire, I have needed more of an outlet than just used circuit boards, parts, and metal inventory.

"You know you aren't supposed to have this extracurricular activity." She gave the door a side glance, but still couldn't pry her eyes fully away from the artistic display. "The time this all must have taken you...How did you get the paint for them? Non-industrial paint hasn't been available since before our time."

"I, um, made it." He grabbed the back of his neck. "With the plants and such from the hillside we used to play on, and with the glue needed for some of the blaster parts. I have everything I need in the shop to make it. So I did. Yes, the Kabiren don't allow for work outside of my upgrades, but this is something I *needed* to do. Surely, you understand that need. *You* wanted to become a Protector to *do* something, and you did it. What I need to do, my outlet, is this."

She interrupted, "But if the Kabiren ever found out about it..."

"They would strip me of my license, and I would be out of a job. I know. Please find it in your heart to keep this quiet. *Please,* Lina."

On the one hand, she had a responsibility, a sworn duty to the Kabiren who trained her. They gave her purpose and meaning, and all they asked from her was for her to care for their ways and follow their orders. Everyone knew there was no room for activities like this;   they didn't have time to revel in the beauty of color or art. The Mentiren could return at any minute and the planet needed to be prepared. They *owed* it to the Kabiren to work solely on technology, not to engage in these frivolous activities. On the other hand, this was *Vargas*, her best friend. He helped her through so many hurdles in her life, extended and over-extended his hand whenever she needed him. How could she not return the favor in his time of need? This was the only way he could cope after the fire, and how could she take that away from him?

Not to mention what would happen to him once the Kabiren knew the extent of this mistake. One offense, they may let slide, but this? This was much more than one offense. Lina looked at several years worth of work around her. Vargas poured his heart and soul into these. They were beautiful, and they were an extension of him. The Scouts would do any number of horrible things to him if they found out. How could she do that to her best friend who would never think twice before helping her if she needed it? He now asked for her help, and her secrecy. Now she could show a tiny expression of kindness and friendship, one that paled in comparison to the many times Vargas had shown her the same throughout the years. With her decision, she could be a good person to him. She wouldn't waste the opportunity.

"Of course, I'll stay quiet, you flout monger. How could I do anything else?" She smiled and winked at him hoping to quell his unease.

His shoulders dropped, relieved. "Thank you." He started clearing out the mess around the room. Lina bent down to help.

"Let me at least help with this, then you can help me with getting that amazing roller home. Deal?"

He smiled at her while placing the parts carefully along the wall to hide his beautiful creations. He nodded in agreement.

"Deal."

23

Dexter

Earth

1 year and eight months since Emma's disappearance

A slight mist clung to Dexter's cheeks, a frigid air that chilled him to the bone. He buttoned his raincoat tighter around his neck. He wouldn't stop his walks now solely because of a tiny lack of comfort. These morning walks were his way of mapping the woods and a kind of homage to the girl who left too soon. He needed to map the terrain and the plant life to get an accurate and consistent picture before his use of the DNA sequencer, and he turned the boringness into an adventure. Any activity that reminded him of her was comforting. Enough time had passed, he forgot to count the days and months, and he felt guilty. He swore never to forget her and always honor her memory, but here he was not able to remember the exact count of days since her disappearance. He'd failed her.

A jarring beep rang out from his tablet, and his instructor's face stretched across his screen. The preview showed the overly-eager face of Mr. Stretcher. Dexter rolled his eyes and answered. "What, Mr. Stretcher? I'm currently mapping out here."

"Glad I caught you, Dexter. Can you spare a minute to come into the lab? I have a surprise for you. A *certain* prototype is finished, and it's beautiful. You need to see it."

His eyes widened, and his heart pumped faster. The sequencer, *his sequencer*, now sat there in the lab. He ended the call and raced through the forest and down the hill to the school. The doors slid open upon seeing his face and granted him access to the lab level. In his haste, he left the wet slick of outside caked on his boots. Twice he almost fell.

He reached the lab, panting, and bent down to catch his breath. "Where…is… it?" he managed to say through his huffs.

"Whoa, that was fast. Did you run the whole way here?" Mr. Stretcher noticed.

"Yes, of course. Where is it?!" Dexter exclaimed through his teeth. He did not like the disapproving tone. "C'mon, man, I'm serious."

"Well, if you would take time to notice, we also have a guest here." He pointed to the other kid in the room. Dexter looked over at the newcomer's grinning face. This kid was barely older than him.

"Who are you, and why are you here?" He looked at his instructor. "Why is he here?"

"Dexter, this is Jericho. He was recently assigned to help oversee this project. He requested to be a part of the beta testing. He has high honors in this program and I think you could benefit from the help. Maybe a few less sleepless nights?"

"I prefer to work alone," Dexter spat out through a clenched jaw. "No offense, Jericho."

"None taken, I assure you." Jericho fiddled with the glass panel display on the armrest and with one swipe maneuvered effortlessly closer to Dexter. "I understand the need for peace and quiet while working. Trust me, I won't be a nuisance. I believe I can be a good resource for field testing, if you'll let me."

"Fine, you can come. Don't slow me down though." He glanced at the wheelchair beneath Jericho.

Jericho scoffed. "Ha, trust me, with how I have this baby programmed, *you* need to be the one to not slow *me* down." He nodded at Mr. Stretcher and the instructor snorted a laugh.

"It's true, Dexter. Jericho is the kid behind some of the recent tweaks in programming, if you noticed. He is the main reason it made it through to testing so quickly."

"But it's still *my* design, right?"

"Of course, the prototype is still your design. It only needed a few small improvements. That's where Jericho stepped in."

Dexter grabbed the sequencer and ran his fingers over the sides of it. He studied the gentle curves. The weight felt lighter than he had anticipated from the plans. It held a faint glow of light around the power up, but it was Dexter's beacon of hope. This was his ticket to find Emma, and he wouldn't stop until he had some answers. "Can I take it out for a test run?"

"Here, sign these forms for release of the equipment, and make sure you return it back to the lab after every test. Got it?"

"Got it." He looked at Jericho. "You ready for this?"

"Let's roll." He raised his eyebrows at his own pun while Dexter shook his head with a smile.

"You done?"

"Never."

Dexter darted out of the lab. He was too eager to get started with testing, and so he headed for the woods. He grabbed some random leaves in the database from his mapping adventures.

"Mr. Stretcher tells me you've been mapping most of the woods in the area around the school and neighborhood. How do you think that will help the sequencer?"

Dexter's mind was lost in his own programming. "OH MY ██████, do you have to interrupt me now?"

"Juuust trying to make conversation," he said.

"If we're going to talk about something, maybe it should be the fact that this project requires a lot of effort and stamina, as I plan on using it the majority of the time in the forest. Are you sure you're really up for the challenge?" He nodded at the chair beneath Jericho.

"You do realize that question is like me asking you how it is possible you worked on the DNA sequencer at your young age, right?"

"Touché." Dexter felt the sting of his quick judgement and thoughtless speech. "So why are you still in a chair? Many kids I've seen have opted for the nerve nanotech to rebuild their walking capability."

"For some reason my body rejected the regrowth. I don't know why exactly, but it has something to do with

135

my specific DNA. So I've tried my best to study all the programming processes linked with my motor. What you may see as wheeling, is more like, umm, floating to me. I'm in perpetual flight." He grinned widely.

"I wonder what it would be like for you on Mars with the terraformed gravity. Have you travelled there yet?"

"I haven't. I'm only a year ahead of you in the MST program. I requested this field specifically because of my interest in it, not necessarily my interest in Mars."

"I'd think you'd jump at the opportunity for any other testing on Mars."

"No. I honestly have more grounded interests. About a year and a half ago, I was puzzled by some news that surprisingly hit me hard. I thought your sequencer would be key to helping solve the mystery. I gather from some chats with Mr. Stretcher you may have the same interest."

Dexter cocked his head. He never met this kid before, and he didn't assume to be similar to anyone else in the Mars program. He rather enjoyed being a loner. He wasn't about to change that now because of some random "mystery" this kid spoke of. They reached the wide forest path. "Beta test one recording." He pointed the sequencer at the pathway and scanned through the trees in one fell swoop. It beeped with recognition of his input. "Huh, those were easy leaves to detect."

"Yeah, who woulda thought, detecting a *tree* in a *forest*." Jericho chuckled.

Dexter grinned. "Okay, so let's try something a bit more complex. Let's try a bird." He scanned through the pathway with a negative result.

"How wide is the range on it?"

"I programmed it to have a two-mile range. Ugh, did your updates decrease my range capabilities?"

"Nah, if anything they would've been improved. Did you program to weed out all the fungi and plantae?"

"Good point. I didn't check if I filtered them out. Let me do that really quick," he said while he fidgeted with the screen on the scanner. He rescanned the area and a small beep of information returned. "We have a bird. Now let's see if this thing can read something more complicated. You up for a game of hide and seek?"

"Sounds like a fantastic idea. I'm in!"

They trekked further into the forest. Dexter programmed in his DNA code and handed it to Jericho. "Give me ten minutes, then come find me." He smiled big and ran off at full speed.

Jericho waited for the DNA code to input and lined the scanner up to trigger level. "Let's see if this thing really works." He sped off into the forest.

24

August

Merah
1 year since E2 contamination

The metal floor of the Kabiren headquarters lobby felt cold and drafty. Emma was due to arrive soon, and August paced. Field training was not his favorite. This would make or break Emma. She performed excellently on her exams and adapted quickly, which was why he recommended her for the position. But he needed to show her way too many sections of headquarters she previously had no access to. His head spun with all the things he needed to do. The general became adamant about Emma taking on the Protector Emulate title, and he needed to see if she could make it. He hoped she would prove herself capable, and he could forego this babysitting. Well, not exactly babysitting, he wasn't that much older than her, but it wasn't a good look for him. He was General Proximate by birth, but this task wasn't going to gain him any respect.

Emma arrived in the field uniform August sent to her quarters yesterday. He nodded at her prompt arrival and approved of her field appearance. Nothing to critique there. Most of his trainees failed their first field day based on those two basic assessments. Her long sleeves covered right up to her wristband, and her empty field belt was fastened tight. He admired her understanding of each piece of attire and its purpose.

He nodded at her. Her hair was tied up higher than usual. "I appreciate you arriving on time today," he said.

"I appreciate the compliment, however unnecessary. When have I been late for any of my studies?"

"Fair point. I was making an unnecessary observation. I will use my words for instructional purposes only. Let's go. We have many areas of the complex to visit and not a whole lot of time to accomplish everything."

He led her toward the elevators at the center of the headquarters building. She had already been issued her personal holo band with limited capabilities unlocked, solely for messaging. Now, he needed to get her other field tools from the lab area. The process was simple with the right cataloguing. Till now, Emma had resisted the process, however with Kabiren systems, it was necessary for the release of her tools from the lab. They were DNA- issued, which helped them keep track of every piece checked out and would allow her to obtain her own equipment. She had resisted so far, but field assignment would be different. Their system worked perfectly, and she needed to conform to it.

They stood on the elevator pad and headed for the equipment lab. "Now, we are heading to the lab for all your

Protector Emulate tech before your first field testing. Every request will go through this lab." They arrived at the lab doors. With a nod at the scanner above the doors, August opened them. "I have been catalogued completely, so my genetic code not only allows my entry into the lab, but also permission to retrieve my specific equipment. See?" As he strutted through the lab doorway, it formed to display rows and rows of gadgets and equipment, and with a click, they were unlocked. The left wall of the room glowed with small discs charging. To their right, rows revealed holobands of different sizes and materials. Blasters lined the back wall and glimmered under the storage lights. He picked up a small blaster, one Emma could easily hold while remaining mobile, and said, "Follow me. The labs have practice rooms so that Protectors can get a feel for the technology outside of holo screen specs."

They arrived in one of the back rooms attached to the equipment center. A small target shield appeared about twenty feet away from them. "Now here, we are going to have a little bit of practice. I'm going to unlock this blaster. I need you to try to hit the target." He handed her the small blaster. The grip still took up most of her hand as she held it, and he wondered if she would even be able to engage the trigger. Emma brushed her hands over the metal like a careful dance, and she examined the trigger.

The target sat further away than it should for a training session, but Emma had proven herself to be adept at pretty much anything he gave her. So here they were: her, ready to learn the ins and outs of protecting Merah, and him, ready to speed her along to the finish line.

She stared down the target with both eyes clear, focused, and squeezed the trigger. Nothing happened. A small piece of metal on the side of the blaster came off. The metal was worn down underneath with lines of continual replacement. He would have to speak to his mother about the patchwork of upkeep in the weapons lab. This was shocking neglect.

Emma examined the blaster when it didn't perform as expected. Her eyebrows raised. The pin-sized hole surrounding the grip had dislodged. She grabbed it by the sides and realigned it. August raised his eyebrows and nodded. *Two minutes to figure out the dislodge problem. Maybe I should have suggested her assignment be in the weapons lab. She probably could teach some of the Scouts a thing or two.* The thought of his little student not needing him to guide her on a small trivial matter pleased him.

She pointed the blaster at the target and squeezed the trigger to a built-up surge. The energy released toward the target, but it didn't hit the mark.

"First tries are hard," August said. "Again."

She pointed the blaster a second time and pressed on the trigger gradually for a harder power surge, and the energy hit the target at the line just outside of bullseye. She scrunched her nose and frowned. "Gah!"

"Good start," he reassured her. "You'll get more practice as you use it in the field. This target practice is to ensure you know how it works and can use it safely."

She scowled at her target, determined. August reached to grab the blaster but two quick surges fired through it. Emma stood with her body squared toward the target. "HA!" She pointed at the two clear target marks. Dead center.

August glanced at the shots and pretended not to be impressed. "Let's hope you can do that when you're actually in the field."

Emma looked back at him. "Then let's get me *in* the field.

August nodded at her impatience. "We need a few more items before we head out and to grab your genetic material for your weapons."

Emma hesitated, looked down at her blaster, then said, "Let's get to it, then."

August grabbed the blaster and returned it to its place in the lab. He motioned for them to make their way out, and Emma followed. They rounded the corner in the hallway to the doors for cataloguing. Emma read the words to herself in a whisper, "Classification Archive." He knew her reluctance to come here. Maybe she was reassuring herself in some small way.

"It will only take a moment." He spoke in a softer tone and hoped it would ease her mind. It was simply classification, routine and nothing special.

They walked through, and August quickly retrieved the acknowledgement releases for Emma to sign. "Here." He displayed them on his holo. "Sign these to show we're processing your DNA to be assigned to the Protector equipment you'll need. I have selected the basic tools you'll need in the field. Your selection will grow as you request more job-specific equipment. For now, these are the only ones you'll need."

"Let's get this over with." She motioned her signature on the holo and stepped forward to the archive technician. The technician motioned her towards the species archive booth, and she stepped in. August's wristband pinged a new message from his mother. "I'll be right outside while you finish up." He motioned to the doors, and Emma nodded at him.

General Proximate August,

Please give a status update on the cataloging of the E2 girl.

General Sotora

August tightened his jaw at the unnecessary message. He was about to send her a status update. Her sending the first message request always made him look unproductive and lazy. She managed to do it. Every. Single. Time.

General Sotora,

Cataloguing of the E2 girl has commenced.

General Proximate August

25

Emma

Merah
1 year since E2 contamination

Emma stepped into the archive booth. It had several panels of white with soft, calming lights built into it and a wider top to make it feel less claustrophobic. A loud whirring started, and the lights flickered in the booth. Emma exhaled a small breath bracing herself for what she'd fought against. There was disappointment in that breath. Her only leverage with the general was not letting them catalogue her. They needed it for some reason, but she didn't know why. But if she wasn't going back home, this was her new life. In order to move forward, this was her only option. She would adapt no matter what they threw at her. Plus, she needed her tech for her training, and she didn't want to be left behind because of a simple task. This was the only way she could prove herself.

The booth's noise hummed to a lull, and the lights went out. The door opened, and she stepped out to be greeted by an archive assistant. A small Amethite held a holo screen in his hand, looking at her data.

"We should have your full results by the end of the day," he said in a monotone without glancing up from his screen. Emma wondered how many times he already said those exact words today.

"Thanks," Emma said, but she was pretty sure the small scientist wasn't paying her any attention whatsoever. She rounded the corner and headed out to meet August.

The doors slid open to reveal a preoccupied August. He mumbled to himself, and when he saw her emerge, she thought she heard him say something like "Finally."

"See, that wasn't so bad now, was it?" He smiled.

"Not at all." She scrunched her nose. "Now when do I get my own tech and not have to bum off you?" She nodded at his pack.

"They should log your information by the end of the day. Did they not tell you that? I'm going to have to talk to them about protocol."

"No no, they did say they'd be finished by the end of the day. Wasn't sure how automated the process would be. That's why I asked."

"This is *Merah*, Emma. The most advanced planet in the galaxies. Everything is automated."

"And I still have to wait until the end of the day? Okay," she pretended to check her wristband notes, "Merah, planet, *very* fast tech, check," and smiled at him.

August snorted a laugh and eased a bit. "Let's go. I received our first assignment."

"Ooh, where?"

"Just a portal assignment with some gardening." Her smile turned into a slight frown.

"Cheer up, everyone gets their gardening orders first. Let's see how you handle it."

"Fiiine, but after I nail this assignment, you better assign a *real* one, okay?"

"Promise."

They left the complex together and approached a roller parked off to the side.

August hopped in and directed her to the secondary seat. Emma harumphed with a slouch. "I thought you were training me. Doesn't that mean I need practice with driving?"

August looked to the side as if contemplating his own death. "You said you hadn't driven before on Earth."

"If I can pass a simple Kabiren piloting program, I'm pretty sure I can drive a roller. You *know* I've gone over the details a million times."

He looked back at her with resignation. "Okay… Once we are out of the city, I'll let you take over."

"Yesss!" Emma exclaimed in a loud shout that echoed through the roller. They sped quickly through the lanes and headed outside the metropolis. She took in the buildings of the city with its glass and metal, harsh angles and mishmashed elements. From afar, the structures lacked a curved look which would have enhanced the beauty and flow into and out of the city. *They probably pieced this place together like they pieced all the other tech they "designed,"* she thought with a frown.

When they reached the outskirts of headquarters, August hopped out. "Okay, as promised, E2 girl," he said, indicating toward the controls, "your turn." He smiled. Emma's eyes shined with excitement. She would finally get to try the new toy she would receive after being a year three Protector.

She hopped into the driver's seat and displayed the control panel. She pressed the starter and set the driver mode to manual. She clutched the holo panel and inserted them into the energy fields. The rush of ignition and power came over her. She expanded the map to the portal location and studied the route. There were several tiered avenues, but one looked the most exciting—and the fastest. She chose it. "Ready for this?" She waggled her eyebrows.

"Ready as I'll ever be," August said in a monotone.

His monotone disappointed her. The only time he showed an increase of interest was when he caught Emma dancing. All these other training sessions had been instruction from a masked teacher. Someone who had a reserved interest in her only because it was his job.

But she was excited to be able to take in the beauty of her Red Planet, of Merah, and from a *roller* no less. She wasn't adventuring in her small Earth forest anymore, getting lost in the tedium of its green hues. She was *living* her adventure. The roller lurched forward with her touch. Emma yipped and edged further along on her trail map. The ride was smooth and reminded her of an ORV, an off-road vehicle, Grandpa let her drive around the fields by his home, back when she could visit his home. Her thoughts of her grandpa faded into a blurred face, the memory lost to the year she had already spent away from him, away from Earth. How quickly memories are replaced by a new life.

The roller whirred through the countryside, or at least what Emma called the countryside. Miles of those same plastic-like blades of grass stretched out ahead of her. In the distance, rocky mountains peaked above the orange leaves. The space between Dvaarapaal and her target was called "Aimetadi" in her Kabiren coursework, and she never asked Lina what the Amethites called this land.

They quickly arrived near the portal. Emma relived her first moments on Merah. The forest enveloped her. It felt like ages ago. She was only twelve when she came here. Now, one full year had passed, she was almost fourteen, and she loved this place. The orange wisps of trees rooted in deep black ground showcased their full beauty. She still wished she could dance among those trees like she could back home. It was what she missed the most. A lump formed in her throat, but she closed her eyes tight and swallowed it down. She had a job to do, an assignment, and she needed to do it well.

"Which portal was logged?"

August looked at his holo band and popped up the request projection. "Here, let me forward it to you. You'll be getting your own assignments soon enough anyway." He shrugged and flicked over the location and job information to her screen on the roller.

She scanned the display for the red dots scattered throughout the map. There were quite a few portals in the area, but the *gardening assignment*, as August affectionately called it, came from a localized dot. An orange glow from the brush obscured her view of a massive silver cylinder ahead of her. She released her hold on the roller, and it stopped dead in its tracks, just before the pile of brush.

"Whew." August stepped out of the Roller.

Emma raised her eyebrows. "We didn't crash. You're fine." She stepped out of the roller, and a thick block of musty, dead smells invaded their noses. "What is that smell, fish? Maybe more like rotten garlic?" Her face scrunched, and she gave August a concerned look. He did not flinch but looked straight ahead toward their target portal. Emma put on a brave face while straining to breathe and pushed aside the orange brush surrounding her. The large portal stood in front of her and beckoned her to approach cautiously. Yellow pollen drifted from the portal to the surrounding grass and trees, only to be swallowed up by the foliage and immediately rejected by it. It looked as if with every speck of pollen there was a drip of poison leaking from the plants, and the leaves cried out every time it met with the painful foreign material. Emma reached her hand out as if to comfort the hurt tree.

"I wouldn't do that if I were you." He held his hand out, blocking hers. "The spores could burn a carbon-based hand right off, and we don't know how infected the tree is. We have to be very careful."

"I'm guessing we need to set up a field to enclose the yellow particles. How wide of a range will they reach? We probably need more than one, right?"

"We shouldn't need more than we have."

Emma looked at the extent of the damage. "Will we need to destroy everything?"

"We can't allow the pollen to expand and cause further destruction. We may have to make the field a bit larger than its current radius; it seems like our video bots were late to detect the influx of particles."

"Does that happen a lot?" Emma asked.

"I haven't looked into the reports extensively, but it may happen more than we realize."

"Well, let's get started." She flexed her fingers. "All right, you have how many deflectors?"

August checked his log. "I logged out three."

"Then we have three to build a massive field." She replied. She looked at her holo map and shook her head. "We might not have enough power to build this large of a field with only three."

August focused into a blank space, sorting through options with the tech on hand. He held out his deflectors to Emma. "See what you can do, E2."

Without hesitation, she grabbed the small cylinders. The tiniest of tech, but pretty powerful according to everything she'd studied about them. They still weren't enough of a charge to handle the area they needed to destroy. If only she had one extra cylinder, then they could encapsulate the total area. She needed to mirror a fourth deflector, but not to interrupt the field. Emma glanced at her blaster, the lone equipment she was allowed to have in her field training, and smiled. She ran around the portal area placing each of the cylinders at a corner around it. She was about to make a large square field to encase the particles; all she needed was a fourth point of power. She held her defective blaster and slid off the small metal piece around the trigger, holding it to a consistent pulse and pinning the trigger down. After she carefully placed it on the ground, she aligned the deflector field and closed her eyes. "Here goes nothing," she muttered, then pressed the trigger into an overload.

The field surged into a pulsating hum. As the surge expanded, there was a loud *boom*. The blaster set off a reaction within the field and decimated all within. The ground shook underneath Emma. Her feet slid across the unstable ground, but her toes pushed her body, and she twirled away from the rubble. Her heart expanded with her unsuspected dance of escape, but as the dust settled, she fell to the ground.

August ran to her side. "Are you okay? Can you get up?" She nodded and straightened up. "You did well. The contaminate has been destroyed. And that's exactly what I would have done." He raised his face in triumph.

"Why do you keep the portals active if *this* is what they do to your world?"

August scrunched his forehead up and shrugged. "Why wouldn't we keep the portals? There are still many resources we obtain from them. Just because there might be a rapid influx of foreign material doesn't mean we stop using the portal's resources."

"So you haven't always had this level of contamination?"

"No. Our sensors on the bots are normally triggered way before we get to this level. Even then, this is the most affected I have seen Merah become. It will be okay. Merah has always been capable of amazing regrowth. It's not worth worrying about."

"I guess I feel Merah deserves better." She calculated the destruction she'd caused.

"*We* didn't build the portals, remember, but have always maintained them—"

"At the expense of the planet," she interrupted.

August snorted and retrieved information on his holo screen and forwarded it to her. "Look at this material. It is licanium, and what is licanium used for, if you can remember from your studies?"

Emma narrowed her eyes and repeated from memory in a monotone, "Licanium is the main component for the creation of deflector fields."

"And what do we need the deflector fields for?"

"Basically everything."

"Yes, so think about that before you judge how we obtain these resources. WE have the most advanced technology in *all* the galaxies. You would do well to remember that."

Emma stared blankly at the shorted deflector field. "I'll go collect the cylinders and my broken blaster." She lowered her head and walked away from him. She needed a small break alone, and a short trek to grab the tech would give her that.

"I'll send the success report. Hurry back," he said and filled out the form on his holo.

"Yeah, you send your stupid report," she mumbled to herself.

26

Dexter

Earth
2 years since Emma's disappearance

Dexter sat in his room piled over his sequencer and notes upon notes of equations. The weekend never stopped him from working on his project before, and it wouldn't now. No matter how nice of a day it was outside.

"You're always cradling that thing like a little baby," Ryan said.

Dexter's thoughts were interrupted by the surprisingly mild insult. He held the sequencer tight in his two hands and scanned through the previous day's testing notes. Lost in the data, he muttered some babbling response, and his brother walked away with a shrug. Ryan's attempt to prod Dexter to annoyance had failed, and Dexter could continue his work in peace.

He studied his notes with several screens open. "I think it may finally be capable of consistent DNA sequencing," he said to himself. A message popped up on his screen.

From: Jericho

Hey, you headin' out today? These terraforming modules are kicking my butt, and I need to get out of this lab!!!!! Can I meet up with you?

His newest and only friend's message was welcome. He knew he was ready to test his baby to search for a very specific DNA and probably could use all the emotional support he could get.

To: Jericho

Heading out in a few minutes. I need to grab something. Meet me in a half hour at the Beakman trail.

He carefully placed his tablet and sequencer in his bag and walked out the door. The last piece he needed for his project was DNA, more specifically Emma's DNA. He hadn't been to the Riley house since she disappeared and wasn't exactly sure what he could find there. Would they still have her favorite item or any trace of her that he could use for his sequencer? He would find out soon enough.

Dexter gulped his nerves down as he approached the house. It was the same distance from his as it had always been, but today it felt like miles long carrying the weight of what he was about to do. He rang the doorbell and jumped at the beeping noise. No one answered. *How thoughtless not to message ahead. Of course no one would be home.* Emma's little sister would be in school, and both her parents were still in the shuttle program. Who knew where they were in between their runs to Mars? Dexter hung his head low and paced back and forth on the porch.

He'd dreamed of today for so long, the day he would finally be able to figure out what happened. He *owed* it to her not to stop here. The neighborhood looked as dead as the house seemed, so he walked around the back. A small branch cracked from behind. Dexter jumped and turned to look. No one was there, so he swallowed his nerves and snuck around. The back porch door could be locked, but he was going to try it anyway. To his surprise, it slid open with a squeaky jarred motion. "Shh," he whispered to the door panel. He didn't need to announce his break in.

The house looked barely lived in. He wondered how that was possible with a seven-year-old living there, but who was he to judge? It also felt smaller to him now. It had been a while since he'd been inside, and he'd grown a foot since stepping through these doors. Dexter quietly crept up to Emma's old bedroom. As he opened the door, he inhaled and closed his eyes, not sure exactly what he would see. The door opened up to a bed, dressers, and a tall mirror. The same sun shone through the window that he imagined she woke up to every morning. Everything was there, in the exact same place from the days she spent here. He shook his head out of memory lane, and started his hunt.

"DNA, DNA, DNA. There has to be *something* here." He opened her closet and rifled through some boxes. One by one he disregarded their contents. Then there they were, in a vacuum sealed box, her ballet shoes. "AHA! These should work. She lived in them." He snatched up the shoebox, raced down the stairs to the back door, and snuck out of the house, being careful to look around and make sure no one watched him. He slipped into the tree line.

He ran harder and faster than he had ever run before to the Beakman trail, clutching the box so tight his knuckles turned white. When he landed at the meeting place, he relaxed his muscles under a tree. *Her tree.* He traced his fingers along the sequencer and calibrated the sensor. The shoe box nestled in the grass and he pulled out a pink pointe shoe. He scanned it. "Pleeeassse find some small piece of her, pleeeease." he begged his tool. The screen spun its yellow wheel, uploading results to his tablet. His foot fidgeted a rhythmic motion, and he waited.

"If that's not pure concentration, I dunno what is," a familiar voice interrupted him.

"Ricco, shh! I'm working."

"Dude, after four months of working together, I can guarantee, I will always interrupt you working." He beamed. "What are you calibrating for today? Rabbits? Or Toads?"

Dexter paused before he answered. His screen returned a negative result, "Incomplete Data". His head hung and a small whimper escaped his lips. Incomplete data meant it couldn't be calibrated enough to find her. He thought about a response to Jericho. He wasn't sure how it would be received that he stole a missing girl's shoes to scan for her DNA, only to come back with a negative result. But Ricco had proven to be nothing but helpful and positive. He took a chance.

"Remember the young girl who went missing a couple years back? Everyone, including Veribo Industries, tried to find her and came up empty?"

"I remember my dad up late many nights trying to handle the negative press for it. That was a bad few months."

Dexter bit his lip at someone only having a few bad months. His torture lasted a lot longer than that, and it still continued. "She was *my friend*. And she has been gone for more than two years... Too long. I hoped my sequencer would give me some answers."

Jericho had a far off look in his eyes, "I know, Dex. I met her the day she went missing." He reached into his chair side compartment, to reveal a small pack. "Here, this is for you." He handed it to Dexter.

Dexter turned the pack in his hands, studying it. He opened the flap to find a tablet, some utensils, school items, and a hairbrush with butterflies on it. His eyes widened as he recognized the contents. "This is Emma's school pack." He hesitated. "Why do *you* have it?" All sorts of horrible thoughts about how his friend came to have Emma's pack appeared in his mind, and he backed away, uneasy.

"No, no, no. I have no idea why she went missing. I met her at school. The day she disappeared she was having a rough day. I tried to help the best I could, but she left her pack and ran out before I could give it back. And then she disappeared, and I got scared to show it to the detectives. I didn't want anyone to think I had something to do with her disappearance. It would have been too much publicity for my dad to handle at Veribo Industries."

A swirl of anger bubbled up and out of Dexter. He couldn't contain himself, "AND YOU DIDN'T THINK TO TELL ME THAT SOONER?" He paused and spoke through quieter, gritted teeth. "I just looked like a complete creep as I *broke into* her house to try to find some viable DNA for the sequencer. And you had this the whole time? Didn't feel a need to tell me? You *knew* her and knew why I built the sequencer."

"I'm sorry, Dex. I didn't really think of it like that. You never talked about it, and I thought you weren't there, you know, mentally, to discuss it. I didn't want to be the first to bring it up."

Dexter looked down at him. It was logical of Jericho to withhold the information, he knew that. But the sting of it hurt as bad as being punched in the gut. He needed to be alone and to refocus on his own purpose, the reason he came out to the woods. "I get it. I really do. I think I need some space today." He directed his friend to the path. "Maybe we can hang tomorrow."

Jericho looked down in disappointment. "Sure, man. I'm here. Always." He turned his chair away and gave Dexter a small salute. "Later." He sped out of view.

"Later, Ricco." Dexter looked back at the packs, his and hers, laying by the tree. "Time to get to work," he whispered. He took out Emma's tablet. It was still charged—Ricco's doing he guessed—and he unlocked it with ease. Words in her handwriting scrawled over the screen in the last app she had open. "Queen of Featherstone and the Red Planet" scrolled across the screen. His heart warmed at a story all but forgotten, at fond memories of exploring the forest, and her wild accounts of the queen and the adventures she wished she could take. Her Dad always told her the stories were secret, but she openly shared them with him. A smile crept over his face... and then he saw it.

A pink butterfly brush with strands of hair curled around the bristles. His breath caught in his chest, and his heart pounded faster. Every muscle in his body tensed, and he pumped a small fist. Slowly, he pulled one long piece of hair from the brush. The sequencer shook in his hand as he held the hair out to be scanned.

He calibrated the sequencer and powered it on. He inhaled a short breath, still not able to shake a slight feeling of being watched, and sorted through the data from the sequencer on his tablet. He paced back and forth, waiting for the scan to finish. He clenched his fist to feel the beads of sweat forming on his palm.

Ding.

The sequencer finished and revealed a giant green circle with a check mark. "YES!" he shouted, scattering the birds from the trees. He jumped up, shimmied his upper body, and crisscrossed his legs in a quick dance. "Wooo!" The sequencer slid from his clutch, and he wobbled for balance so he wouldn't drop it. "Finally, a DNA match," he said while he patted the sequencer. "Okay, baby, let's go find her."

He gathered up his things and placed them all carefully in his backpack. Sequencer in hand, he started his trek on the path that pointed away from her tree. The sequencer returned a "Possible DNA Match Proximity" notification. Dexter continued further down the path and continued his scans. He headed toward the forest center. Eventually the pathway was lined with boulders lying askew, as if they had been thrown from the hills on his left and right.

As he busied himself with the sequencer screen, his foot suddenly met with water. A pool of water had developed in the middle of the deteriorated path. "Where did you come from?" He looked up toward the source of the small flowing stream. He balanced on the boulders and made his way up toward the large walls of limestone. Large cracks surrounded the water flowing through as if they were on the verge of breaking the whole wall of limestone next to him.

He peered into the cracks. The water drips suddenly pierced through and rushed out of the wall. Rock and water shot out from the opening. "Whoa!" Dexter jumped backwards to avoid stumbling from the sudden rush of tumbling rocks. His feet scrambled over the rubble. The water forced open the wall to reveal a small tunnel. He pointed the sequencer inside.

Beep. Beep.

"Positive DNA Match."

Dexter's heart pumped faster at the green indicator. Thoughts flashed of Emma running in the woods—her laugh carrying on the wind as she found her way right here, to this spot. "She was here. Right here." He bent down to inspect the tunnel.

A small dark patch of brown dirt streaked across the side of the tunnel. From the pattern of the streaks, it looked like dried blood, barely legible but there. His pulse throbbed in his neck. He needed to follow the blood marks. If he crouched down, he could manage it. He shoved the sequencer in his backpack and flung it over his shoulders. In a crouch supported by both hands, he maneuvered his way through the tunnel following the tiniest of brown streaks to arrive at a large open cave.

The opening allowed him to stand. He rose and his face was met with a slap. "OWW!" Something hit him hard. SMACK. Another on his back. "What is going on?!" he yelled into the echoing cavern. Suddenly a rushing wind flew around him. Several smacks to his body made him stumble forward until he tripped on a hard metal cylinder and face-planted in the middle of it.

He crouched into a ball, stuffing his head into his legs and closed his eyes. His body was pummeled by hundreds of fluttering objects. A red light pierced through the cloud of dark creatures, and whirring noise began to pulsate.

An invisible pressure forced his body tighter in his stationary ball. The pummeling had stopped but the noise grew louder. He looked up and saw bats held in suspension above him. The wet smell of the cave slowly dissipated, and the red light overwhelmed him. His pupils shrank in the brightness of the light. He glanced down, aware of a strange feeling in the pit of his stomach... and the cave disappeared before his eyes.

The fading cave was replaced with dark trees and a burning red sky.

Dexter blinked to clear a film of dust covering his eyes. The bats, in a panic from their move, flew back and forth and crashed into him. A faint echo of shooting rang out through the thick of the trees. Dexter ducked down from under the fluttering mess of bats to see where the shooting came from. He thought he saw a small purple figure standing behind a tree.

27

Lina

Merah
1.5 years since E2 contamination

L ina trudged up to the E2 portal again. This was her fifth
time being sent there in three months. She shook her
head at the cloud of black in the center of it.

"Huh, the pfoteros are in mass quantity this time. Guess
I have to keep dropping them one by one," Lina said to
Maut while ridding Merah of the flying rats with her blaster.

"Feel like helping me out a bit?" She nodded toward the
pfoteros, and Maut jumped up.

Maut's back legs lurched him forward, flying up to
catch one, and he threw it to the ground. Lina blasted it into
nothing. As the rest of them dropped out of existence with
each press of the trigger, she muttered, "Good riddance."

Behind the rush of the cloud, Lina saw a crouching figure. As she drew closer to the portal, the figure held up hands, the same way Emma did when she first met her. It stood slowly and grew tall with the rise of its body and finally, its head. Lina's eyes met it determined and focused. She held her blaster high and focused. The creature had a lot of the same features of her E2 friend, but this wasn't her.

In a steady and strong voice, she yelled at it, "Why have you travelled here, creature?"

Lina and Maut slowly walked closer and closer to the portal platform. She held her gaze steady while the creature's face contorted in a rather confused fashion. She thought maybe it didn't hear her. More loudly and slowly she asked, "What is the reason for your travels here?"

The humanoid shook its head, rubbed its eyes, and squeaked out, "My name is Dexter. I'm not here on purpose. I was searching for a lost friend of mine." The creature held up its hands.

Lina squinted at the response. "And *who,* might I ask, is your lost friend?"

He looked down, shifted his weight, and eventually said, "Her name is Emma. She's been missing and in my search for her, I ended up here."

Lina peered at him. "And how would you describe this friend of yours?"

"She is tall, with light blonde hair and skin lighter than mine, and eyes that are so piercingly blue you would think they were from the sky… but not this sky of course. And when she smiles at you, it is in such a way that you know with every fiber of your being that she cares about you." He stared off into the distance. Lina thought he looked sad.

"This creature must care a great deal for Emma," Lina whispered to Maut, studying Dexter's face. She cautiously lowered her blaster. "I believe that you have no ill will toward this Emma, but why did it take you so long to find this planet?"

"*This planet...?* I don't even know what planet this is!"

"Your friend Emma is here. This planet is Merah, also known affectionately as the Red Planet."

"Merah, the Red Planet... wait... You know who Emma is? SHE IS HERE?" The creature huffed in an excitement Lina had never seen before, then paused for a minute. "If she has been here this whole time, why didn't she come home?"

"She can't go when there isn't a way."

His hands went up. "Wait, wait...there's no way back to Earth?" His fingers pressed against his forehead.

"I'm afraid not. Emma searched for it for some time before finding out she couldn't get back home."

Dexter looked down at the ground. "So that's why she's been lost for so long." He looked up at her. "Can you take me to her?"

"I can get you in contact with her. She may be on assignment, but it can be arranged. You'll need to come with me."

Dexter stepped off the portal cylinder to follow Lina and there was a sudden loud whirring noise. "BEHIND ME!" Lina grabbed her blaster from its place and aimed at the platform. Dexter hopped off. The portal activated for a short amount of time, and Lina was quick to blast the one small winged creature that came through, but there stood another taller creature, looking a lot like the one standing behind her.

"Ryan?" The first creature exclaimed toward the portal.

Lina lowered her blaster. He seemed to know this incoming one. She eyed the two exchanging looks from each other, to the forest, and back to her.

"Who is this, Dexter? Where are we?" Ryan muttered.

"This is... I actually don't know your name," he looked at Lina.

"My name is Mylinah, and this is Maut." She pointed to her winged friend, glancing between the two creatures from E2. "Who is this one?" she nodded toward Ryan.

"Thank you, Mylinah. This is my brother Ryan. Although I am a bit confused as to how he is here." He looked toward the platform where his brother stood. "How did you get here? I barely know how I got here."

Ryan looked down toward his shoes and kicked a small pebble off the platform. "I followed you into the cave. And to be completely honest, I've actually been following you all day."

Dexter squinted at Ryan like he didn't understand his own brother. Lina never had siblings, so she didn't understand the complexity of their looks, but there had to be something extra going on because she couldn't tell if these were friendly or fierce glances.

Ryan shrugged and tilted his head back to look up at the sky. "I was bored, okay? And you've been going off with that Jericho kid and are never home. So, today, I thought I could sort of end up in the same spot, and maybe, I could, umm, ask to help you in your work. Maybe?" His smile beamed at Dexter, and he waited.

"This is the longest exchange of greeting for brothers I have ever heard in my entire life!" Lina said finally. "We need to be on our way, Dexter, and you, Rrrriiiiaaaan, will also need to come with me, if your plan really is to help your brother." She motioned in the direction of the forest.

"Well, he's stuck here like me, so he might as well come." Dexter raised his arms in a shrug and then waved his brother forward to join them. "Let's go."

"Finally!" Lina exclaimed, slightly exasperated with how much time she had to expend on this mission. Now she had two additional problems from E2. The first one she handled perfectly well, if she could say so herself, but this one was something entirely new. These ones were on a mission. They weren't here by accident like Emma. Lina had to stall to figure out what to do. She disregarded the message she had started to Emma. She needed to buy time until she could discuss matters with the general about how to handle these two. She did have Vargas close by. He may help her host them and give her some time.

Lina led the way away from the portal site on a mostly silent walk back to the village. Her two companions awkwardly gawked at the surroundings and then at each other, only to quickly return their gazes to a random tree. There were words hidden in those looks, but Lina couldn't decipher their meaning. After a grueling journey of silence from the portal site, they finally arrived at the village.

"Wow, this is a quaint little village you got here, Mylinah," Ryan said.

"Yes, it is small and old." She scrunched her nose in disgust.

"Where exactly are we going?" Dexter asked.

"I have a friend in this village who I believe will be able to take you in while I'm away."

"You're going away? I can't come with you? I thought you were taking me to see Emma," Dexter said, annoyed.

"I said I can get you in contact with her; I didn't say meet her. She is most likely on a trainee assignment and not available, but I'll try my best to get you in contact as quickly as possible. And you staying here with my friend will be the quickest way possible."

Dexter darted his eyes at her. "You keep saying she might be on 'an assignment,' what exactly does that mean?"

"Emma has joined the ranks as a Protector Emulate. And you can ask her more about it when we can make contact with her. She's been doing very well in her assignments from what I hear."

"So she's doing well. I'm glad to hear that," Dexter said in a low voice. His tone hinting that he did not mean it, which made her concerned about the truth in the other words he said.

They arrived at Vargas's place. Lina had messaged him back at the portal, so she knew he'd be home. He answered his house comm slowly, *as per usual*.

"Hey Lina, c'mon in," he said muffled while chewing.

They entered through the door with Vargas rushing to clean up his food generator and kitchen. He raced down the hall toward them and gave her a quick smile.

"Look at you, Lina, bringing me more strays." He winked at her.

"Yes, yes. Can you see to these strays while I head back to headquarters?"

"I already said in my message that I could."

"Are you sure?"

"Yes, go. Let us have our own meet and greet," he snarked.

She looked toward the strays. "Dexter, Ryan... Vargas will house you while I'm away. Please be as needy and demanding as you require. He actually likes the needy." She raised her eyebrows at her friend. She motioned for Maut to come and quickly left them on their own; she needed to be smart about their presence here on Merah. While Vargas had his own secrets, she hoped she wasn't pushing her luck when it came to him keeping hers.

28

Dexter

Merah
3 Earth years since E2 contamination

Dexter exhaled a long and slow breath while the three of them sat in the middle of Vargas's house. They tapped fingers on the furniture and bounced knees in anticipation. Dexter finally broke the silence.

"So Vargas, does Mylinah normally drop off people randomly at your place?"

The creature snorted a laugh. "Yeah, not recently though. I haven't seen anyone else since the E2 girl came."

Dexter hesitated before asking, "When you say E2 girl, do you mean Emma?"

"Yes of course. I believe this was the first place Lina brought Emma after she came through the E2 portal. Lina said in her message you were looking for the girl. Were you friends with her?"

"We were friends back on Earth. Then she disappeared. I have spent almost three years trying to find her."

Vargas looked at them with a contorted face. "But Emma has only been here for a year and a half. You said there have been additional years on your planet, more than ours?"

Dexter and Ryan looked at each other confused. "Wait, so it's only been a year and a half that Emma has been here?"

"Yeah, that's about right."

Dexter thought about the agony the past three years had given him. How nice it would be to have only experienced half of that time. Part of him hated that he was forced to live with the pain of loss for a longer time than Emma, but the other part was grateful his friend was mostly spared. Ryan interrupted his thoughts..

"So Vargas, does everyone of your species have big ears like you?"

Dexter shoved Ryan and tried to cover for his brother's behavior. "He means, really, that we haven't seen any other of your species here on this planet so far. You're a different species than Mylinah, right?"

"Yes, there aren't too many of my species on Merah; I actually think we're the only ones, in this village anyway. I'm Pinneat. My parents came through a portal to work here on an agreement with a Kabiren Scout after hearing about the advanced technology they'd built. They came thinking they'd keep their work quiet per the Scouts. Merah is an amazing planet, with a lot of tech, but it has its secrets it wants to keep I suppose."

"So your parents work with the native species on this planet?"

"Lina's species, the Amethites, are the original species of Merah. The Kabiren are just the most recent to gain access to Merah due to some treaty." Vargas shook his head in disappointment. "I use the word treaty loosely."

"Why does everyone want to come here? To Merah, I mean?" Ryan asked.

Vargas scoffed at the question. "Oh wait, you are serious? Merah is *widely* known for unimaginable techno-logical advancements because the Kabiren here are developing some of the most advanced technology in *the entire universe*. And the only place to be part of that, is here, on Merah." Vargas shrugged his shoulders.

Dexter and Ryan looked at each other with gaping grins. Dexter turned to Vargas. "So when can we see it?"

"See what?" Vargas asked.

Dexter smiled, stood up, and looked out the window. "Everything."

29

August

Merah
1.5 years since E2 contamination

From: Protector Emulate 1

Re: Assignment 59

Please, please, please, August! Let me handle this one on my own. It will take me, AT THE MOST, three days to process the assignment, and you have so much going on in your lab recently. Don't you want to be able to focus on the new secondary portal systems? I know you haven't figured out the circuit attachment yet, and you want to finish it. Can you please assign me a roller to take care of it?

"Oh, she makes a valid argument going alone on this one," August chuckled to himself while scanning the assignment requests. It was a simple assignment, and Emma proved herself more than capable on many jobs so far. He tried to think of the worst possible outcome of her taking one by herself. He couldn't decide if the possibility of her death on an assignment would be worse than facing the wrath of his mother if he didn't finally figure out this attachment. He had difficulty with so many of the new plans recently that he wondered if the Scouts were going a bit crazy bringing him all these different ideas for retrofitting the portals. The assignment Emma requested was only a plant life-cleanup assignment, shouldn't be too difficult for her, and it had an extremely low danger rating. Why not?

To: Protector Emulate 1

Re: Assignment 59

You have my approval. Go for it, E2. A roller will be available upon your departure from headquarters. Happy hunting!

He retrieved the two most recent logs on his holo screen and sent a roller request to the tech department at the departure station for Emma. She should be able to log out the roller with her imprint. This would be the appropriate time for her to test out her ability to check out tech. She would be on her own soon enough and would have to get her own equipment anyway.

"Ahh, freedom," he said. He spent the night in his lab and traced all of his plans into his portal graphs. No matter which way he worked it, they didn't quite fit. He had no idea where these new ideas came from. He selected the Scout number for that particular file.

"Hmm, Scout 659 entered this file four days ago. Let me see if I can backtrack any missing logs for this." He pounded away at holographic squares of files and dragged them forward so he could scan them. There were multiple attachments to this particular assignment, but they were tagged with an "irrelevant," or unimportant, popup. Irrelevant files were locked, but they kept coming up in his recent searches.

He remembered asking his mother one time if they really were irrelevant files, as they were marked, then why were they encrypted and locked instead of deleted? He was met with an hour long 'discussion' regarding the importance of *all* the files in their possession and how their species were excellent record keepers and that would not stop under her watch. Ensuring   all files were catalogued was the Scout's job, and whether or not they were important was not for him to care about. "If it's locked, it's not for you," she'd said, and he left it at that.

Now he wished he asked more questions about the locked files he always found somehow attached to his work. This being the fifth time he had to rework some tech he'd received in the last month, which included additional files he didn't have access to.

An intrusive voice echoed through his lab. "Have you finished your work on the new secondary portal systems yet?"

August smoothly and swiftly refreshed his work station to show the new systems he started on earlier in the morning. His mother had a way of sliding into his work at a moment's notice. To be fair, he was always working on something she needed to be updated on; therefore, he lived every moment of his life in expectation of that voice.

"I'm very close to finishing it. The new plans are more challenging than I originally anticipated. But if I crank it out, they should be ready by the end of the week."

"That won't do. I require the updates by the end of the day tomorrow. There are some things that have come up, and they require immediate completion. Do better."

"Why do they need to be completed so soon? Did something happen?"

His mother gave him an icy glare. "We should *always* be quick in the expansion of our knowledge and technology. The glory of our people is *dependent* upon it. You know this."

With that rousing speech, General Sotora left him in an empty lab with a feeling of inadequacy. He glowered at the holo screens of information surrounding the new plans but now was determined. He filtered his files for all those locked files, and viewed the rows and rows of data. If he needed to "do better" then the fastest way would be in those files. The additional information definitely would give him insight to the specs in order to ensure the new portals are created in the time frame given to him.

How about I run a simple decryption on the "irrelevant" files as a whole, and maybe I'll be able to get more information from them, he thought to himself sorting through the files. He never tried to directly disobey his mother, but she had given him two options: disobey, or fail.

Run Decryption Program A-39

Error- T54330-220

"Stupid." He dragged his hand down his face to wash away the idea that a simple program would decode a complex problem.

"Okay. Now let's try a new code to break this lock. Maybe my old one would work." he whispered under his breath while he tapped at a file from the old days of his hijinks hacking his instructor's holo in school. "The necessary coding to poke a hole in these locked files has to be in one of my old files. I definitely remember a significant amount of information I was able to obtain the last time I used it." He quickly dragged the code over to the locked files.

Run Techra - 17c

Running

Access granted.

August jumped out of his seat and pumped his fist into the air. "YES, I finally got access!" *Now I hope to not be disturbed by the prying eyes of Scouts wondering what I'm doing looking at these locked files*. He transferred the unlocked file copies from his holo screen over to his private computer he safeguarded back in his training days when he didn't want his instructor to know what files he stole.

"All right, let's see the most recent 'irrelevant' file attached to this project." He cracked his knuckles in hopes of a sprawling data dump, but instead was met with a small video file. He furrowed his brow, and his heart slowed from disappointment. He braced himself and opened the video.

His holo screen displayed a 3D image in the middle of his lab. He saw what appeared to be one of the Scout's diplomatic missions on Regaodjen, a planet in the Jrakan region of space. It looked like it had the same tag as the files he worked on for the portals. He had heard the Scouts were praised for their efforts in obtaining the technology from this mission. His mother told him that the Scouts had amazing diplomatic skills in order to work out new tech deals.

The video continued to show images of the Scouts approaching a small family from the Regoadjen planet. A small one, who was maybe three years of age, happily played with their toys in a corner of the lab while the parents greeted the Scouts. The first Scout, burly with a square jaw and deep red eyes, initiated the diplomacy.

"I am sure you know of our interest in your work," he said, glancing at the lab casually.

"We are aware of your many attempts to share technology. Your last representative here was, well, she was very convincing. However, as we have expressed on multiple occasions, there simply is no need for us to add your technology to our current system. We are close to being fully developed and running. There's nothing further you can do for us that would entice us to come work with you. We obviously have not made that clear enough. So now we're hoping you understand us—no."

The second lanky Scout winced slightly at the negative response, but the more burly one stayed steady in his gaze at the small family. "I see," he responded slowly and succinctly. "Let me rephrase our request. See, it isn't actually a request. It's more like a requirement." The Scout looked over at the young one in the corner playing. "You have so much to continue your work for, over there," he motioned at the child, "and I'm sure you are aware of the consequences of refusing a requirement from the Kabiren."

"We have heard whispers, but we sincerely hope you're capable of maintaining your honor with our planet. You have gained multiple resources from us, and you know the only way to keep those resources is to maintain a good relationship."

"Of course we want to continue with our wonderfully built friendship and would never think of doing anything to jeopardize what we have worked so hard to create." The Scout paused slightly to assess before continuing. "However, you need to think long and hard before refusing this offer and what your actions could potentially do to our *friendship*."

The small Regaodjen family stood firm. "We've made our decision, and we ask that you respect it before we get the council involved."

The second Scout with thinned hair and a scrawny body nodded with an icy stare. "We thank you so much for your time and hope you understand our eagerness. We appreciate you even considering working with us. And as always, we hope you will change your mind."

"We appreciate your offer, but we won't work for you. Please leave."

The scrawny Scout quietly slid a small cylinder next to the lab system, and it attached itself. The angle made it impossible for the family to see; it blended perfectly. The

Scouts bowed and then exited the lab. "We thank you for your time."

"We hope you have a safe return home." The family bowed a stern goodbye.

The video showed the family continuing to work, moving about the lab. The young one played in the corner while the family gave them a small kiss before returning to their work. Seconds turned to minutes, and there was a soft beep that came from the cylinder. Suddenly, a large blast engulfed the lab. The video stopped and was replaced by an image of Scout one seated with a report in front of him.

"We were able to get all the information we needed during this mission. Our condolences have been sent to the Regaodjen council for the unfortunate accident at the lab, and it looks like they have accepted our explanation of what happened. Any trust that the council lost after the Nerezza's actions during her last meeting with them has been repaired, and we will be able to have a working relationship with them going forward."

August stood with his mouth agape. He could not process what he just watched. The stories he heard about the Scouts and their diplomacy for this mission were completely based on lies. There was no diplomacy in what he watched. There was barely any negotiation.

"What did they mean exactly when they spoke of the Nerezza being there on a mission?" He wandered through the video a second time. August stopped and stood by his holo screen. There were so many other files, all with tagged "Scout mission documentation," and each one matched up with every design project he and others had worked on. He wondered what horrors he would find in those thousands of previously locked secrets.

He closed his eyes and randomly grabbed at one of the others. The 3D images flowed out through the lab with vivid imagery. Another senseless murder after failed "negotiations," this one on a planet he couldn't name. This is what General Sotora had called "skilled talks." However, there was no skill, no display of working with others in these files. He continued to go through five, ten, fifteen different files, all ending the same way—with destruction and theft.

"Of course," August eventually breathed out in an undertone. He clenched his jaw and slowed his breath. "The Scouts are too dense to actually work through a problem. They only know one solution for everything, violence."

He scrolled through the seemingly endless amount of files in his possession. One last documentation tagged as "Nerezza Incident" went across his holo. He furrowed his brow and bit his lip looking back and forth through the empty space of his lab.

"Might as well." He admitted to his curiosity and selected the file.

This video took longer for the 3D processor—a much larger file than the rest. The video of a pixelated forest on Merah appeared and slowly came into focus.

In the video, a girl who appeared to be a few years older than him stood near a portal site. Next to her were several Mentiren and Amethite fighters, each with their own phase imager, allowing them to take on another race's form, shielding the girl. The scene was familiar, only he didn't remember Amethites being there. He had seen it growing up in his training. The Nerezza, destroyer, helper of the Mentiren, steals valuable information from headquarters and is ended swiftly by General Sotora with her army of Scouts and what are now known as Protectors.

But this scene looked slightly different. The general had not arrived yet, and the Nerezza spoke.

"We need to prepare for a fight here. We're not sure how soon the General will find these portals. I'm almost certain we were followed by Scouts."

An Amethite with a long beard standing next to the Nerezza spoke softly to her and darted her eyes toward the edge of the forest. "Are you *sure* you secured the last portal location and deleted it from the Kabiren systems?"

"Yes, they will not be aware of the final twenty portals. But we have to make sure we destroy the portals *completely* before they are found, and we must leave no trace. Otherwise, they'll be able to find the missing planets, including my own, Featherstone."

"My queen," a Mentiren with long arms and legs and skin that looked like cobblestone said while bowing to the Nerezza. "We need to be quick if we're going to be able to finish our plan. Some of our people have spotted the general closer than we like. It seems she and a small army are ready for a fight."

The Nerezza furrowed her brow and stared at the ground, lost in thought.

August paused the playback right on the face of the Nerezza. There was Emma's face. He *thought* she looked similar to the Nerezza. Lina had said as much, but now seeing the Nerezza, there was no doubt of some sort of a relation between the two. "Could this be why the general is so interested in my reports on little Emma?" he wondered.

The video continued.

"We may have to bring the others sooner," said the Nerezza.

"How many have made it through?" replied the lanky Mentiren.

"About fifty, but we have no way of knowing their condition or the condition of the planet until we arrive. Are the rest of the Mentiren ready for evacuation?"

"Yes, dear queen," the Mentiren replied solemnly.

"I wish we could help the rest of them too, Allayea," the Nerezza spoke softly. "Once we are able to regroup, we *will* reassess, and we *will* return."

"I know you have promised as much, and with the time difference, it will not feel that long for them. But what if the portals fail before we have calculated? The code to break down the portal systems is being inserted into their systems as we speak. What if we can't get back?"

"You're forgetting who's with us. Whatever you think of them, the Mentiren have learned from their mistakes and will be able to recreate their portals, even if it takes more time compared to here, we will have the plans." She revealed a hidden storage device.

The small Amethite nodded in agreement and looked up at slowly approaching figures. The girl tensed and raised her hand in defense of the Nerezza, only to be relieved to find several straggler Mentiren approaching with their equipment and a few small children.

"Please hurry, we don't have much time!" the Nerezza implored them, guiding them to the shiny metallic new portal. The first of the families climbed the ladder and stood on the cylinder, ready for the red light to surround them and carry them to safety.

Without warning, six blaster shots were fired in their direction, striking two of them down and the portal pulled them through, off and away from Merah.

"Everyone down!" the Nerezza shouted at the small band of creatures. Several Kabiren Scouts and Protectors arrived in the distance while shooting a barrage of blaster shots toward them. The Mentiren approached the Nerezza swiftly.

"Please, my queen, you need to come with me," he shouted into her ear. She looked at him, defiantly shook her head and gestured toward the incoming fire. He whispered something to her that the video didn't capture. She nodded quickly and ran toward the portal, but in the commotion the video lost her image. The general suddenly appeared in the midst of the heavily armed Scouts and Protectors. They quickly closed in on the rebels.

"Halt!" she ordered her small army. Then addressing the remaining Mentiren, "Where is the Queen of Featherstone?" They all stood in strong silence. The general glared into each face, held her blaster toward the closest one, and fired. She turned to the Scout on her left. "I don't have time for this. Destroy them all." The Scout nodded. Several of his comrades spread around the portal and surrounded those waiting. They set charges all around.

A large implosion ripped through the Mentiren and Amethite rebels. When the dust settled, there was only destruction. It left nothing but black dirt and charred bones. The video file ended.

August stood in the middle of his lab with his head down. He most certainly saw the destruction of the remaining Mentiren and the Nerezza, but they called her the Queen of Featherstone. So that is what she was called off-world. The Queen of Featherstone *deserved* the name of

Nerezza after what she did. *Why does that sound familiar?* This video was different than what he grew up being told. There were Amethites with them as well. It certainly looked like they were all working together toward something. "But what, exactly?" August asked himself. His brow furrowed, and he shook his head in disbelief. He knew the general had destroyed the corrupt Mentiren race. They had taken advantage of the Amethites for far too long, and the general needed to remove them from the situation before further damage could be done. But it looked like this file was when the last remaining Mentiren were destroyed. *How could ANY Amethites work* with *the Mentiren, after how they were treated? They were all there together before the general arrived. I need to find out more, maybe there are additional files.*

August's holo screen pinged a notification message from his mother.

To: General Proximate August

Please retrieve the E2 girl for me immediately. Update me upon her arrival.

General Sotora

"SHE JUST TOLD ME I NEEDED TO FINISH THE PLANS!" he shouted, enraged. *Right when I see her destroying Mentiren and Amethites together, she asks for me to bring Emma to her… Does she want to destroy her as well? How could I do that? I need to know more.*

He inhaled and exhaled, inhaled and exhaled. He knew he would have to be on his way to get Emma, but needed to look at the files longer. He quickly transferred the files to his portable holo screen. She wasn't that far away, and this outing could provide a bit more time for him to be able to scroll through these files. He wouldn't have his lab's 3D rendering on the road, but at least he would be able to scroll through the endless amount of files tagged under the Nerezza for further review. He grabbed his pack and requested his roller. Hopefully he could find out more information in the files, but for now he needed to go clear his head.

30

Lina

Merah
1.5 years since E2 contamination

The roller came to a halt at headquarters. Lina hopped out and patted the top. She blew a kiss to her gift and headed toward the front doors of the monstrous building. Her heart pounded in rhythmic beats faster and faster as her feet glided through the front doors. A familiar face raced toward her, and she waved and smiled at her friend. August focused squarely ahead and didn't see her as he made his way toward the doors.

"Where's he going in such a hurry?" she whispered to Maut on her shoulder, but she shook off the embarrassment of the wave not returned.

She took the elevator up to the general's floor, and every time she did this, her veins pulsed with anticipation.

General Sotora had that effect on her. She knew she was doing the right thing in bringing this problem to the general, but her legs wobbled ever so slightly walking down the hall to her office. She motioned to the guard by the general's entrance.

"She is expecting me." She straightened her body and focused. He searched through his holo log and nodded her admittance. "That will have to wait out here." He pointed to Maut.

"It's okay, buddy. Stay here." She placed Maut on the floor by the guard and walked through the entryway over to the general. The general glanced back and forth between her holo screens and scrolled through what Lina thought were endless data logs. She paused in the office to allow the general some time to notice her presence. "Ahem."

Without looking up at her, the general spoke. "You made it here quickly, Protector 42. I normally do not allow such abrupt visits due to my workload, but your message did sound urgent. What is it that you needed to discuss with me in person?"

Lina held her breath slightly and felt a sinking in her stomach. But she punched it down with a swallow and started with her dilemma. "On my last assignment, I had an incident. My assignment was issued as a cleanup of pfoteros; however, I was met with more than I expected. Another creature from E2. One who claimed to know, rather well actually, the girl from E2 we know as Emma. While I was determining the reason for this creature's presence, another one, claiming to be the first creature's relative came through the portal as well."

The general turned toward Lina with a stern face and an icy, gritted tone. "And where are all these creatures now?"

Lina sank smaller in her spot and lowered her head. "They're with a friend." She lifted her head slightly. She was met with a sharply clenched jaw and flared nostrils.

"What is the purpose of a Protector, 42? "

"To ensure the safety of Merah."

"And do you feel that continuing to allow creatures through the portals is living up to that purpose?"

"Well, no, not exactly. But I felt that seeing as they came from E2—"

"Just because you made one decision that ended up for the benefit of Merah, does *not* mean that making the same decision under differing circumstances is wise." The general boiled into a rage. "You have *failed* Merah in continuing to allow the additional creatures to continue living. I ask that you swiftly correct your own problem *as we have trained you to* before I have another Protector complete your assignment for you. Remember, you can easily be removed as a Protector and added to the services line."

Lina cowered under the words. *She's right.* Her dream, her work, could all so easily be taken from her if she continued making these mistakes. "Yes, general. I should have handled this situation already, and I'm sorry I brought it to your attention needlessly. I will return and take care of it."

The general softened her glare slightly. "I know you are a good Protector, 42. What you did on the Monsuta assignment..." She paused and grinned. "Well, how you handled the surprise rebels was admirable, considering who was among them."

Lina stared coldly at an empty wall behind the general. "My parents were in alliance with the rebellion. They tried to stop me and my fellow Protectors when the portal opened on the Monsuta assignment. I protected Merah, as I will now."

"That is good to hear, 42. I know you will do the right thing with your assignment now."

Lina nodded and turned to leave. "Do you wish me to complete my assignment with the girl from E2 as well?"

"I have my own plans for her. My son is ensuring her return to headquarters, and I will take care of her."

"Then I'll leave you to it."

Lina bowed and left the room quickly. Her feet and legs again began wobbling. She pushed them to move faster with Maut scurrying to keep up, and she found the closest evap room, entered it and hung her body over the nearest waste disposal to throw up. She rose to return to her assignment, but her body forced her to maintain its position, slumped over the disposal. Slowly, less and less food bits left her body, and they were replaced solely by lurches and gags. Her stomach soon stopped its quivering, and she raised her head. Maut nudge her knee and she used the dark colored piece of her coat to clean her chin and stood up.

"Time to work," she whispered to Maut. And he followed her out of the building to her roller to complete her assignment. Merah would be protected by her, no matter the cost.

31

Emma

Merah
1.5 years since E2 contamination

The roller hummed when Emma started it and displayed her location map. The first assignment she took on by herself was a complete success, if she could say so herself. The foreign material was contained, and she did it in less than the time she had quoted August. He commended her on her actions, and she hoped that meant he trusted her more. Now there was an entire day she could use for her own adventures before she needed to get back to headquarters. She considered the options. "Where should I venture to today?" She examined the village dots on the holo map.

A message popped up.

To: Protector Emulate 73

There is an adjustment in plans. Please discontinue current assignment and meet me back in my lab.

General Proximate August

"There goes my free day," she groaned and paused in thought.

Well, maybe not completely. The Valley of Euphony is not very far from headquarters, and I do have a roller. Enough to get there to see it and return to the lab without August even knowing I veered off course, she reasoned. *It's one place I still haven't gone on Merah.*

The dot on her holo screen glowed, and she envisioned the vastness of the valley. She hopped in her roller and put in the coordinates. As she drove, she recalled the stories her father told her at night, which included a beautiful valley with huge, rocky mountains around the sides. At the center of it, a large lake of thickened turquoise water pooled. An urge to see it settled into her stomach. It was the favorite place of the Queen of Featherstone upon her arrival to the Red Planet. Her father always let various details slip of the queen's travels here. As far as Featherstone was concerned, it was abandoned by its queen. Emma's father sprinkled small details into his stories. "Oh, the Red Planet is held as a high favorite of the queen's" and "See this lake here, Emma, it mirrors the center of the Valley of Euphony, the most beautiful place ever visited by the Queen of Featherstone herself. Beautiful arched trees lined the way to it."

Emma never asked her father what exactly happened to the Queen of Featherstone. She loved the mystery of her beloved story and never wanted to spoil it with a final ending, and her father enjoyed the light in her eyes while he let these small secrets escape. Now, though, as she drove to the famous Valley of Euphony, she wondered if she should have asked him about the source of his stories. The roller turned onto a worn path as the holo map pointed her in the direction of the valley. Trees on both sides of the path reached over her to each other's side. Their limbs grasped each other creating perfect arches. How could she have known the stories she had grown up with were not imaginary, but rather, events and places that were real? But what was their meaning to her? To him? These places and backdrops of stories that were so real he had to have been there. So who was he exactly?

Emma held back a tightness in her throat and water in her eyes. She tried to hold onto the old memories and shake away any uncertain feeling in the pit of her stomach. The dark orange trees in the distance parted to reveal a deep valley. Just north of her, the rocks and field burned their fiery orange. She halted her roller next to a tree and hopped out. The light from the suns parted through her widened view. She moved in a rhythmic motion and hummed to the rushes of the wind.

The path abruptly ended, and Emma caught herself before she fell into the vast lake before her. She plopped down and drank in the soft motions of the turquoise lake. She knew it wasn't water—there were no naturally occurring bodies of water on Merah. This liquid was different, thicker, near blood-like in consistency. It shined with a brightness of neon from the reflection of both suns. The lake surrounded by burning waves of orange brush was a masterful piece of natural artistry, and Emma found herself wishing she were a painter to be able to remember the scene.

"This will have to do." She gathered the scanner from her sack and captured the sight. "Hopefully August can render this in his lab so I can have this valley in 3D."

"I'm pretty sure your portal assignment was about two villages in that direction, E2." A voice startled her, and she peeked behind her to see August pointing in the direction of her first solo mission. Her heart pounded in her throat, and she stood frozen. His last message was to meet up at Headquarters, not here. Yet, here they both were. Did he follow her tracker here instead? *Play it cool.* Her gaze turned to him, and she smiled with a mischievous glint in her eye.

"Okay, you caught me, August. I got your message to meet up, but I finished my assignment early and decided on a quick side trip. I've wanted to visit this place my whole life and really, it was on the way." She smiled nervously. "Please don't put this on your report to your mother. I would like to not fail on my first solo Protector Emulate assignment." She clasped her hand over her mouth.

August looked at her with narrow eyes, and a tiny smile creeped out. "Don't worry, I won't include this little side trip on my report, if you don't tell my mother I was here either." He chuckled. "I'm actually kind of avoiding her at the moment." He stopped himself short and looked out at the lake.

Emma could empathize. "See, I always had the opposite problem. My mother was always the one avoiding me. At least yours is invested in your life and what you do."

"That level of interest is exhausting. The general is highly invested in what I do, so much so that every little change or adjustment in a project, I am expected to immediately accept and complete. Like I'm some cog in a machine that is expected to take all commands without any time to question what exactly I'm doing."

"See, at least you have a mother who is interested. Mine was always out the door on another supply run. I barely saw her, much less talked to her. I have questions, for both my parents, that I will never be able to ask now." She looked at August and his slight furrowed brows and frown. His concern made her eyes prick. This was the first time she was able to fully feel the weight of her words. She slumped onto the dark sands and melted into them with a shivering body and a whimper.

August slowly dropped his lengthy figure and sat next to his crying student. He breathed slowly, loudly, and Emma could hear every calm breath he took. The thick, lapping water splashed against the sand, and the calm, steady presence of her mentor called her out of her tearful spiral. Tiny grains of sand stuck to her wet, tear-ridden hands. She used her arm to wipe her cheeks dry.

"It seems we both have mothers who keep us in the dark," he said.

Emma looked up at his puzzling comment. "You have so much contact with your mother; I always assumed you had unlimited access to the general's brain."

He stared off into the distance before muttering in a low whisper, "I think I found some troubling information, and I don't know exactly what I'm going to do with it."

"What did you find?"

"A recording of something that happened a long time ago. I always figured the feud between the Mentiren and the Kabiren was simple. The Mentiren were so domineering, treated the Amethites horribly, and were not to be trusted. Now after what I've seen, I'm not sure that's the whole story."

"It's not a good feeling to sit with, is it?"

"No, it's not."

"What makes you unsure?"

August motioned toward his holo screen projector but paused for a moment before he dragged up his most recent file. "The video won't be as good as in my lab, so it may be a bit choppy." He motioned for the file to play.

Emma stared at the grainy video, trying to make out the figures and shapes that stood around a portal she didn't recognize. "Are those Mentiren soldiers?"

August nodded. "With an Amethite and the Nerezza."

Emma furrowed her brow. "Wait, wait. THE Nerezza? I haven't even seen a picture of the famous Nerezza. This should be good." She glimmered in expectation of seeing the face of the traitor and destroyer in the fabled lore of Merah.

The young woman in the video was initially hidden by her companions. Emma couldn't quite make out their faces. She wished they were back at the lab and could see the figures with clarity. "Is she the Nerezza?" She nodded toward the young woman in the video.

"Yes," August replied.

Emma gazed intently, but then, the Nerezza spoke. Emma's eyes widened, and she leaned in toward the holo to hear better. "That voice...I *know* that voice. That is *my mother's* voice." Her heart quickened at a blurred, younger version of her mother.

August looked at her with brows raised. He leaned in, "Are you sure?"

"That's absolutely her voice. Sounds younger, but definitely her. How was she here, on Merah?" She spoke mostly to herself while watching her mother move and gesture. The same tilt of her head and commanding voice showed through every frame of the video. Emma shook her head while her eyes searched the screen for answers to her many questions. *Why is she here? Why didn't she tell me any of this? Is this why she was always not around? What does this mean?*

"Wait, can you back up and replay that part?" She directed August to a few frames back. He dragged the video back to replay. Then she heard the words of her mother on the holo.

"Otherwise they will be able to find the missing planets, including my own, Featherstone." A figure approached.

"My queen."

Emma reached for the holo and paused the screen. "My mother…was the Queen of Featherstone? My mother…was the Nerezza?" Everything clicked into place. The in-depth stories her father told her of a queen that stared at her in the face. Her heart pounded in her chest.

"That must be why my mother wants a close eye kept on you. You're the daughter of the Nerezza!" August pointed to her shocked. "Wait, you really didn't know?" He frowned. "How could you *not* know?"

"I told you, my mother and I rarely spoke," she looked down at the ground and swallowed. "But my father talked to me all the time about the Queen of Featherstone. He told me so many stories, I grew up *loving* the adventures of the queen. I dreamt of adventuring exactly like she did. I had no idea they were real, let alone *a piece of my history*."

August nodded but wouldn't take his eyes off the screen, "You do look incredibly like her. I definitely see it now, seeing you next to the projection."

Emma peered at the screen and started the video again. It showed a younger version of her mother, alongside Amethites and Mentiren escaping through a portal. Not exactly information included in her Protector training, or her childhood. But she wondered, "What's that portal they are using?" she asked right as an explosion completely destroyed it. "My mother apparently wasn't destroyed in that blast. But where did the portal lead?"

August replied, "From what I can gather, it was a newly built portal. There's no information on the planet they went to other than it was almost empty, needed major atmospheric work for people to live there, and was the entry portal used for E2."

"Is it normal for entry and exit portals to be on separate planets?" Emma inquired.

"It's not normal, but some off-world portals were built in separate locations, to keep them more hidden. The Mentiren didn't always like to announce their coming and going on a new world, and two portals right next to each other are definitely obvious."

"I wonder if the entry portal for Earth exists?"

"If there is, it's not showing in our logs."

"So it is *possible*."

"Maybe. We need to investigate further." He furrowed his brow at the idea.

"Okay, let's go back to your lab. Maybe there's more information there we can gather." she suggested.

August shook his head. "We better find a quieter place than my lab in headquarters. I have the bulk of these video files on my holo screen. We need a place to be able to go through them freely."

Emma thought about the places she felt completely safe, at home and "quiet" as August put it, while on Merah. They were few and far between, but there is one place she felt the most comfortable. A small house with a kind host in the first village she ever saw. "Lina's friend Vargas has a place in the outermost village. I think he would be happy to have visitors," she said with a cheerful smile.

"Let's go." And he motioned for her to lead the way.

32

Dexter

Merah
1.5 years since E2 contamination

Dexter's eyes darted back and forth between the small Boden scurrying in the distance and the deep veins of a purple flower whose head could engulf his own. The sky burned its deep red, and the suns stood high in their places. Dexter's senses were in overdrive. The dizzying surroundings captured all his attention. The expansive forest and the small village where they stayed held enough information for a human from E2 to study for his lifetime. He knew this planet would be his future, the same for his brother who annoyingly followed him here.

"Not a bad planet to be stuck on, right brother?" Ryan shoved Dexter on the shoulder.

Dexter snapped out of his daze abruptly. He shook his head. "You do realize that we won't ever be able to get back home, like ever. Or is that thought too big for your little head?" He shoved his brother.

Ryan shrugged and looked at their mutual friend who was engrossed in drawing a picture in the black specks of ground. "You know what I mean. Right, Vargas?"

Their friend looked at the brothers but held his hands up to stay out of the quarrel. "I'm only here to give you something to do while we wait for Lina to get ahold of Emma." He paused. "That and to take a break from my shop, so don't include me in whatever this is." He pointed between the two brothers and went back to his drawing.

Dexter walked forward off the beaten path. The tree to his right bled an orange so deep his eyes couldn't look away though his legs continued to walk.

"Watch out, Dex!" his brother called. Dexter turned while his shoe came loose on the ground. He struggled to gain balance and slid down a sudden slope, falling on his hip with loose pebbles dragging his body. He clutched at the dirt and sand, but they melted through his fingers and he continued his descent. A rough hand clutched his wrist and tugged hard using his weight to offset the slide. Ryan's firm grip combined with Dexter's heel dug into the side of the cliff stopped the fall, but they couldn't move. If Ryan jostled him, Dexter would lose his footing. They were stuck.

"VARGAS! VARGAS!" Ryan shouted, and he tightened his grip around Dexter's wrist. His wrist joint slowly separated with every adjustment on his supporting heel. He winced, and his muscles slackened.

"No, little brother. You hold on." Ryan spoke in even but determined tones.

The cliffs around Dexter blurred into a fog and everything went black.

Dexter's body lay flat on the ground with an aching appendage at his side. Two worried faces sat directly next to him. A small breath escaped Ryan's mouth. "Only you would pass out after dangling from a cliff for like *two* seconds." He threw his body down on Dexter, grabbed his neck, and squeezed tightly. "Welcome back, brother." He whispered into Dexter's ear.

"Probably should have been paying more attention when you mentioned cliffs, Vargas," Dexter sat up and shook his head. "Ow." He winced when he tried to put pressure on his hand.

Vargas grabbed at his hand to examine it. "Yeah, paying attention when I discuss a deadly dropoff nearby probably would have been a good idea." He released his arm with a nod. "You'll be fine. We just need to get back to the house. I'll be able to tend to your injury there. Can you walk?"

Dexter tugged his body up, but staggered. His wrist and ankle throbbed, but he was able to put his weight on his foot. He nodded and limped on the pathway. "Let's go."

Dexter jumped at a loud notification from Vargas's holo screen.

"Looks like your day is going to get better really soon!" Vargas said with raised brows.

Vargas read through a message. "A certain E2 girl is heading to my house as we speak." He smiled. "It'll be nice to see her again. It's been too long."

A cold, creeping sweat expanded through Dexter's palms. He wiped his hands quickly on his side, cleared his throat, and said in a forced calm tone, "You mean Emma is heading to your place now? How long do you think it will take her to get there? We should probably move faster right?" He wiped his hands on his side again.

Ryan and Vargas looked at each other and chuckled. "Yeah, we'll move as fast as your fainting butt will let us," Ryan blurted out, and he smacked his brother's shoulder. They all began walking, Ryan and Vargas keeping pace with Dexter's surprisingly quickened stride.

It wasn't long before they arrived back at Vargas's home. Dexter's eyes darted and searched every nook and cranny of the house. No sign of Emma anywhere. He sat down, defeated, and his ankle and wrist throbbed again. He winced and rubbed at his injuries.

"Ah right, I did say I would tend to those when we got back," their host mentioned while leaving the room and returning with a small silver case in hand. He held out a device, pointed it, and scanned Dexter's wrist and ankle. "Hold on one moment."

He held his finger up, walked to another room, and returned with two pieces that looked like Roman armor. One piece was shorter and thinner. Vargas clasped the piece of metal around his wrist, and it tightened to a perfect fit.

"Can you move it or put pressure on it?" Vargas asked.

Dexter put out his arm and leaned against his hand.

"Wow, this feels great. I don't feel any pressure at all," Dexter replied in awe of the mechanics surrounding his weakened hand. "Is the other one for my ankle?" He reached for the larger metal piece. Vargas handed it to him, and he clasped it onto his foot. This one too tugged tighter at his ankle, and he winced.

"Oops, sorry." He ran to another room and brought out a second brace. "Here, this one should fit better." Dexter grabbed it and adjusted it around his leg and foot.

"Ah, much better." He stood up and rocked back and forth on his foot. "Almost as good as new."

"Keep them on for a couple days, and you should be back to normal."

"Awesome." He stretched out his appendages and dragged his hands against the thin metal pieces wrapped around his wounds. They felt stronger and more whole now that they had a little help. "Thanks, Vargas."

"Of course." Vargas bowed his head slightly. "Anything I can do to help. Plus, I can't have you a mess under my care when Emma comes along." The front cam turned on to display two obscured faces. "Speaking of…" Vargas walked over to the door.

Dexter listened closely at Vargas greeting his visitors. "Welcome my friends! Emma… I didn't realize you would be bringing the General Proximate along with you." Vargas's voice went sharp and direct as opposed to his normal jovial manner.

A soft voice replied. "I'm sorry, my friend."

The air left Dexter's lungs completely. There wasn't enough space in his chest for his heart that raced and jumped like mad.

He inhaled deeply and purposefully while she continued, "I was trying to be as vague as possible. I'm sure the general or her Scouts keep track of my messages, and I didn't want her to be aware that August was with me." Their footsteps came closer and closer to the room where he and Ryan stood. He steadied his breath and brushed his fingers through his hair.

Vargas continued, "Well, I'm certainly glad you're here. Lina must have finally gotten ahold of you." Emma paused in the archway and turned to face Vargas; her back was all that Dexter could see. "What do you mean? I haven't heard from Lina in a few weeks. She has been out on assignments, as have I."

Vargas paused before he started again. "We have had a development from the E2 portal this week."

Emma straightened her back. "What sort of development? Did something come through it?"

Vargas scratched his head and held his hand out toward the guests in his living room.

Dexter tensed every muscle in his body and braced for her glance. Emma looked up toward the boys from Earth standing in Vargas's living room. Her gaze slowed and paused at Dexter, and he drowned in the bright blue eyes he had been missing for years. Her face was somehow smaller than his, but still held the same look of adventure and whimsy he remembered. He marveled at how much she looked the same, but only a bit of age had shown in the face he saw every night when he closed his eyes. Emma furrowed her brow and studied his face.

"Who are you?" She glanced between the brothers, confused.

Dexter's throat dropped to his stomach, and he swallowed a large, dry gulp.

"Emma, it's me." He held her stare in an invisible embrace. She took small and slow steps toward him, holding his gaze. The corners of her mouth turned down. "There's the upside-down smile I've missed so much."

Emma's eyes widened.

"DEX? Is that you?" she exclaimed. She rushed over and threw her arms around him in a giant bear hug. "How is it that you're taller than me now in just a year and a half? I barely recognize you."

"Emma, I'm fourteen. It's taken me almost three *years* to find you. I refused to give up, and now you're finally here; you hardly seem real, yet the same Emma I remember." He smiled as he hugged her.

She let go and backed away, but only slightly. The distance seemed too far. He wanted to stay in her small sphere of space.

Her face contorted at what he said. "So you mean to tell me there is a *significant* time difference from Merah and Earth?" She looked back at August standing in a tall silence. He looked like a brute. "August. Did you know this?" she demanded as she moved toward him.

"I've never been off Merah, so no," he replied.

Emma walked toward him and as she did, Dexter reached out his hand to stop her, but pulled it back. "You're saying that the possibility of time variation never occurred to you in all your time spent working on the portal plans?"

August looked between everyone in the room. "I guess I knew there was a possibility, especially considering the rapid aging of the Scouts upon their return from missions, but they are the only ones who go off-world. The time difference wouldn't affect anyone else," he admitted.

Emma's gaze hardened. "Anyone else until now. Do you realize I've lost three *years* of my life back on Earth?"

"Does it matter though, when you could do nothing about it?" August replied.

Emma lowered her head. "I guess it really doesn't matter now." She sat down on Vargas's chair in the living room. "It would have been nice to know that my world was significantly outpacing my existence here." She cradled her knees and laid her head in her lap. She looked so small tucked into a ball; Dexter couldn't bear it. He knew what he could do.

"Hold on one second. I have something for you, Emma." He ran to grab his pack and riffled through its contents. He grasped the satin pink shoes he held safely in his pack. He removed the small ballet shoes and laid them softly next to her. "Here. Thought you might want these."

She picked up the light pink ballet slippers and studied every inch of them. Tears welled up in her eyes, and she stood up to bury her face in his chest. "Thank you," she whispered through her light sobs. "Thank you." He wrapped his arms around her and held her tightly.

"Oh, quit your crying, we are *all* stuck here," Ryan interrupted. Dexter glared at his brother's ill-timed comment, but he wouldn't let Emma go, as long as she needed him.

Emma let go of Dexter and wiped her eyes. "Shut up, Ryan," Dexter whispered.

"No, he's right. It's not just me stuck here now. It's both of you, too. And Ryan, I didn't know that was you. It's good to see you." She sat down on the chair and put her ballet slippers on. "Excuse me for a moment." She made her way toward the kitchen. Swift motions and sounds of tapping came from Emma leaping and spinning around. "She always was a beautiful dancer," Dexter thought aloud.

"She really shouldn't be doing that." August made motions toward Emma to stop her.

"No, don't. She needs this. It's the only way she can clear her head," Dexter said.

"Fine, but she must be more careful." August looked toward their host. "Do you at least have shades, so that your entire neighborhood doesn't see her display? I'd hate for a random Scout to come walking by. Too dangerous."

Vargas nodded and brought up house instructions on his holo. The rooms went dark momentarily while they switched to indoor lighting.

"Why is it dangerous for Emma to dance?" Dexter inquired with slight disbelief.

Vargas quickly replied, "The Kabiren do not really like this type of self expression."

"Quite frankly, they are useless, and therefore are... discouraged," August chimed in.

"Yeah, a death sentence is definitely being 'discouraged,'" Vargas snorted.

Emma glided into the room, still in her light pink shoes. "After much thought, we have to look further into the video files we brought, August. The only way I'm going to be able to figure out my place in all this will be to learn more about my past. The only way I can do that is through those files of my mother. Can we download them into Vargas's holo screen so we can get a better view of them? We need all the help we can get to sift through all the video files you have."

Dexter peered at Emma. *Did she just say she would learn about her past from here?* he thought to himself. "Wait, what about your past is here?"

Emma looked down at the ground trying to find the right words to say. "My mother was here on Merah. August found encrypted video files that show her, when she was younger, helping the evil alien race who were not kind to the Amethites before the Kabiren arrived."

"To save the day, mind you," August interrupted.

"That we know of, August. You saw the video. As it stands, my mother was helping a well-known murderous race, but there were also Amethites there too, and they called her the Queen of Featherstone."

Dexter gasped outright. "Wait, you mean the queen from all the stories your dad used to tell you? I thought those were just silly fables, stories he told to get you to go to sleep at night."

"I thought so too, but it seems like those stories were all about my mom, Featherstone, and here. The detail is astounding, from the trees to the sky. I know this place, as I know my own home. This is the Red Planet. This was where my mom trekked. And this will be where I find out about what she has done. August can we please upload the videos?"

August scrunched his nose at Emma. "Are you *sure* that the files are safe... here?" He studied Vargas, Ryan, and Dexter.

"I have a separate computer system that's completely off of the main holo grid." Vargas winked. "Untraceable."

"Your files are safe. Trust me." She looked at him with eager, imploring eyes.

"Fine, Vargas, is it? Can I upload these files to your home tech?" He showed the endless list of files to their host.

"Yes, I have enough space for that amount of data. You'll need to upload it over here though." He motioned for August to follow him.

"I'll come too. I'd love to see this tech," Ryan said, following them quickly.

Finally alone, Dexter turned to Emma, "Soo, what's new?"

The corners of her mouth turned down, and she smiled in her upside-down way that only he noticed. "You first. I think my story will take longer." She chuckled. "Plus it'd be nice to hear about things from home." She looked off into the distance for a moment.

"All right." He smiled and started to tell her all the thoughts he had saved up for her.

While they whispered, there were moments of laughter and more tears. Her laugh penetrated him. All his moments of worry melted away at the sound. But they were perfect moments to Dexter for they all led him here. It felt like Emma never left, and he was home.

33

Emma

Merah
1.5 years since E2 contamination

Emma sat across from her old friend she barely recognized. He was a breath of fresh air, a glimpse of home, and for the first time in a while, she breathed it in again. The amount of time that passed for him paled in comparison to hers. As he spoke to her, his words dripped with sorrow and loss. It was all her doing. The accidental discovery of the portal and her trip to Merah had left his small world broken. She never recognized how much space she took up in his world, and the realization pressed upon her. Her actions, however unintentional, created a kind of obsession in her old friend, built out of loss and grief. The words poured out of Dexter, and she tried to understand the immense effort he put into finding her, effort she was not sure she would have maintained had the roles been reversed.

"So you were able to finish your work with the DNA sequencer in *less* than three years?" she asked, still trying to wrap her head around the time difference between them and the feat of production from the boy she remembered. He could not possibly be the one she had left not that long ago.

"I actually have it with me. It was safe in my pack when I found the portal." He retrieved his beautiful design.

"You made this all by yourself?" she asked, grasping at the sequencer and slightly grazing Dexter's hand in the process. Her face felt momentarily heated; she assumed it was from the new tech she held in her hands. *I'm obsessed with tech just like the Kabiren now.* "What did you use for it to be handheld?"

"That probably was created by Veribo Industries after you went missing. It was the last piece I needed for the sequencer... Veribo could easily take it to Mars after my initial beta testing." He paused and chuckled a bit. "Which I guess they won't be able to do, since I have the only sequencer here with me... That will probably set them back a year or two."

"What were they planning on using the sequencer for on Mars? It doesn't really seem to be relevant to the terraforming timeline we were taught in my classwork." Emma wondered how Veribo Industries could possibly have approved such an expensive project when there were so many others waiting for approval.

"Maybe they really did want to find you. Even though the detectives gave up rather quickly in your missing persons case," he said, a touch of anger in his voice and his eyes dimmed.

She couldn't bear to see that pain in his eyes. "Hey, hey…" Emma spoke softly and moved her head into his eyeline. "But *you* found me."

He looked down at her smiled, and his eyes softened. "Yes, and I'm so glad I did."

Emma paused. Thoughts of Dexter searching for her swam around her mind; she blushed and briefly ducked her head down. She looked back at him and was glad that she still could make him smile through a dark thought. There were times he had that same look in his eye. That look which held the sadness of the world always returned after a fight with his family, or a shove at school. He needed a friend, and she was happy to be the one who could pull those corners of his mouth upright again. Only she knew the amount of times he got *her* out of the black hole of existence. These small efforts she took toward her friend's happiness paled in comparison to the invisible tally she kept of all the ways he helped her. Now she just hoped she did the same for him.

August interrupted her thoughts, "We're uploading the video files. There are more than I initially thought, and this guy Vargas has a very slowww system. It makes me wish we found a better place with a faster holo system." He paused after realizing he interrupted them and stood back. "We have about one hour before it finishes." He left, back to his work.

"Well, we have a bit of time. Feel like an adventure?" she chuckled and raised her eyebrows.

"Lead the way, Daughter of Featherstone." He held his hands out in front of him.

She leaned in to yank her friend up. "Don't call me that," she whispered in his ear and grabbed his arms. "My name is

E2 here, seeing as no one can seem to remember 'Emma.'"
She dragged him up. "C'mon!"

They quickly moved to the door, and after it opened, Emma hollered into the back room, "Vargas, we're heading out for a bit. See you when we get back. Let's go." She pushed Dexter out the door.

"No, wait!" August called out but they were already out.

Their walk started in town and they made their trek around the village toward the bright orange forest.

Emma broke the silence when they passed through the shuttered rows of kiosks. "I'm sure you've already visited the market with Vargas to see his shop?"

"Yeah, it's a great little shop. So many cool things. I was still processing the small wristband holo capabilities a whole day after seeing it." His voice trailed off.

Emma opened her mouth to reply but struggled to find the right words to say. A muddled combination of words were about to escape her mouth, but she clamped it shut. She knew she would sound ridiculous. Their slow walk to the forest turned silent, and Emma wished she had the ability to say exactly what she was thinking. They reached the beaten path heading into the forest. Now they were at the edge, and her feet itched to explore, but now she was curious if her friend felt the same. She wondered at his thoughts while he took in the glorious rich colors. His footsteps behind her were louder and heavier than she remembered. Here was the same kid who she pitied for a supposed fragility, and now, he stood tall behind her with such sure footing. Her pity may have been misplaced. A small tendril of guilt wrapped around her heart.

"Here we are." They reached one of her favorite trees. The burning orange and large deep roots grew through the ground as if they owned the dirt beneath and the sky above them. The tall roots reached up and around the hillside in waves. Emma sat on a particularly worn root stump. Dexter followed her lead and sat down next to her. Time had already slipped through their fingers, but still they watched the waves of the trees and the scurries of the animals.

"I can see why you like it here," Dexter finally whispered. "You found your very own tree to replace the one back home, so no need to go back to it," he said with a small quiver in his voice. He swallowed to clear it.

Emma looked at him with her face scrunched. "What's that supposed to mean?"

"Nothing."

"No, continue please, with accusing me of basically not wanting to come home. If you can remember, I have no way home. I *tried* to find one from the highest source there is here, the general, and there's none to be found. A portal back to Earth *does not exist*."

"Yes, yes I know. You say that, but—" He stopped himself.

"But what?" Emma tried her best to pry at something she was certain he held back.

Dexter dragged his fingers through his hair. "It's just that, for a year, there *wasn't* a way to find you, and eventually people stopped trying. I couldn't take it, losing you, one of my best friends, and not knowing what happened to you, it gutted me…But *I made a way*. I figured it out and… it…it doesn't really feel like you tried all that hard to come back home. You're too busy with this new life and now being—what did that guy call you?—'Protector Emulate.' What even is that?" He looked down at the ground and kicked his metallic-encased heel into the ground.

She played his words through over again and settled them deep in her stomach. There were few times where she felt pure anger in her life. Once when she was little, her baby sister dragged a sharpie marker across her favorite barbie and then proceeded to drop it out of the moving car. Second, when some boys in her old neighborhood kicked a small, wounded lost puppy. And now, this. This was anger. She felt it deep in her chest. An old friend now accused her of the worst, of not trying. The amount of time she spent scouring the logs she had access to, the assignments she went on and hoped that somehow the general was mistaken, and she would see a portal report for E1. The exit portal. The *nonexistent* exit portal. She knew it didn't exist, and she tried everything she could to find it. But Dexter, her best friend, didn't believe it.

Her voice shook, "Do *NOT* compare your apparent 'success' in finding me with what you have seen here and thought of me in what, a day? My level of effort is not tied to success measured by you. My world *ended* when I came here, and I needed to act practically. I moved on with the circumstances I had and did my best. Just because you haven't been here to see my efforts doesn't mean I didn't try," she huffed and stood, determined to walk away and leave him there.

"Wait, wait. Please don't go," Dexter said in soft and soothing tones, the kind of tones he used whenever she sat under her tree and cried back home. They were deeper and stronger than she remembered, but they still held the same calming air. She turned back toward him and his shoulders sunk. "I'm sorry. It's hard for me to see you become this entirely new person on an entirely new planet, while I have been stuck in a memory of you for years." His shoulders shook trying to stifle his emotion.

The knot in Emma's stomach returned to her throat, and she sat down next to her friend, leaned her head on his unsteady shoulder, and let her own small tears fall. Her own unfortunate events that led her here did not prepare her to understand the repercussions of it. The bouts of homesickness were quelled by constantly learning something new about Merah. She didn't have the time to fully process her disappearance. But her friend, who not only had time to fully process it, still felt it deeply. Dexter dragged her back to the day she arrived and the hopelessness she felt.

"Sometimes we can hate what we've lost, but still love what we find. I'm glad you found me," she spoke softly. "I was beginning to think no one really missed me. Thank you."

They both stared off into the vast distance of twisted trees and melting suns. The day was beginning its descent into night with its red hues turning purple. Emma felt his every breath with the rise and fall of his comfortable shoulder.

"I didn't really mean what I said. You were always the smart one. It seems hard to believe you, of all people, couldn't figure out a way to get home," he admitted.

Emma sat up slowly. "I tried; I really tried. There were so many logs in Merah's system I searched for some sign of E1." She held her hands out in frustration with not only her situation, but her utter failure. She had no way back to Earth, and it gutted her.

"Well, I guess we all are stuck here then. Let me tell you though, that sky, beautiful.

It's what I imagine the sky on the surface of Mars looks like."

"You mean you never got the chance to see it for yourself? I thought fast track students had their field trip there before final assessments?"

"Mine was scheduled for next week," he laughed. "Just my luck to get lost right before my first off world exploration field trip. At least here, I can look up at the sky and pretend I'm on Mars, the colors are mesmerizing!"

Emma chuckled, "Yeah, I'm sure Mars is great and all, but Merah is something else entirely." Then Emma had a tiny thought. A trickle of an idea that she never entertained, because she honestly never saw a connection. The stories her dad told her about her mom flooded back. He always said that they met while on his first shuttle run to Mars while he spoke about her beauty and how easily they conversed, but one thing he never really mentioned was exactly *how* he met her.

Her mother never spoke about her life before Mars, and Emma was beginning to finally understand why. Maybe because it never really began in that system before Mars. In the video August found, her mother *was* escaping through a portal—she assumed it to be a long lost portal to Earth that was never rebuilt, but maybe it wasn't a portal to Earth she went through at all... Maybe it was a portal to *Mars*.

Emma stood quickly and turned to Dexter. "You brought my entire school pack with you right? The one my pointe shoes were in?"

"Yeah."

"I might have an idea to get home, but I need to get back to August." Dexter stood up and nodded. "Then let's go, E2."

34

Lina

Merah
1.5 years since E2 contamination

Lina's meeting with the general replayed in her mind. There was a tough road ahead. Normally she crushed all her assignments, but this one seemed insurmountable. She wished with all her heart that she had destroyed the E2 boys when they came through. She'd messed up, broken the Protector code when she let Emma live, and now she was in a grossly dangerous habit. A habit she needed to break.

She slid through Harimanne's village quickly and quietly en route to her own village. "Maybe a brief visit with an old friend would help," she said to Maut, laying in the seat next to her. Harimanne had a knack for always being able to say the right thing at the right time. She needed that. The roller passed the main street to Harimanne's quarters, and Lina needed to double back to get there. She should have decided on this visit quicker and wouldn't have had to deal with traffic in the village center, right at midday rush. It was torture waiting to get through all those people heading toward the market.

She hurried through the street only to notice some Scouts at the far corner of the pathway. They looked similar to the ones she'd seen as she left the general's office, but she couldn't be sure. They were so hard to recognize individually. As she sat in a crosswalk for passing pedestrians, a small Amethite girl, six or seven, walked along the road with a little wooden block carved into a figure. She couldn't quite make it out, but it reminded Lina of Emma. She smiled at the girl slowly passing, then suddenly the girl twirled and leapt around the crowd, spinning in a circle with incredible grace. Lina sucked in a breath at the display. Her eyes darted around the square. She noticed the wonder and joy that came from the small girl, and she smiled.

Lina's smile drained from her face when two Scouts rushed through the passing crowd right toward the little girl. She screamed at the top of her lungs watching them grab her. The girl dug her heels into the ground, pulling her arms out from underneath the Scouts' grasp. She slid out from their arms and ran to evade them, weaving in and out of the crowded market. The Scouts initiated their shields and shot up a sound wave emitter, meant to immobilize a crowd, and everyone in a five-foot radius fell down flat, including the small girl. The dazed village dwellers shook their heads in confusion. The Scouts nabbed the girl and carried her motionless body to the transport shuttle site.

Lina choked back a tear but rode on past the crowd. "Reckless girl," she whispered to Maut. No one had ever made such a public display so blatantly in front of Scouts before. "That's what happens when you break the rules." She couldn't help but blame herself. In some way, this was her fault. She let Emma into Merah. Here, she failed to protect the Amethites—a mistake she couldn't make again. "Sorry, Maut, no visit with Harimanne today. I have an assignment to do."

Lina turned the roller back toward the path, out of the village. It was time for her to finish her assignment. She had no choice but to protect the people of Merah. It was her only job, and she couldn't fail.

35

August

Merah
1.5 years since E2 contamination

August tapped his fingers impatiently on the table and watched the processing bar fill to completion for his video files. He never used such a slow computer, and he wondered if all the villages experienced the same levels of tech speed. He never really thought about the limitless access he had at headquarters and his family association that let him take whatever he needed whenever his lab needed it. The length of time this upload took made him want to put his head through the wall.

Vargas walked in. "Need any help with the files? Or some tea?"

August groaned. "No, I don't need anything, other than this unit to process faster."

Vargas backed away with a nod.

"Yes, finally!" He selected a random video file.

Flickers of light were cast around the image of a Kabiren, and the video blinked in and out of focus. Out of the corner of the holo screen, a figure that looked like the Nerezza slid into view quietly.

The Kabiren bowed and spoke in a hushed tone. "Good evening, my queen." "Were you followed?" said the queen with a quiver of worry.

"I wasn't followed by a Scout, but I cannot say the same about security bots. They would have no idea why I'm here though."

"True, our plans have managed to stay concealed, for now. Do you have the most recent portal locations and plans?

"Yes, here." He handed her a small holo screen. "The entire file is on there, and it has been deleted off the main computer."

"Will they notice they're missing?"

"Only if they search for them in the next three hours. The program is rewriting as we speak."

"Great. Where are we on the Cal Project?"

"Unfortunately, not as far as I'd like. The lab has additional safety units being added and rotated daily. It makes me think they're aware we're planning something."

"Good thing we kept our plans separate. We may have a mole on the Cal team. Please do further inquiries."

"Yes, my queen."

The video file faded out to static but August did a keyword search for "Cal Project." Two videos returned with a partial match. His finger itched to play the next one, but it was met with a warm cup of tea from Vargas.

"Thank you," he said gruffly.

"You're welcome. Have you found anything interesting yet?" Vargas inquired with almost too chipper of a tone.

"Yes, I hope Emma will return promptly." He checked his wristband with a holo map showing her indicator dot. "She's close by."

As he finished speaking, Emma, with Dexter close behind, scrambled into the home and grabbed at a bag, revealing an old square piece of tech. Her face lit up when it powered on, and she dragged her finger across its screen, until she stopped and pointed to something displayed.

"Aha! There! August! Can you pull up the portal locations and an overlay map from the video of my mother you showed me?"

"Yes, why? What are you looking for?"

"I'm looking for the location of the portal my mother used when she left Merah. In the stories my Dad used to tell me about Merah, my Mom frequented a mountain with deep silver circles etched into them. I think that is where the portal to my solar system is. Do you think we can find it?"

He displayed the file. "We should be able to. But odds are the blast destroyed it. I don't know why you'd want to find it. Here." He grabbed the file and displayed the map overlay through his holo screen. "Huh." The map location for the video did not have a valid portal location displayed. "That's odd."

"What?"

"I'm not finding a portal log for this specific location. According to this, it doesn't exist."

"But we saw them leave through the portal. Even if it was destroyed, there should still be at least an old log, right?"

"Yes, there would be a log, and I have location markers here. But the plans for that specific portal are not showing anywhere. What are you thinking?"

Emma looked back toward Dexter. "A very wise friend told me that he thought it hard to believe that with all the tech Merah has, we can't find some way back to Earth. It reminded me of the stories my father used to tell me when I was small. I never heard about my mom and her life on Earth. Most of the stories all start when they met on Mars. So maybe, there isn't a portal to Earth…" She paused.

August inhaled a quiet gasp, following her lead. "Then the portal she may have used was not to Earth, but to Mars."

"Yes, exactly. If we can somehow find a portal near a hillside or mountain with those silver circles, maybe assess the damage, if it still exists, we might be able to rebuild it."

August was excited at the thought of building a portal. He had finished so many plans, he could easily try his hand at a portal that was already in existence. Just maintenance work with a twist. "But what about time? My mother is definitely going to notice something is up if we don't return to Headquarters shortly."

"Isn't there any excuse you can give?" she pleaded.

He searched his own training logs from his old assignments. There was a cleanup assignment that required a significant amount of time to process during his trainee days. He could mirror that assignment in the system, volunteer Emma for it, and that might give them the right amount of time. He typed in the assignment request into the main Protector server. "That should do it. Emma, please accept that assignment immediately."

Her wristband pinged the brand-new assignment. "Ugh, a gardening assignment. We're going on a gardening assignment?"

"It's the only kind I could think of that would take the amount of time we need. And no, of course we aren't going on a gardening assignment. Let's hope they think we are though."

There was a plan forming but they needed to carry it out quickly. "So we leave in the early morning, okay?"

"Sounds good."

Dexter shifted behind her. "I'm coming, too."

August huffed. "There really is no need. We'll be fine."

Emma interjected, "Dexter is very resourceful; he would be an *asset*, not a hindrance."

"Fine. We leave at suns-rise."

A chime at the front of the home stilled them. There was no way the Scouts could know what they were planning already. So the fact that there was a visitor only slightly bothered August. He would have to make an excuse for them, and he would have to do it soon. Vargas's excited tone and cheerful welcomes could be heard in the processing room, and he and his guest walked through to the back.

"Look who has decided to join us today." Lina and Maut slid out from behind him and waved.

"Are we all on vacation today?" She looked around at everyone seated. "So what do we have on our plate today, my friends?"

"Emma and I actually have an assignment to begin tomorrow morning," August quickly replied.

"Was it that big cleanup assignment that came through? I saw the general notification pushed out to the Protectors, but Emma accepted it first." She raised her holo notifications on her wristband. "That's going to take you all a looong time. That's not a day's task."

"They can manage it with *my* help," replied Dexter, and he glared at August.

"Yes, yes. Emma's friend is coming, too," August said, sounding slightly disappointed and waving in Dexter's general direction.

Dexter glared at him before he addressed his attention to Lina. "What happened to getting me into contact with Emma, Mylinah? She didn't even know I was here."

Lina shifted her stance. "I do have other important things to attend to besides being your messenger. I had to get to headquarters on Protector business. I knew you would be well cared for at Vargas's home while I handled my job first."

This was the first time August heard of Lina being at headquarters recently. She normally wasn't tasked there, so whatever Protector business she could have possibly had there puzzled him. Emma looked slightly uncomfortable before she opened her mouth.

"You *knew* Dexter came through the E2 portal, and you *didn't even message me*?"

Lina moved closer to Emma and put her small hand upon Emma's arm. She peered up at her with sincere eyes. "I was not sure you were prepared to meet someone from E2. I also had no way to verify what Dexter said was the truth. I wanted to be able to devote the appropriate amount of time you may have needed from me. So I handled my headquarters business first before coming to you. You can understand, right? I wanted to be there for you, in person."

Emma looked down at her small friend and smiled. "Thank you, Lina." She patted Maut's head. "You too, buddy." Emma brought her attention back to August with raised brows. "We really could use all the help we can get. Please bring up the video files. Let's see if there's more information we can find about my mother."

August hesitated with the growing crowd in the room. There was so much he still didn't know and no way he was going to ask his mother about it. He tried to count the number of lies she told him, but they piled up into a tangled mess, and he stopped counting. He studied the faces of everyone in the room: Emma, Lina, Vargas, Dexter, and Ryan all eagerly anticipating his next move. He needed help. If these secrets spilled over too quickly, there may not be enough time to mop them up, and he couldn't risk the loss of control. Emma had her own reasons for wanting to search through the video files. Family curiosity and a chance to get home seemed to rate high on that list. He wondered what kind of deep connection drew a line so strong that the pull would be irresistible. Emma had that attachment to Earth. Did he have that bond to Merah? He contemplated the E2 girl he had come to know over the past year and a half. This friend of hers, Dexter, a brave soul with a strong heart, happened to be a pull of that heart, and August found himself wishing he too had such a connection. Now he had the opportunity to have faith in something. It wasn't something that came easy, but he trusted the E2 girl.

"All right, here we go." He replayed the files he showed Emma first and then the most recent one. They all watched, intently searching through the videos. Lina shifted her shoulders straight and glared intently with a furrowed brow as they played.

"Man, it really is Mrs. R. Right, Dex?" Ryan popped his head out of the back of the group. August became even more uneasy about the amount of people in the room, but he might need every single one of them,

"She's younger, but that's definitely Emma's mom." Dexter looked at the videos closer.

"Yes, we've established it's my mother," Emma said. "But what does that mean? What was she doing here on Merah? How did she get here? And how exactly did she get to Earth? These are answers we are looking for here, focus."

"Maybe she came here by a portal?" Dexter rubbed under his chin.

"But why come at all? Why insert yourself into all this?" Emma waved her hands around.

They all shrugged at each other with uncertain faces.

August rubbed his eyes and stopped the video files. "Okay, I think we have gone through all we can tonight. We'll learn more after investigating the portal location tomorrow."

"We should turn in. Vargas, think this tiny place can house all of us?" asked Dexter.

Vargas smiled, "If you are okay with being floor dwellers, then absolutely!"

"While sleeping on the floor is mighty tempting, I think I'll take my leave to my own quarters and rejoin you in the morning. Have a good night. C'mon, Maut," Lina said and they departed.

36

Dexter

Merah

1.5 years since E2 contamination

Dexter sat across from Ryan on Vargas's floor. Ryan's feet crept closer and closer to his brother's face, and Dexter's tiny nostril hairs twitched with every close encounter with them.

"I know we're trying to sleep in a small space, but could you not creep so close to me, Ryan?" he whispered and then shoved Ryan's feet away from his face.

A small snort escaped his brother's nose but he lurched awake. "Sorry, dude," he muttered. "I can't help where my feet end up if I'm asleep." He yawned, his mouth opened wide. "What time is it anyway?"

"Shhhh. Don't wake Emma." Dexter pointed to Emma slumbering in the chair across the room. "It's still the middle of the night."

"Okayyy. Geez. I thought I *was* being quiet. Why do you always have to attack me?" He tugged his blanket tighter and turned over.

Dexter sucked in a breath and sat up. "Attack *you?* You think I always attack you?" he whispered forcefully.

"Yes, you do. No matter what I do, it's always wrong, or stupid and I'm so sick of your arrogant attitude."

"Me? Arrogant? C'mon, Ry."

"But you are! You were always way too busy for me, or anyone else who wasn't named Emma or Jericho or Mr. Stretcher. Too busy doing more scholarly things than spending time with me. You left me at home with Jeff and Chad, and I had to endure their merciless torture."

"What do you mean *you* were tortured? You were always in on it. Way more than them! I had to throw myself into school to be able to get away from you."

Their whispered breaths stirred Emma, and with their increased volume, she turned in her sleep.

Ryan paused, and after being reassured of her continued slumber, he continued, "Of course I had to be in on it, Dex. Do you know what they would have done to you if I hadn't? Trust me, anything I did to you pales in comparison to what they were capable of doing. And I wasn't about to let anything happen to you. Not on my watch." Ryan turned in the opposite direction, refusing to look him in the eyes.

The darkness veiled his brother's face, but through the shadows, Dexter caught a glimmer of a tear in his brother's eye. His stomach sank, and he sat motionless, unable to formulate a reply.

"Let's get some rest. We all have a big day tomorrow," he laid his head back down. This time he didn't mind the feet.

37

Lina

Merah
1.5 years since E2 contamination

Lina flumped down in her chair upon arrival at home. She felt the trek from headquarters in her bones. The rush to complete her assignment, only to be confronted by witnesses, was quickly quelled. Worry lines in her face grew deeper. The Nerezza was Emma's mother, and the Queen of Featherstone, she heard the words straight from her mouth. That must be why the general has been so interested in Emma. Flashes of Mentiren and Amethites protecting the queen swam around her mind. She searched her holo for records of the queen. Nothing. There was no way that any Amethite would work with a Mentiren, especially to protect a thief like the queen. She was bad, everyone knew that. The Amethites *never* would have helped any of them.

Would they?

Every Amethite knew the stories of the queen and how she threatened the safety of all on Merah. An image of the young girl in Harimanne's village laid out flat and motionless after her imitation of Emma's dancing flashed before Lina's eyes. *That* is what Emma and the Queen of Featherstone's influence have over Merah. Distractions that tore the Amethites focus away from their goal. Merah was the most technologically advanced planet in the universe, and it was her job to not let any contaminates disrupt that.

The videos August played had to be fake. There was no other explanation. She chose to be a Protector of Merah, and she would continue to do that with this assignment. Finishing her E2 assignment would be more difficult than she originally thought. Not a lot of opportunity to get rid of the two E2 contaminates. Maybe tomorrow would be her only chance, but she knew so little of their plan and feared further inquiries. Emma had been suspicious of her hiding the boys' existence, but seemed to accept her explanation.

There was a small certainty that August and Emma had not informed the general of their plans. The general said Emma was not her responsibility; August had control of the situation, but he didn't seem too interested in bringing Emma to headquarters. This job was basic, but the location of the job was suspect. She hadn't gone further than the E2 portal site for an assignment since she took her Protector post. She lacked clarity, but maybe a message to the general would fix that. She opened her message holo:

To: General Sotora, From: Protector 42

Arrived at location to finish E2 cleanup. Complication has arisen. General Proximate August and Emma also are at location with Protector assignment plans that will lengthen my assignment completion. Going ahead with plan completion at the first available opportunity. Please advise should my assignment be adjusted.

A small trickle of sweat beaded on her brow while her hand hovered over the send command. She hoped this complication would not affect her Protector status, but really, her assignments could not get more basic than they were already. And who knew, maybe a successful completion of the E2 assignment would garner a higher tier, or maybe her own shuttle and an assignment at headquarters. That she could live with.

sent

Lina tossed and turned in a sleepless night.

The tips of the suns peeked over the horizon and light cascaded through the small window in Lina's room. She forced her body up, slid out of bed, and put her clothes on. She adjusted her long-sleeved shirt over her wristband and rolled out her Protector storage unit from beneath her bed and stared at her assigned equipment. The specialty holo screen with information chip and the blaster were a given, but there was also a small knife buried in the corner. Such an ancient tool, but one that had proven useful in the past. The last time she used it stayed in a memory she couldn't quite quell. She reached for the tool, but paused only to grab it and stuff it into the depths of her bag. Maut gnawed on a corner of the bag. She wiggled and tugged her boots on and tapped her door open. She escaped into the morning air. "C'mon, Maut. We have a big day ahead of us."

Her roller was parked outside, and her stomach grew tighter and tighter as she drove the path to her old friend's home. She took this path frequently, but this time seemed different—it had a sense of finality. She brushed off the feeling and arrived at Vargass' with a painted-on smile and shifting eyes.

"You made it!" Emma smiled at her.

"Well, it seems like you all are right where I left you. Did any of you sleep last night?" She smiled.

"We...we did not. Okay?" August peeled his eyes away from the video file he had up on his holo to quickly swipe it away.

He didn't need to do that. Lina didn't need to know what was in those obviously faked videos. No video of the *supposed* collaboration of the Amethites and the Queen of Featherstone made any difference. Emma's mother or not, she was a destroyer and a thief on Merah, and Lina would ensure those qualities remained flushed from her beloved planet, always.

"So are we heading out soon, or what?" she quipped. "Assignment time is upon us."

"Let's go over our plan," August said.

Emma stepped forward. "We need to make sure we can gather as much information as possible from any remnants of the portal." She viewed the map on her holo screen and pointed to a deserted area.

Lina looked at her own map of the same coordinates and again, it showed nothing. "Where exactly is this portal we're going to look at? Cause my holo's got nothing—"

Dexter interrupted, "Emma thinks the portal her mother used to leave Merah was in that location."

"So basically we're going solely on hunches here." Ryan laughed, and Dexter shot a glare at him.

"It's not a random guess," August said. "From my calculations and Emma's description of the hillside and silver circles, this is the most probable location for the portal in the video of the queen. I mean, Emma's mom."

"So what kind of information do we need?" Lina asked.

"We need to see if there is anything remaining from the portal, anything we can use, so August can try to rebuild it," Emma chimed in while loading her pack with snacks. Dexter looked at her and chuckled. "What?" she asked.

"Nothing. You and your love of food, as usual. That hasn't changed one bit."

Lina scrunched her brow at their banter. A food obsession was not one that should be glorified or even encouraged. The general would not approve. Yet, her supervisor, just let it go on as if it were normal. He spent too much time with her, and Emma rubbed off on more people than Lina originally thought.

They all squeezed into their rollers. These machines were built for three people at the most. However, their group managed to get everyone into two of them. The less in the carpool, the better. Vargas and Emma hopped into August's roller. Lina motioned for Dexter and Ryan to join her, and they quickly jumped in. Too easy. They were like trusting

Vadeeren animals, the ones who came at the slightest call or whistle to their own death as the next Amethite meal. Dexter and Ryan were under her control, and she could carry out her mission without a hitch. Her messages dinged.

From: General Sotora, To: Protector 42

Complication understood. Hold off on completion of original mission in regard to the additional E2 intruders. Continue with my son and the E2 girl, and report your findings throughout your journey. Do not disclose this request to your party.

Lina pulled at her cheeks.

"Something wrong?" Dexter asked.

"Thought I left something back home. But we're good." She started up the roller to follow August.

She was so close to finishing her job, but her throat tightened. The threads of her mistake still laid bare and unfinished, and she was now asked to leave them open. The image of the young girl from Harimanne's village rushed back into her mind. She would never again let Emma or any of these contaminates influence another Amethite. She tightened her grip on the roller's controls and started the drive.

August set a scatter beacon from his roller ahead. He didn't want anyone else to track their location, and the beacon's field was big enough to scramble both of their rollers' trackers. August definitely knew how to cover his tracks, and Lina would have to be careful to keep him in her sight, otherwise she could lose them. If only she'd thought to grab the map location for her roller before they left. It was a careless slip on her part that made her entirely too dependent on August's roller. She didn't like that.

They made several stops along their trek. First, a stop to relieve themselves after being cramped together for several hours. Second, to order some sheet metal at August's request for delivery upon their return. Lina was relieved when she knew they wouldn't both need to haul it in their already cramped rollers. And lastly, to grab some food at a local market tucked away in the outskirts of their region. This was way past the portal sites near Porta that Lina had frequented, and it felt a bit foreign to her. She never realized there had been portals this far out and didn't truly believe of the existence of one, even now. There weren't stories told of assignments out here, ever.

The valley stretched out far and wide across the horizon. The day slipped away during their trek. They would have to camp out in the valley because there were no lodgings nearby. August's roller veered off the path and turned to the west. There weren't any worn paths, and the roller pressed its way over leaves and unpacked dirt. There were several moments Lina wasn't sure her patched-together roller would make it through, but she knew Vargas was excellent with machinery, and he had put his heart into her machine. At least he was with them and could tend to it if it broke down or dirt got stuck in its igniter.

Once the hum of the roller stopped, the clicks and chirps of the night surrounded them.

"This seems like a fairly covered spot in the valley. We should set up camp here," August said.

"Did we bring enough supplies for camp?" Emma replied in a worried tone.

"I think you brought enough food three times over." Dexter nudged her and laughed.

"Ugh, stop flirting, you guys," Ryan said, clearly annoyed at their ever-growing friendliness.

They set up camp. The heat generator warmed them as they sat around its core. Emma's small blanket barely covered her shoulders, and it slid a bit. She shivered and tried to stretch it over her body. When it dropped from her shoulders, Dexter wrapped his side of the blanket around her, and they held out their hands to the warming unit in silence. They were all tired from the ride.

"Well, I'm going to retire." Lina stepped away from the party. "See you in the morning." She slowly made her way to her sleeping pack and lay in the dark with Maut curled up at her side. She pulled up her messages on her wristband and typed a rather boring report to the general.

From: Protector 42, To: General Sotora

Location pings set up from current location. Several unimportant stops made, except one to purchase a significant amount of sheet metal. Unsure about its use for now. Will update upon arrival at the coordinates followed by General Proximate.

Lina let out a deep, quivering exhale. Tomorrow would bring answers that would hopefully satisfy the general so she could complete her mission. She fell asleep on the hard, uneven surface. It was exactly the discomfort she deserved for what she was about to do.

38

Emma

Merah
1.5 years since E2 contamination

T he suns' heat rose over the valley in pink waves, stretching out from over the hills.

Emma shivered from the chill of the cold ground and scooted closer to the nearest form of heat her back could find. That heat generator felt warm, and she sleepily snuggled closer to it. It calmed her shivers and was incredibly soft for a hunk of metal. A cozy arm curled itself over her. Emma's eyes shot open. Dexter's arm was wrapped around her as he slept. The chill outside was not welcome, so Emma stayed put until the suns rose higher. She closed her eyes, waiting.

"Wake up, everyone! We don't have much further, but we have a lot to do once we get there," August boomed.

Emma's eyes opened slowly. She had fallen back asleep. Dexter's arm shot up from around her when he realized where it laid. His cheeks turned bright pink. "Sorry," he muttered, shaking his head, and he started to pack up his blanket.

Emma stretched and ran her fingers through her hair. Everyone else shook their blankets out and splashed some water on their faces. It was early but they needed to leave. They packed up their things and got into their respective rollers. They stared back at each other through the glass and metal windows. A small smile crept across Emma's face, and Dexter smiled back. She looked down in her seat and hoped that no one else saw her burning cheeks.

The terrain was fairly smooth the entire way to the location. They slowly came to a stop, and August's roller beeped its arrival there. No clear path laid ahead toward the portal, because the brush had grown into twisting fences. They would have to cut through in order to get anywhere.

Emma and Vargas hopped out of the roller while August checked his holo screen.

"I'm fairly certain we need to head north," August said.

"Are you sure? This doesn't really look anything like the video we saw, August," Emma replied.

"It was completely destroyed in the video and the terrain has been regrowing. Who knows what it could look like now?"

"True. Let's go." She threw on her pack and twirled ever so slightly on her toe.

Ryan was trying to hold in a laugh, but it burst out.

"What?" Emma paused for a response.

"You look ridiculous, always hopping and twirling around," Ryan said. Dexter socked him in the arm.

"Hey! It's true. You don't see anyone else dancing at any given moment."

Emma dragged her toes over to Dexter's brother and glared at him. "Just because you don't understand something, doesn't mean it's ridiculous. Plenty of people have different outlets, and dancing happens to be the one I love."

"And it happens to be adorable," Dexter whispered under his breath. Emma pretended not to hear, but her cheeks flushed pink again. She turned in the direction they needed to go and walked. "Leave her alone," he whispered to Ryan, watching her walk away. He left Ryan and followed her.

"Dude, I'm kidding!" Ryan hollered, running after them and throwing his arm around Dexter's neck just behind Emma.

"You know I do really like her, right?" he said quietly when he thought Emma couldn't hear.

"I'm sorry; I think I get jealous sometimes. You left me alone at home with tweedle dee and tweedle dumb, and they were relentless. I hated that you had somewhere to go and I... well I didn't." His voice cracked.

"Well, now you are stuck with both of us." Dexter lightly jabbed his brother in the stomach, and they laughed.

Emma smiled slightly, pretending not to eavesdrop. She was glad to see a real relationship forming between the two brothers. After last night, they needed it. Because Dexter was right; they were all stuck together. But she hoped she would somehow make it right.

"Stop, Emma!" August ran ahead of her and stopped short. His holo revealed a small trigger of light expanding across their path. "Don't move. This may be a trap. Let me see if I can overload its outgoing signal." He typed a few codes into his holo and the beam dimmed. "Okay, you should be good."

"What sort of a signal is it?" Emma asked.

"Not sure exactly. All I know is they can be used to trigger anything from a message to a weapon."

"Someone wants to know who is here?"

"Would seem so."

"Who?"

"I have no idea. But keep your eyes peeled. We could be walking into literally anything."

"C'mon, let's go. We must be close to something at least." Emma stepped over the dimmed beam and continued forward. Lina and Vargas came up behind them unaware of it.

"Tread lightly; someone's interested in whoever comes here," August hollered back at Lina and Vargas.

"What?" Lina replied.

August pointed at the now clearly visible signal beam. They slowly stepped over it. They joined closer together just in case there were additional signal beams or something else to catch them off guard. Emma walked further and dug her heels into the soft dirt creating a small pathway for the others. The trees parted slightly, and she hopped over a boulder to reveal a large meadow. It was picture-perfect and exactly like the video, although a little overgrown. The meadow and hills rolled in waves of grass. The hills around them began to get larger and steeper before they saw them. Etched in the stone were circles of worn-down silver.

"Can you pull up the video again? Maybe it will help us with where to go," she called back to August.

He nodded and jogged closer to her so they could review the video. The holo showed the queen passing a small clearing, one that looked similar to the one they were in. They had to be close. A tiny worn path lay ahead of them, and it would have gone completely unnoticed had Emma not been specifically looking for it. She followed the small path to where it abruptly stopped. The rest of her party trailed behind her and noticed the empty area.

"Sooo, what are we looking for exactly here? Because this looks like a bunch of nothing," Ryan said.

Emma brought up a scanner on her wristband. "Lina, August, can you help me?" She started scanning the sections around where they stood. Lina and August both joined her in scanning, each taking their own section and working in grid patterns to slowly work toward Emma.

August returned a beep. "I may have something over here." He peeled away purple vines entwined on the ground. They all joined him and kicked and yanked at the vines. Emma's hands slid over a small piece of metal lodged in the dirt.

"Here! I think it's here," she yelled with clumps of dirt and weeds all around her. Everyone dug deeper and each revealed a small rounded corner of metal. "This is it!" Emma peeled back a small panel on the weathered portal platform. The circuit on the portal, if it was still intact, would show an entire backlog of information they could use. "August, can you come to this side? I think I have the circuit house over here. Can your holo access it? My wristband doesn't seem to be able to. But it might be completely dead."

August jumped over to the circuit panel and flicked open his holo. It beeped with a sudden access to the circuit. The holo returned the circuit information. This model was different, to be sure, but it had to be the one used by Emma's mom. August initiated a full information-retrieval program, and the holo sped through lines and lines of information.

They scrolled through dates and times used lists, to intricate plans for additional panels in the platform. It revealed a treasure trove.

"Yesss!" Emma hopped into a twirl. "This is more information than I thought a portal was capable of containing."

"It must be one of the most recent portals made. I haven't seen any of them this advanced," Lina said, blinking toward the ground. Her shoulders sank slightly.

"I wonder why we don't have any of these records though. There clearly is a portal here. Damaged, sure, but we should have some record of it," Emma replied.

"Not necessarily. Before we defeated the Mentiren, they did manage to destroy some of their records. Maybe the information for this one was deleted before we took over their logs." August said.

The download took longer than Emma wanted it to. She searched around for where Dexter and Ryan wandered off to. She thought they mentioned something about going to find a place to go to the bathroom. She hoped they wouldn't linger far away for too long. There was so much information from the portal to download. Lina mentioned people rarely came out here. She smiled and looked briefly at her friend. Lina busied herself checking her wristband but looked up at Emma smiling at her.

"What are you busy with over there?" Emma asked her.

Lina shuffled from one foot to another and looked around the clearing quickly. "Trying to find something to do as we wait. And how long, General Proximate, do we have before this thing is finished?" she asked.

"Not long. The space on my holo is filling up. Either the information stops, or space for it stops. We won't have to wait much longer," he replied with a shrug.

"I'll go check on the boys while it finishes up. Maybe they have something better to distract me." Lina held out her arm to Maut, and they both darted away.

"I do hope they haven't wandered too far away. We need to be able to get back and analyze all this data quickly. We have barely a week before we are supposed to get back to headquarters and report to the General," Emma muttered, concerned.

"We'll be fine, Emma," August chuckled. "No other Scouts know we're here, and we're almost finished."

"No, other Scouts we *know* of," Emma said.

They scrolled through endless pages on August's holo. Either way, it was going to be interesting processing it. There were so many coordinates, dates, and plans showing in the circuit, Emma was excited to be able to see it. Her curiosity about what it contained revolved around her mother and Mars. She hoped it would have the exact arrival location and the date she left through the portal. It would put Emma one step closer to her mother and home.

A small whistle whirred through the breeze around them. Emma looked at August. "Do you hear that?" August poked his head up and listened closely. The whistle grew louder and louder.

"Run!" he said, jerking his holo from the portal. He grabbed her arm. His large gait made it difficult for her to keep up, but she ran hard and fast. A loud explosion blasted through the air, destroying the clearing and what was left of the portal. The pulses from it shot toward Emma and August, knocking them down to their knees. And the pulses kept coming. Every time she tried to raise herself from her knees, she was hit again, pushed to stay stationary on the ground.

Out of the trees came two of the oldest Scouts she had ever seen. Wrinkles creased their faces and hands. One held a square box emitting blue pulses of light. The pulses increased and were now directly aimed at Emma and August. They couldn't move while the blue pulses pushed them down. The Scouts stood above them with their blasters drawn.

"General Proximate, it looks like you are far off course from your assignment," one Scout said. "The general is not pleased with your choices as of late." He nodded to his comrade.

"What exactly are you doing out here, boy?"

August's lips remained motionless, but his eyes glared a fiery determination. His mother had to have been watching them, had to have sent these Scouts. Emma knew he would be resolute in his silence, but what about the others?

The others! Dexter. Emma hoped he was far enough away from the blast. For him to make it all the way here only to end up in the blast radius of an evil Kabiren Scout would be the worst end. She hoped with all her heart that he was okay, even if she may not be.

The Scout aimed the blaster closer to August's head and spoke again. "Time is ticking. Answer the question."

"There are definitely more of us than there are of you, so I would watch where you point that blaster," August said in a huff.

The Scouts looked at each other and laughed. Emma and August exchanged confused looks.

"C'mon out, 42. We really need to see these numbers," the Scout shouted into the air.

Emma's eyes widened, unable to believe what she was seeing. Dexter, Ryan, and Vargas slowly approached with their hands raised. They were pushed forward by the point of a blaster, and Lina held it tight. Maut's teeth clenched at Ryan's pantleg.

Emma gasped. Her first friend on Merah threatened the life of her oldest friend on Earth. Emma looked away to hide a silent tear. Lina could never do something like this, yet, she was betraying all of them.

Emma's heart pounded. Lina must have relayed their position and plans to the Scouts. There were no visible bots, and no one else was aware of their plans. Vargas interrupted her thoughts.

"Why are you doing this, Lina?" he asked quietly.

Lina's gaze faltered slightly but she quickly raised it high. "My job is to protect Merah. Not anything else. Those from E2 are a danger to Merah, and I am destroying the foreign contaminates," she said while pointing the blaster at Dexter and Ryan.

The brothers quickly glanced at each other, and Ryan slyly mouthed "moose," then let out an annoyed whine. "UGH, I can't believe I followed you all the way here for THIS, Dexter. This is all your fault."

"ME? MY FAULT! You think EVERYTHING is my fault! But you know what, it's not. You're just an idiot with nothing else to do." Dexter shoved him with a jab, and Maut loosened his tug.

"That's it!" Ryan yelled as he hurled himself at Dexter, and they fell into a tumble. Dexter punched Ryan in the stomach, and Ryan held Dexter's throat. The Scouts ran over to quell the commotion, leaving Emma and August unguarded but still forced to the ground by the blue pulses from the square cube held by the Scouts.

August pushed his arm through the pulses and into his pack, drawing out a small, round cylinder. The deflector field powered by the cylinder would generate a nice protective shield from the pulses, but Emma wasn't sure it had the range to protect all of them. Either way, she hoped August would act quickly. She was ready to pull her blaster the moment it triggered.

Dexter and Ryan had their arms at each other's throats now. Dexter was pinned by his older brother, and they were screaming. Lina stood watching the scene. "Stop!" She held out her blaster, her aim slightly faltering because she couldn't focus on which of the boys to shoot. The Scouts partially redirected the pulse beam toward the boys, and they were stuck in their throat-bared positions. Lina jumped onto Ryan's neck to peel him off of Dexter and tugged him out of the pulse beam with one hand while the other grasped her blaster. Ryan kicked backwards forcefully to shake her loose, and they landed squirming on the ground. A Scout ran up and grabbed Ryan by the neck with one hand to yank him off of Lina. His blaster discharged twice in quick succession, and Ryan, with clouded eyes, slumped motionless to the ground.

"NOOOO!" Dexter exclaimed, and he tried to yank free from the pulses. Emma couldn't look away from Dexter, and she watched him scream. But she had a job to do, and she grabbed her blaster while August, in one swift motion, ran up behind to discharge the deflector field. With Dexter released from the pulses, August grabbed him and pulled him to his feet, while Emma held her blaster aimed at the Scouts.

Vargas quickly ran up to the Scouts, grabbed the pulse trigger, and redirected the blue pulses toward them.

Lina remained pinned by Ryan's large body, struggling and unable to move. Emma, August, Dexter, and Vargas banded together, and they ran as fast as they could out of the clearing and into the brush. Emma hoped they would be able to get enough distance from the Scouts and Lina, but their rollers were in the opposite direction. There was no way they would have the time to circle back around. They had to find cover fast.

Vargas hollered back toward the breathless group. "I sent a message for help from some friends. They should be here soon. C'mon, this way." He cleared the brush out of their way, and they ran toward a flat rock formation beyond the trees. Their feet kicked at the stone as they approached the flat, opened area. Vargas paused and looked at his holo screen for pinging messages. His holo lit up yellow as they reached the rock formation.

A loud sound rattled above to reveal a large shuttle hovering over their location.

It landed light as a feather, and they all followed Vargas into the hatch, "Don't worry! This is them! C'mon, we have to get out of here!"

They entered the hatch, and the shuttle pilot lifted them all off into the sky. They made it. All but one.

39

Dexter

Merah
1.5 years since E2 contamination

A small corner on the wall of the shuttle contained a piece of bulging metal. Dexter fixed his attention on this slight imperfection, and he didn't move his eyes from it the whole flight. He felt the warmth from Emma sitting next to him. She rested her hand on his arm. He couldn't look at her right now. He couldn't even look away from the scrap of metal that carried them to safety. He was safe, his brother was not.

Images of the day flashed before him as he saw his brother nudge him slightly to ready him for a moosing match. Ryan created the perfect distraction for their escape, but it cost him his life.

Even in his last moments, he still protected him. A lump formed in his throat that he feared would never go away. Ryan is the brother Dexter loved to hate. Or rather Ryan *was* the brother he loved to hate. That would never feel right. It was all his fault. Ryan was there because of Dexter's unending need to find Emma. He followed him right into the fire, and only Dexter came out unscathed. A small level of comfort only came from the idea that if they were unsuccessful in their plan, his family would never have to hear of his death.

The shuttle floated lightly in the air before it landed on soft ground. They didn't travel far, and he wondered if they were a safe distance away. But Dexter had no energy to question Vargas's friends. They all looked to be Kabiren and Amethite, but he didn't care. He vaguely heard Emma and August mumbling something about not being sure they were safe amongst themselves, but he couldn't be sure. The exit hatch of the shuttle opened, and Vargas and his friends motioned for them to venture forward.

As they rose and exited the shuttle, they entered a large cave. It was fully lit, yet it looked completely encased by rock. He wondered at the source of the light. They moved slowly and cautiously but headed toward a carved-out room with several benches of rock placed around a glass table held up by stone. If you looked too quickly, you wouldn't see that it was a large holo screen. On the rock walls were paintings of mountain peaks and the burning orange trees of Merah. Another wall of swirls and dots blended together in an interconnected web depicting multiple planets. A dance of red lines connecting them all. Vargas kindly motioned them to sit down and wait. There was a slight musty smell from a draft wandering into the room with a soft sound like a whistle on the wind.

Emma and August exchanged concerned looks when a tall Kabiren entered the room. He imagined this one was a Scout, as he had the presence of one as described by Vargas and Emma. The stern look he maintained as he entered soon melted away to a smile.

"Welcome, friends," the Kabiren with long hair addressed everyone and then turned his attention to Vargas. "I appreciate you reaching out to me."

"It's great to officially meet you," Vargas replied.

"Wait, I thought you were friends?" Emma whispered.

"We are friends," the Kabiren said with a chuckle. "I needed a small painting commission to spruce up this dreary site down here. Vargas obliged before we moved in. I had heard he was a wonderful artist, but this, this is something else entirely!" The Kabiren noted the landscape-colored walls.

August sized up the man. "What is your name and rank? You don't look familiar."

The Kabiren shook his head ever so slightly, and he typed information into his holo to turn off his phase imager. Suddenly there was no longer a Kabiren Scout standing before him, but rather another humanoid that looked very much like himself and Emma. He was almost human, except for his long arms and legs and the way his skin looked like cobblestone.

"So, you're the E2 intruders the general is so worried about." The man examined Emma. "You do look exactly like her. I didn't know if I believed it when our drones captured your image. But the catalogue records prove it.

You're the queen's daughter." He bowed in Emma's direction. "You have her eyes, princess." He smiled, raising his head up.

Emma wrinkled her forehead. "I have no idea what you mean. I only recently discovered my mother was called the Queen of Featherstone, and I know about Featherstone from bedtime stories told by my father, not my mother. So you'll excuse me if I don't really care... And don't call me 'princess,'" she huffed.

"My apologies. I wasn't aware that you weren't informed of your heritage. This must be overwhelming to you." He paused for a moment in thought. "My name is Veribo. I was the one who sent a message to your mother on Featherstone asking for help with Merah. I became responsible for the safety of your mother. She traveled from Featherstone to Merah in hopes of helping end the feuds here. I was with her before she disappeared through the portal that was destroyed in the Kabiren attack. She was supposed to return to Featherstone." He looked down in disappointment.

Emma squinted in confusion. "My mother and family have only lived on Earth, not Featherstone."

"Right. Allow me to explain. The portals were a brand-new technology we developed after deciding to help Merah with the black hole situation. We created Cal to pull the planet out of the universe and away from the black hole. But that left us with a problem—the planet would be completely isolated. So, we created the portal system to give the Amethites a way to go off-world. Now there are only two hidden portals left. The locations of the last portals were stolen from the Kabiren when the Queen departed. Any hope of starting those newer portals also lies with you, Emma."

Emma's eyes widened. She backed up against the cave wall and shook her head. "What do you mean it lies with me? Nothing you're saying makes any sense. There's no way my mom was hiding secret portal locations somewhere. That wasn't her. That wasn't our life!"

"This must be a lot for you to process, princess. And I wish I could lift the heavy burden you already bear, but we need your help. Before the last of the Mentiren—as they are called here—had escaped, as part of their agreement with the Amethites, they programmed the newest portals so the only person who could access them was the queen. She left in a hurry before she could turn over the access to someone here. Royal DNA is needed to unlock the portals. Your DNA is the key we need to find the portal to Featherstone… and to Earth."

Dexter looked up suddenly upon hearing the word Earth. "What do you mean finding the portal to Earth?"

"Unfortunately, we only had a small amount of time before the Kabiren came to build additional portals on other worlds, which is why we were stuck guessing where your mother would end up. We narrowed down the possibilities of planets they were connected to and came up with three: Featherstone, Earth, and Mars. When she realized what happened, she sent me a message, but it takes a bit of time for messages to go between planets. I was quite upset when I found out where she ended up. But it must mean that portal she used was either for Earth or for Mars."

"Why would there be an entry portal for Mars and Earth? That seems like a huge waste of resources to have two portals in such close proximity," Dexter said.

"We Martians wanted it that way. In case there were any problems with our portal, we would have a second option to a close planet in the system."

"Wait, Martians? There are no Martians on Mars. Veribo Industries has had ships and terraforming stations on Mars for years, and we've never heard of any lifeforms there. Wait, *VERIBO,* you're the founder of Veribo Industries... you're Martian?

"My apologies if this is difficult for you to hear. Or if you misunderstand me. Your mother has been sending messages to me and Featherstone from Mars all this time. But you have seen the Mentiren in the video logs, right?" Veribo asked.

"Yes, but they were all destroyed by us," August replied.

"No, they most certainly were not destroyed. I'm sure that is what the general would like you to believe. Mentiren are still alive and well. Only in other systems outside of Merah, we are known as Martians. You cannot tell me you believe the Kabiren are so mighty that they destroyed all of us? The others escaped through whatever portals they could on that last day. I hoped they would return with Featherstonian reinforcements. And yes, I started Veribo Industries with the intent of eventually including Earth in the portal expansion program. I'm glad to hear they've indeed included you in their updates. There was so much research lost on that last day, I hoped they would have continued with the portal project. But something must have gone wrong."

"Why did my mom insert herself into all of this? Just because you asked her to?" Emma said.

"I sent the message to your mother asking for help because after the Kabiren arrived, our work on the portals stopped, because we were too busy warring with them. They saw the technology on Merah and wanted it for themselves. It took a while for her to come because she couldn't convince anyone else to help us. You see, Featherstonians strongly believe in peace and want to preserve it for themselves. No one else wanted to get involved, no matter how desperate things got here. So, the queen came herself, undercover of course. But that was quickly blown."

"Why did she steal the portal plans? She's known as a thief and destroyer because of that."

"She realized how powerful the Kabiren were growing and how dangerous that was. She didn't want them having the plans or the final portal locations because she wanted to protect Featherstone, Mars, and other planets from being taken over like Merah. She's actually quite the hero."

Dexter and Emma caught each other's glances of bewilderment. So much new information had been given to them, they didn't know what to think. Their entire lives had been in service of Veribo Industries, and now it was likely that Veribo Industries had lied to them. Plus, all the news about Emma's mom was mind-boggling. But a piece of the puzzle was missing; Dexter couldn't quite process everything, and he saw the same confusion on Emma's face, the one he had seen so many times when she was about to spiral.

"Excuse me, please," Emma lowered her tone, shot up, and ran out of the room.

Dexter shook his head. "That was too much at once for her." He ran out of the room to follow his friend. Emma had almost run out of sight, but Dexter caught a quick glimpse of her direction, and he sprinted toward her. "Wait, Emma, please!" he called out into the echoing caves. He came upon her, curled up in a ball in the corner of a musty rock formation. He dropped to her level watching her tuck her face into her knees and cry. He sat motionless, wanting to reach out to her every second he sat near, but he didn't. It took every ounce of energy in him to only breathe and sit there. He hoped it was all she needed. There was a sort of comfort from just knowing that someone is nearby. He would be that solid comfort for her, always.

Emma wiped the tears from her face with her sweater. A deep breath escaped from Dexter's lips. "I'm okay, really," she whispered. "It's too much for me right now. I mean, I can understand my mom not telling me all of this. And now I know why she spent so much time on Mars. But we never had those deep conversations you always see moms and daughters having in the movies." She paused. "I wonder what that's like. But my dad, why didn't he tell me all of this?" She shook her head, and the tears welled up in her eyes again.

"Hey, hey," he whispered back. "Maybe he didn't know everything *to* tell."

"Or maybe he only told me what he thought I could hear."

"Yeah, you're really proving that you're amazing at handling things. Wonder why he would think you wouldn't be able to handle it, as you sit here… on the floor."

"Shut up," she replied with a shove and sniffed. "I'm a fragile soul."

They both burst out laughing, which echoed through the cave. Dexter felt relieved that Emma's episode didn't last too long.

"C'mon, let's get back to them." She stood up and held out her hand to him, and he took it with pleasure.

They walked back to the same carved-out room where they left their friends. There were lowered voices around the holo table when they entered the room.

"I'm sorry, princess... I mean Emma, I didn't realize the pain I could cause you." He bowed low. "Please forgive me."

Emma waved her hand. "No need to apologize. It's fine. All necessary information. Now, how can I help?" She plopped down on a bench and rested her head on her clasped hands, studying the holo screen displayed above the table.

"Thank you. There was a lot we were unable to finish because of your mother's unexpected departure. The general caught on to our plans and forced us to quickly get her to safety instead of finishing what she promised the Amethites."

"What exactly was the promise to the Amethites she didn't keep?" she asked.

"*Couldn't* keep, dear Emma. The general had us cornered at one portal. We had to use it, otherwise the Kabiren would have had all of the remaining portal locations. We couldn't allow them access to additional worlds, they had already stolen so much. They still do. But that was plan B."

August adjusted his shoulders. Veribo did not seem to notice the sudden thickness of the air. "Am I correct in thinking that all here are considered your friends and can be trusted, Emma?"

She nodded and replied, "You can trust all those with me. We have been attacked by the Scouts, and I don't even really know *why*!" Her voice echoed around the cave walls. Dexter sat down next to her on the bench. The cold penetrated his good leg.

"It can be assumed that the general knows you have a plan of sorts. The video bots are everywhere and catch more than you may realize." He pulled up a map on the holo table, sharing multiple blinking red dots in constant motion.

August, sitting across the table with his fingers steepled, nodded his head in agreement. "I think we finally got that from the video files we discovered. There's a lot that's recorded by the bots, but much of the information captured by them is locked to the other Kabiren. Most don't have the knowledge we've obtained from the video files."

"Then it's safe to assume you saw something you shouldn't have, and the General is having her Scouts do some cleaning."

"But against her own son?" Emma nodded her head at August.

"I don't know if you've noticed, but family loyalty is not one of General Sotora's strengths. You must have threatened something for her to go after you all. Why were you at the portal?"

"We were there in hopes of downloading the original plans for the portal Emma's mom used, or just some more information we could use," August replied.

"We wanted to be able to maybe rebuild it," Emma said, "to get my friends and I back home." She looked at Dexter, "I mean, my friend and I, back home." Her brows stitched together in worry, but Dexter shook his head. It was not the time for her concern.

"I see. And, August, what was your plan after it was built, and they were gone?" Veribo asked.

August didn't respond but blankly stared at the painted wall behind Dexter.

"I see. So how much thought have you all put into this plan of yours?"

Dexter responded with words Emma and August couldn't find. "We knew we had to do something, and this is what we came up with. It was our only hope."

Veribo looked at them and smiled. "I admire the effort you put into your plan. But it's not your only hope. In fact, you have more options than you realize. There are two remaining portal locations; I'm fairly certain now they're for your Earth and Featherstone. And with your royal DNA, Emma, we can finally activate them."

Emma looked at Dexter with bright widened eyes and her upside-down smile. They both raised their eyebrows and said in unison. "Let's get started."

40

Lina

Merah
1.5 years since E2 contamination

The general's office looked larger than before, or maybe, somehow in the time since she was here last, she had gotten smaller. She stood hunched over next to the Scouts who had dragged Lina here. Dexter's scream when Ryan fell still rang in her ears. She swallowed down a lump in her throat.

The general entered her office without looking at the three that stood before her. Lina stood to attention. General Sotora sat down, then calculated and reviewed the video bot footage from the mission.

"And what is your plan to mitigate this mess?" she asked without taking her eyes off the screen.

The Scout with deeper wrinkles shuffled in his stance in front of her desk. He must not have ever failed a mission this badly before. His voice cracked. "Well, we have bots out scouring the last known location of the shuttle, and we're still calculating where the shuttle went and possible hiding places for the rebel Scouts."

The general glared at them, "They are not rebels, they never were proper Scouts. They are intruders with phase imagers who need to be dealt with." She glanced up at the Scouts. "Immediately."

"Yes, general, we'll find them." They both nodded and one trailed his hand over the holo map on her desk to search. General Sotora swatted it away.

"You may leave. I want them found...today." She waved them away. Lina backed toward the doors.

"I need to speak with you, Protector 42. Stay, and let them go." She nodded toward the Scouts, and they exited her door. She displayed a video on her holo screen in front of Lina. Bots replayed clips of her failure.

"You have gravely disappointed me. You were trained to be a Protector, yet, you let all these intruders into our world...into Merah. It is *your job*, and it is your only job." She shook her head.

"I know I have failed you," She looked from the video to the general, "but I won't let that happen again. Now that I know the consequences of my actions, I can promise you it will never happen again." Her words were firm and direct, and she knew within her heart she meant every one of them.

"You have one final chance to make this right." The general pulled up a red dot on her map and flicked it to Lina's holo.

Lina nodded. "Yes, absolutely. Anything you ask, I'll do."

The general pointed at Lina's holo. "There is a small abandoned portal that is of no importance. But our little E2 friends may think something of its significance and head there. I need you to go there, and protect it. Do not let them activate it." She viewed her holo screen with a map of the outskirts and flicked the location to Lina. "Here is the location. *By any means necessary*, do not let the little portal be activated."

Lina bowed deeply. "Yes, of course, General Sotora." She noted the portal location. "This portal isn't on any of my updated maps."

"Yes, well, the queen, being the little thief she was, stole some hidden locations of portals. This one we only found recently, which is why we need it to be guarded. Can you handle that?"

"Of course I can. I'll head there immediately." She backed away toward the exit.

"And, 42," the general said. "This is your last chance."

Lina exited the office trying to hide her shaking hands.

41

August

Merah
1.5 years after E2 contamination

Emma peered down at the location maps with an intensity August only recognized when she studied her coursework. Martians and Amethites alike bustled through and around the caverns. Their footsteps echoed throughout the walls. Veribo motioned and directed each of them to their task. The two portals on the map were not too far apart, but that didn't necessarily make them close either. They had no way of analyzing where the portals led from their location, and it would require Emma's physical presence at each to enable them. The Martians made sure to lock down the last of the portals before their escape. They were crafty like that. Maybe that's why they weren't completely destroyed like August had been taught.

He shook his head to escape his thoughts. He had been lied to, over and over again, that much was for sure. But the extent of the truths told by Veribo was even less certain. He hadn't the time to verify anything. All he could do was believe the videos he saw, and Veribo didn't oppose any of those.

Emma interrupted the doubts that crept into his mind with a nudge. "So if my mother got the Martians out and back home through the Mars portal, why did you think she never made it back to Featherstone?"

August shrugged.

Veribo shifted his eyes from August to Emma. "It was always the plan to try bring Featherstonians back here as reinforcements. At least that was the agreement as I understood it. Our plan was rushed; we didn't have a lot of time to prepare for after leaving through the portal. Something else must have gone wrong. As I said, the queen was unable to fulfill her promises fully."

"What was the other promise, the one she had made to the Amethites?" August asked, and he leaned up against a smoothed ledge of rockwall.

Veribo looked August up and down and narrowed his eyes.

Emma interrupted the silence, "August is *my* friend; I would ask that you answer his question because I'm wondering it myself." She stretched her neck up and narrowed her eyes at Veribo.

Veribo cleared his throat. "The queen promised the Amethites inclusion, not segregation from the universe."

Emma looked at August with one brow raised, but August just cocked his head and asked, "How is it segregated?"

"Ahh, I forget General Proximate, that you were born here and are not fully aware of the specific location of Merah in respect to the universe."

"This is true," he replied as he sat down on a bench surrounding the table and peered at Veribo.

"Haven't you ever wondered why the Scouts return more aged from their missions? Or why the sun Cal sometimes flicks out of existence, only to return moments later? These are common occurrences, if you are looking for them."

The Scouts were always referred to as the Old Ones by the Amethites. He figured it was a sort of nickname, not actually referring to them being older. But the more August thought about it, the more he noticed the subtle wrinkles that grew on the Scouts whenever they returned from a portal mission off world. *So Dexter wasn't lying when he told Emma more time had passed on Earth than on Merah.* But inconsistencies with Cal, their second sun? That was not possible. He shook his head. "Cal does not flick out of existence." He looked at Emma. "This is ridiculous."

Emma interrupted, "I've witnessed Cal blipping. But when it happened, there was nothing in the logs or my coursework to explain it. I assumed I was seeing things."

Veribo smiled with pride. "Cal is the power source for Merah's position in this little pocket dimension. Modified portal space stations, set up around Cal, were created to harness the massive energy and exert additional gravity on Merah, essentially pulling Merah out of sync with the rest of the universe and away from that black hole. As you know, the portal systems have been breaking down, this also includes the stations around Cal. When the portal stations cycle through the energy, they basically reboot, and it looks to us as if Cal disappears. When the system was created, it was done out of fear. We calculated a cataclysmic event approaching the planet, and Merah needed protecting, the Amethites needed protecting. This was the only way we Martians knew how to protect them. We shifted them out of the universe and worked together to create the portals as the only access points into this dimension, but did not realize the consequences. The Amethites eventually expressed a want to return to the universe in a new location when it seemed that the danger had passed, and the queen promised them such."

Emma looked down at her shoes, and her shoulders fell. "How could my mother promise them that?" she asked in a quiet voice.

"Princess, your mother had excellent diplomacy skills and could gather almost anyone to her cause. With enough people, we could succeed in a plan for the Cal station," Veribo answered.

"What was the plan for Cal?" August asked.

Veribo glanced between the two of them. "The plan was always to basically turn it off—to disengage the space portal stations, and cut off the ground station from its power source which would return Merah to the known universe."

Emma looked at August, and he shuddered. Were they really capable of destroying all that was built to protect? It would obviously have repercussions for the many who have been born on Merah since its activation. "Did you calculate the projected result from that much change in gravity?" August asked.

"Of course we did. And yes, there would be difficulties initially, but we calculated only a small increase in gravity therapy for those ones, and the Amethites signed off on that."

August glared at Veribo. "I find it hard to believe the full consequences of destroying such a massive star system has been fully studied."

"Of course not *fully* studied. There wouldn't be enough time to fully study anything regarding the return of an entire planet to the universe. All we really have to go on are the reports of the Amethites that were here before we created it. So many of them are gone now, but their accounts are solid. They all led us to the conclusion that the need to rejoin the universe outweigh any possible initial difficulties."

August scoffed and left the cavernous room. In the hallway, he kicked the sturdy wall, shaking a nearby light fixture. A small Amethite passerby quickly turned away and speed-walked in the opposite direction. He didn't want to hear Veribo's words. Cal was too great a power source to no longer be harnessed. How could anyone want to do what he suggested? He had done so much work on the portals. Now it would be all for nothing. The portals and the countless hours he worked on them would be worthless.

"Please come back, August. I need your help." Emma's small voice echoed in the cave. He looked back toward her.

"I'm not helping to potentially destroy Merah. There's no proof this won't negatively affect all of us living here now, and we can't guarantee that whatever threatened Merah back when the portal systems were created, isn't still out there."

"We don't really know what to expect, other than what we've been told. But if this is what the Amethites truly wanted, maybe it is really what could save Merah, not destroy it."

August lowered his head down and dropped to his knees. "If what Veribo says about Cal is true, that means my whole life has been a lie. I haven't helped the Amethites to have the best tech in the universe, I've helped keep them from it. My work to sustain all of the portals has just been so my mother and her Scouts can steal other species' ideas and then skulk back here where they don't have to face any consequences. I have always thought Merah's special hidden location *is* what keeps the Amethites safe. If that's gone, what will happen to them, and me?" His voice faltered.

"Maybe the Amethites don't need anyone to save them." Her words were soft and sad. "I happen to think every Amethite I have met while here is very capable and not in need of saving. And if you let them make their own choices about their planet, I think you'll be in a much better position than you are now."

August's stomach twisted. She was right. He never thought about the effect of his own existence on Merah. It had always been his home, but somehow now it wasn't. Cal's power had always been such an integrated part of this world, but he needed to think about the Amethites and what they wanted, not what he thought they needed. Emma had a knack for reasoning, and could make an uncertain darkness bright with her soft tone and kind heart. He was glad she was there, and with his next words, he tied his fate with hers.

"You're right, so what are we going to do?"

Emma's eyes lit up, and she smiled. "I think we should honor my mother's promise to the Amethites and restore Merah to the universe."

"What about the Earth portal? Once the Cal portal control station is destroyed, I'm not certain the portals will work anymore. There may not be enough time to get you home once my mother gets wind of what we're doing here. We'll almost certainly be captured."

"I may not be able to make it home, but I can return this home to the Amethites, and I will honor the promise my mother made to them. No matter the cost." She looked back toward him and smiled. "Eager to get rid of me, eh?"

"On the contrary, I fear my life would be immeasurably more boring if you were gone." He laughed.

"Let's get back to Veribo. We've got some plans to make."

42

Dexter

Merah
1.5 years since E2 contamination

The cave room wall was visibly wet. It silently dripped collecting condensation at the ceiling. One thousand two hundred and forty-five. One thousand two hundred and forty-six. One thousand two hundred and forty-seven. Dexter counted each drop. He should be with his friends as they made their plans, but his heart wasn't in it. Back home he was annoyed with the nonstop irritation that was his brother. But now, he somehow *felt* spaces in his heart which were no longer full. All those bad memories, not so bad now, haunted him. His soul was menaced by the time stolen from him and his brother, time he only began to embrace on their adventure here. Merah had taken not only his friend, but also the life of his closest brother, and he didn't know how to mourn.

"I'd ring, but there are no door notifications down here apparently," Vargas muttered from the doorway. "Mind, if I come in?"

Dexter motioned him in. "What's up?" he asked, trying to seem unphased.

"I was coming here to see how you were doing and to share with you my sadness at the loss of my guest and your brother. I will mourn twice for your world's loss. He saved our lives, and he will be remembered as brave."

Dexter nodded through a lump in his throat. "Thanks."

"I also wanted to give you this." Vargas handed him a small frame. Makeshift paper stretched across wooden sticks held an abstract figure made up of colors and lines. It was Ryan's face; he could tell from the sharp lines drawn around the space he assumed was a chin. Ryan always had the sharpest of jaw lines.

"Th..." Dexter started, but trailed off into a sob. His body shook, and he dropped to the ground and scraped his metallic knee covering on a jutted rock.

"Here." Vargas worked on the broken piece of metal on Dexter's leg. "There, much better." He knocked twice on the kneecap.

Dexter let a laugh escape his lips. "I didn't realize I'm basically the Tin Man." The musty air dried his face. "Thanks, Vargas. Your gift is wonderful. I will treasure it always." He stood up and shook some dust off his pants. "Can you catch me up on what I've missed?"

"Emma seems to have some pretty ambitious plans and could really use all the help she can get. But it would be best if we joined them for their explanation. I would not do it justice, my friend." He smiled and motioned them to head out.

"Well, now I'm intrigued," Dexter said while they made their way to the cavernous room. When they entered, Emma and August were lost in a holo display. The table showed an area somewhere on Merah, but with his lack of experience, he had no clue the location it showed. Emma pointed to different areas.

"So if we have two groups here and here, we should be able to get to the Cal station and the portal at the same time."

"Yes, but there is still the problem of which portal to get you to. There are two left, and we won't know exactly where one leads until you are physically there to unlock it, princess."

"Well, let's use an educated guess. You said the last portals were for Earth, Featherstone, and Mars. We have figured out the Mars portal was destroyed, so that leaves us Earth and Featherstone. Did the Martians speak of what formula they used to build the portals? In my mind, the next portal out from Mars would be for my home, right?"

Dexter's chest swelled. Home. She said home. It was possible to get her back to Earth.

It was still home to her. He smiled sadly and looked back up at *his* home. There she was standing in a solid and knowing stance. She looked confident and ready to set her plan in action. And he would help her do so, whatever it took.

"I think, princess, we'll have to assume the spacing of the portals gives some clue of each portal's ultimate destination. The next one out is... this one." He pointed to the next portal to the north. "Which actually is pretty far from Cal's control center. I'm not sure we'll have enough time to get you to it, no matter how quickly we deprogram, or destroy, Cal's main control center. Not to mention what we have to do to the backup portal system."

"August, could you work with Cal's hidden code to potentially put the destruction on a delay?"

"I can, but our mere presence there will cause a stir, and the code will not be so hidden once the general really starts looking for it, no matter how much of a delay I program into it."

"If we use the phase imagers to hide our species, we'll be harder to spot," Veribo interjected.

"Easier to ignore at least," August replied.

"Then let's get to work. We need to do this as quickly as possible. We only have the element of surprise." Emma glanced at Dexter.

"We'll get right on it, princess," Veribo bowed.

"I told you, don't call me princess."

"Yes... ummm... Emma," he replied.

Emma walked toward Dexter the paused.

"Come with me." She grabbed at his arm. The meeting room with the large holo table started to close in around them as they moved to the hallway just outside. Emma's hand still tugged his arm, but he let it remain. They passed by lights hammered into the cave walls strung together by cords and wires until they saw a section of two empty metal seats. They nudged them together and plopped down.

Emma removed her hand before sitting down, and Dexter held back a frown. "Are you okay to come with us tomorrow?" she asked with a furrowed brow.

Dexter dropped his head. There was no way to convince her that his pain wasn't real, but he couldn't let that stop him from helping her. She always saw right through him. "I can't pretend I'm not sad. But Ryan's not here, and his being gone can't affect our efforts to get home. I'll do whatever you need. Just say the word." He side-eyed her with his fingertips resting on hers.

Her cheeks turned pink, and she looked intently at something across the corridor, twisting her hand so that his fingers could fully envelop hers. She held her gaze across the room but inched closer to him. Her head dropped slightly to rest on his shoulder, and she tucked her arm under his. "I really am sorry about Ryan. I know you weren't close, but sometimes in death we lose the potential of what could have been, and that's worse somehow." She breathed out the words in her perfect way.

"Mmm," he hummed. "And I'm sorry about Mylinah. She sounded like... well, she sounded like your friend."

Emma nodded. "She was the first person I met on Merah. She helped me find my way around here. I still can't wrap my head around what she did with the Scouts. The Lina I know would never do that. But then again, I haven't been here that long. Maybe I really don't know anyone."

He looked down at her and slightly grazed her chin with his finger, directing it toward him. "Hey, you know me. Don't doubt yourself because of one misjudgment. First impressions aren't always revealing."

"I know. I...I'm usually a really good judge of character. Lina was special, and fun, and she had kindness. I *know* she had kindness. I don't understand what could make her do that."

"You may have to be okay with not knowing. We don't always get the chance to know someone's intentions, and we have to be okay with that."

"I know you're talking about Lina, but you knew Ryan. He was your brother. Good and bad, he was family."

Dexter let a solitary tear stream down his face. His lips grazed the top of her head with a sigh in uneven breaths. Emma reached her hand up and let it rest on his cheek. Her thumb rubbed the wet line across his face and dried it with a graze of her finger.

"Tomorrow we at least get to see how it feels to destroy an entire generation's way of life on one planet, before hopping off world to return to ours." He cleared his throat and swallowed the tightness in it.

Emma nodded, "I hope it will be what they really want. My mother was known as a destroyer when she left. I wonder if I'll be known as the same."

They sat in silence before they stood together. Dexter took her hand, not wanting to let go. *There's no telling what will happen tomorrow.* He turned to Emma and reached down to hold her face cupped in his hands. Her eyes had dark circles around them. He placed his forehead to hers and wanted nothing more than to close the gap between them. He was already exhausted, but this restraint he maintained while his heart was about to burst from his chest was more than he could handle.

"Goodnight," Emma whispered into his ear and placed a small kiss on his cheek before stepping away from him.

He closed his eyes tightly. ████, he loved being home.

43

August

Merah
1.5 years after E2 contamination

T he clambering of the shuttle ripped through the passenger space. Newer models didn't have that incessant noise. He would have to fix that after they were done getting Emma off Merah. Metal pieces shifted and vibrated around the occupants stirring and pacing. So few of them he met personally, but Veribo had vouched for them, and Emma subsequently did, too, so he had to be okay with them. This was her plan, and it needed to go off without a hitch. August glanced at a young Amethite in front of him. So small, but eager to help as he grabbed for a tool to seal up the vibration they heard. *Phew*. Emma and Dexter sat with barely a crack of space between them, their fingers intertwined. His eyes darted away from the personal moment.

"We are getting close," Veribo spoke through the comms.

"Prep time," the Amethite said, hopping up to initiate his phase imager. He looked exactly like a Kabiren Scout. The display wasn't exactly perfect. The phases that changed the Amethite to look Kabiren, ran through their display every fifteen minutes but when each cycle ended, there was a tiny glitch that could be seen.

"Hey, come here." August motioned for him to come over. The Amethite complied. "Can I take a quick look at your imager?"

"Sure, be quick though," he said, disengaging it and handing it to August.

He removed the outer casing quickly and looked at the contact marks on the turnkey inside. They were slightly worn down from use. He grabbed a small stray piece of wire from the shuttle wall and wrapped it around the contacts before replacing the casing. "Here, try it again." He handed it back.

"Is it okay?"

"Hold on." He waited for the first fifteen minute cycle to finish without a glitch. He held up a victory fist. "Yes! It's better."

"Thank you. I was told the parts were old. Now I won't die!" the Amethite chuckled.

The entire crew of passengers nervously laughed along with them. It was surprising how many of them supported such a task, with such a great potential for risk. Here there were Martians, Amethites, and a Kabiren. He, a Kabiren, being the most technologically advanced of all the species in the universe, was currently about to destroy all capability for that advancement, in spite of the potential consequences for themselves. His race only acted with this much haste when it involved the creation of technology, not the destruction of it.

They left the portals open for so long and never once considered destroying them, even through the multiple retrofitting problems and contaminates. There was so much to gain, it was worth the trouble of training and employing the Protectors to take care of whatever problems arose. But now, if he was successful, that all would end.

The shuttle vibrated in a landing sequence on the outskirts of the hidden Cal control station center.

"All right, here we go," said August, swinging his body out of the shuttle door. Emma and Dexter were right behind him. They all were a bit too eager for his liking. He wasn't sure what they were walking into, but he knew that if this control center was what Veribo said it was, then they would have to deal with their fair share of Scouts. He hoped they were ready.

They trailed each other and fanned out so as not to create a stir. The large metal doors to the entrance were supposed to be cut into the side of the looming mountain overhead, but the environmental holo display concealed them by showing only solid rock ahead. Trees obscured the pathway to it, too. August tapped a button on his holo band. The rock wall in front of them disappeared into thin air. Thick interlocked metal doors were held clasped shut by a robotic mechanism. Multiple bots overhead scanned and recorded every movement. They would have to be quick and precise. There was no telling how much they would blend in with the phase imagers, but they were here to try.

August walked up to the control center door and pinged the now visible cam with his wristband.

A voice came on the video monitor, "What do you need, General Proximate?"

August cleared his throat lightly. "Yes, I'm here on coded orders from the general, requesting access to speak with your highest-ranking technician available."

The video monitor clicked off with silence behind it. August checked on his friends behind him and hoped they wouldn't be noticed upon his entry. The video monitor clicked back on.

"We don't have any coded orders for your arrival. Unfortunately, we cannot allow access."

"Well, that's too bad *you* don't have the orders, but fortunately, I do have them right here. Sending them now." He found old inspection order approvals from his mother and quickly changed the date on them before transferring them directly to the entry technician. The monitor audio clicked back on.

"Fine. We will allow you limited access. Please follow the lighting cues to the nearest lab. Tech Jirasot will be with you shortly."

The doors slid open and led him into the facility's bare gray hallways. He attached the micro scrambler, meant to constantly upload a fresh code to the robotic arm that controlled the doors, to the side of the doors in a swift motion. The slanted dimmer lights transitioned him inside to reveal a much darker center than the daylight outside. His eyes adjusted to find the indicator lights along the hall. He made his way farther down the hallway to a small room to the right of the entryway. He waited in the room for the tech to come in, shifting his feet back and forth.

Someone entered the room. "Well, General Proximate, what can I do for you? I see there are some orders from the general that require your presence, but I can assure you, everything is running smoothly at Cal Opps. I didn't realize the general cleared you for access to this facility yet. Very few Kabiren are allowed to be in here." His eyes narrowed at August.

"You saw the orders from the general herself, so obviously I'm approved to check on your work here. Don't worry, I'm sure you have a handle on the power processing unit as well as your expertly trained tech teams. I'm only here to do a quick run through of the facility and make some notes to update the general. Please lead the way to ensure we make it through the facility in an efficient manner. Tech...?" He paused for the technician's name.

"Tech Jirasot." He bowed and finally replied, "Yes, right this way." He pointed toward the direction of the building's center. As they exited the room, August glanced at his wristband. His location pings were functional, but he did not yet see Emma's pings indicating she was in the building. He hoped his scrambler worked, and they were able to sneak into the facility, but there was no indication they had yet. They would need a bit more time.

"Can you show me the cooling room for the processing unit first? This was one area the general was deeply concerned about." He tried to have as casual a tone as possible.

"That is all the way downstairs in the basement. I thought you said you wanted a quick run of the facility?"

August scowled at him. "You mean to tell me that one of the key elements to keeping this facility functioning was put in a location that isn't immediately accessible should anything happen to it? This seems to be a greatly inefficient design oversight." He looked down at his holo screen, entered a few notes, and shook his head.

"Well, General Proximate, the facility was originally created by the Mentiren... So we aren't personally at fault for the design of the Opps Center, but we've done an excellent job maintaining it, despite the problems." The tech shifted his walk slightly so as to put some distance between the two of them. August silenced a chuckle while walking behind the tech. They stepped onto the elevation pad to bring them to the basement area. He checked his holo band again to reveal several pings. Emma and the rest must have gotten in. "Phew," he muttered, and immediately stopped breathing once it escaped.

"What?" the tech inquired.

"Nothing. Have we reached the cooling terminals yet?" he responded forcefully when the pod came to a halt with a ding.

"Yes, right here. While there's a distance between the cooling towers and the processing unit, we have excellent transportation allowing us to get where we need to go. In spite of the distance, we are able to function according to the general's standards," he said and they disembarked the pod.

The room holding the cooling towers blew frigid air around them. August tightened his muscles in an effort to keep from shivering. The two cooling towers blasted intense cold air through vents that shot upward.

"Is there a leak from the main tower piping?" he asked, trying to keep his teeth from chattering.

"No. The pipes need to stay cool so as to not interfere with the quality of the air traveling toward the processing unit. The amount of power the Cal portal space station collects and transfers here needs this cool air in order to be processed. The entire facility would overheat and wouldn't able to power the rest of the portals on the planet if it was a degree warmer. So we maintain the cooler temperatures outside the piping as well. Just in case." The tech paused, receiving an incoming communication.

"Technician Jirasot, please return to the main processing unit. Your presence is required urgently," a voice bled through his comms so August could hear.

"It looks like I have a pressing matter to attend to. Please come this way." He led him to the transport pod and walked toward the facility's main exit. "Here is where I leave you. We'll reschedule your tour for a more convenient time." He bowed and started to walk away.

August quickly hollered at him. "Halt! I *require* a full tour, which would include whatever emergency you're trying to run to without the general's knowledge. So, I order you to take me with you." He towered tall over the tech and glared sternly at him.

"As you wish, but please hurry, there's some sort of problem at the processing unit." He took off into a jog and headed toward the center of the facility. August followed his stride closely, and they were soon at the main processing unit.

Multiple holo screen projections completely enveloped the massive room. The glowing from the screens made him feel warm and fuzzy. Each holo system displayed a different code-run program. One for the Cal power collection, another for distribution, and it looked like a third showing the motion of Merah's orbit. No other planets or stars were shown on the projection though. The design of the unit and the code required to map out and project everything in the room, all required a level of ingenuity he could barely wrap his head around. *I wish I built something this cool.* He would have loved to poke around here for a few hours to marvel at the sheer brilliance of it. He dragged his eyes away from the main unit, and they fell upon three figures held at blaster point in the smallest corner of the room.

The tech dropped the holo screens from projecting and lit up the room to the fullest brightness. He shielded his eyes from the light to let them adjust after being in the dark for so long. His chest sank. There standing with their hands up in the corner of the room, were Emma, Dexter, and Veribo.

"What do we have here?" the tech snarled to the Scout security while he glared at the intruders. "It seems like we have some unauthorized access. What are each of your names and ranks? Because I can guarantee none of you are assigned to my teams." He checked his holo logs of the crew assigned this week and chuffed. "As I thought, none of you are assigned to this center." He paused. "No one will speak? I guess I have no choice then." He motioned to his security. "Blast them."

August steadied his chest and placed his hands together. He loudly and noticeably started to clap, a slow clap. They all stared at him quizzically, including Technician Jarisot. "I have to say I actually am surprised how quickly you found my team, Tech Jarisot." The tech looked back at the intruders when August pointed to his friends. "Part of my inspection included testing security measures for this facility. I'm impressed with your ability to find them, even with their phased imagers."

Tech Jarisot looked back and forth between August and the intruders. "So this was a setup?" he asked in a voice that faltered in a disbelieving way.

"Yes," August responded. "I trust you'll release my team to my care." The security team lowered their blasters slightly before raising them again.

A familiar voice entered the room from the doors. "Well, well, my son. You seem to have been up to an awful lot here. Now, would you please tell me what you, the little E2 pests, and the ever-evasive Martian are doing here?" The general's words were in the form of a question, but her voice was a command. He knew that voice all too well.

"Yes, mother, I mean, general. I'm here with these ones as a lesson in training facilities." He stammered through the explanation.

The general clicked her tongue several times, like she was scolding a child. "You really shouldn't assume I am so stupid as to believe that trash pile of an excuse, child." She shook her head. "I don't know exactly how you found out about this center, but I assume it is best that you do now, being my proximate. You probably have realized what this place is, and why it is important to us?"

"Yes, it is the command center for the portal stations collecting energy from Calypso, our sun—which is responsible for Merah's location in the universe."

"Not only location, my boy, but the gravitational pull we can exert on Merah. It allows us to not only experience time at a different rate than the rest of the universe, but also pulls us aside dimensionally and keeps us safe from all those who would try to know our secrets and steal our technology."

"It seems like we don't have any real secrets or technology of our own, only those we stole from other worlds," he said through gritted teeth.

The general stood back from him and smiled. "You have learned a great deal more than I anticipated. You must have accessed the locked files. How cute. You would have known them in time anyway. But I am rather bothered by your actions with such knowledge. You realize the uniqueness of this world and yet, you choose to do what? Insert some ridiculously easy to find code to destroy the operating program for Cal? The one thing that is still ensuring your future, and the rest of Merah's future? I doubt you have had time to think this through fully, son." She smiled wistfully at him, a smile he had only seen from her three times in his life. First when he passed portal programming training. Next, when he had gotten frustrated with the portal program he was working on, and then cracked it five hours later. And now. He frowned at his mother's valid points. There was a hastiness to his actions. He hadn't fully thought about what would happen to the Amethites if he and the team succeeded. He opened his mouth to defend himself but looked pleadingly to Emma instead.

Emma piped up in her small voice from the corner of the room. "You don't deserve to have Merah. Go back to your home planet!" Her voice was steady and unfaltering, and the smile disappeared from the general's lips.

"What did you say, E2?"

"You heard me. The translator is working fine. I said, 'You. Do. Not. Deserve. Merah. Go home.'"

"There is no home. It's gone. Merah *is* our home. And what in your minuscule experience has led you to believe we don't deserve it, girl?"

"Sometimes those with the most removed experiences can have a more complete world view. And I stand by what I said. You have only exploited Merah, and countless other worlds, and that ends *today*." She signaled Veribo, and he nodded.

Red lights whirred around them, and the warning system enabled.

> *Please make your way to the nearest exit. Building system overload. Chance of survival if present, 0%.*

> *Please make your way to the nearest exit. Building system overload. Change of survival if present, 0%.*

The repetitive warning was deafening. It distracted August from his search for his team. Emma, Dexter, and Veribo rushed out of grasp of the security Scouts and toward the doors. He called out to them while multiple holo environments lit up and were displayed over the entire room. Flashes of trees and rock were projected as shooting up all around him. Different landscape features on Merah flashed as random projections in the control room. One second he was teetering on top of a black tree root and the next he held his body back from falling off the Cliffs of Stad. Holo displays of buildings near headquarters suddenly appeared around him. It made walking almost impossible.

August held onto the only wall he could feel, tripping over his own feet. He closed his eyes and an arm reached around him to tug him toward safety. He opened his eyes to reveal his mother right above him. She dragged him out of the control room and along the long hallway. He blinked through flashing lights and shouts.

They stumbled together through the exit doors, the walls of the mountain around them shaking like a volcano about to erupt. August's legs wobbled and tripped over the rocks spilling down and around them. His mother yanked him up into a shuttle, and the doors closed in around them. The engine on the shuttle choked while the alarms still blared outside the shuttle doors. The pilot pounded on holo screen buttons reigniting the drive on the shuttle. It whirred to full power, and he quickly lifted the shuttle to a hover. A loud explosion boomed. Their bodies jolted with the rush of a shockwave from the control center's blast. Small shards pelted the shuttle armor. August looked down at his mother still gripping onto his arm. Stuck in a shuttle with the one person he hated the most. The shuttle pulled further away from the destruction and into a humming quiet as they made their way back to headquarters.

He dropped his head down and looked at the floor. "I didn't know what I was doing," he said to his mother, his voice faint and words slowly strung together.

The general patted his arm, "I know dear. At least all is not lost. The backup processing unit for Cal portal is housed elsewhere. You have done no real harm. But we will have to see what we need to do with that E2 girl. At least before she left she used her DNA to unlock Cal's systems for us. We can now run it however we please from the secondary location. But I think I may need you to work your retrofitting magic on it to get it up to snuff to come close to the original Cal computer."

Of course, that's why she saved me. She has more work for me to do. Pictures of a future of him huddled over his holo screen in his lab constantly working flooded his mind. He grimaced. A sudden beep escaped his wristband and projected three dots moving away from him. There was one thing left he still could do, and he hoped he was lucky enough for it to work. "Yes, general." He slowly looked up at his mother. He nodded his head and revealed his saved holo band locations. "E2 is heading here; she is looking to reprogram the portal so it can be used again."

The general smiled. "Then I guess it is very good that we already have someone there to greet her."

44

Emma

Merah
1.5 years since E2 contamination

"We can't just *leave* him!" Emma shouted to Veribo and Dexter while they tugged her onto the shuttle. She fought and writhed to break free from their grasp. After all August had done for them, they left him. It wasn't right, and it wasn't fair to him.

"August has done so much for us!" she yelled through a sore and cracked voice. "We can't leave him."

Dexter tried to hold onto her fighting body, but she peeled his arms from her and shoved him away. She curled up in the middle of the shuttle floor. An Amethite carefully placed a blanket over her, and she shivered through tears. Dexter sat in the nearest shuttle seat he could find. She could feel his concerned eyes on her. She didn't want concern. She breathed in and out, in and out. The slow breaths slowed her tears and stopped her shaking body.

Veribo's voice reverberated around the shuttle, but she glowered at him. "Princess, please, princess." She raised her head slightly to see where his voice came from. He kneeled next to her body and pleaded with her. "Please, I know this is hard. But my first concern is your safety. The general will not harm the proximate. He is too important to her for her to do that directly. He'll be fine. You, however, would not be, if you were caught."

"They had me. I was in training for over a year, and I was fine. I would be fine." "You were ignorant of your heritage when you were training, right?"

"Yes."

"But now that you know who you really are, it makes you dangerous in the general's eyes. And she will not hesitate to destroy all that you love along with you." He nodded in Dexter's direction.

Emma's heart sank for Dexter and bled for August. She raised her body up and looked ahead. "Was Vargas's team able to reach the secondary location?"

"Yes, princess. They uploaded our destructive code the moment your DNA released access."

Her muscles relaxed. "Well at least I was able to fulfill my mother's promise and Merah will slowly return to the universe away from the black hole. Now about my protection…Are we almost to the portal site?" She spoke quietly but firmly.

"Yes, we'll be there momentarily, Veribo smiled. "We'll get you home soon, princess."

Emma walked toward Dexter. There was still concern in his eyes. He always held the worry of the world in those eyes, even when he was small. She hated that she had been the cause of it this time. She sat down next to him, slid her arm under his, and leaned onto his shoulder. She was home with him.

The shuttle creaked during the landing. It needed another patch. Veribo announced their arrival at the portal. "We have arrived, but we have to hurry." Dexter and Emma trailed behind Veribo, exiting the shuttle and following his motions to move forward.

The shuttle landed in an airy open part of the outskirts of the forest. The shades of trees on this side looked more amber than orange leading to the portal site.

Trees glowed through the sunlight, and they were all blinded by the brightness. Soon they reached those familiar metal cylinders. Veribo swung the dormant cylinder's control panel open and motioned Emma to come to it. She placed her hand in the panel, and he filled the screen with the code in the holo display to redirect access. The portal hummed a broken hum. It hadn't been used for a long time, and it sputtered and whirred a bit, but it seemed functional.

"Checking now for the destination of the portal." Veribo said, but halted and stared ahead of them at a blaster pointed at Dexter's head.

"Why have you stopped? We need to know where this portal—" She stopped mid- sentence as she saw Lina's blaster directed toward Dexter, and Maut next to her with teeth bared. Her chest lurched, but she steadied her voice as much as she could. "Please, Lina, don't hurt him. He's already lost his brother. You want him gone as well?"

"Of course I don't *want* him gone." Lina slumped at the accusation. "I have sworn to protect Merah from the perils of the outside worlds, and you all have already taken so much by your presence here, I'm not supposed to allow it to continue. It's my job as Protector to keep Merah safe from contaminates like you all."

Emma looked straight into Lina's eyes. "Have you ever wondered *why* you're protecting Merah from outside worlds?"

Lina shifted, "Of course. The entire planet would be destroyed if we let foreign contaminates in. You've not been here that long, and your influence has already caused death and destruction. We cannot have it here."

Emma held her hands up. "I don't know anything about the death and destruction you're talking about, but think really hard, Lina. Am I the cause of the destruction, or is it the Kabiren? By training Protectors to destroy all life that comes through the portals, by destroying all avenues of self expression, the Kabiren have not succeeded in protecting Merah, they have *stifled* it. The ingenuity and friendship and joy that I've seen in you and in all other Amethites, now that is the beauty of Merah. And I wish the universe could see it."

Lina lowered her blaster and whimpered. "But I betrayed you all, and it led to Ryan's death. There's no beauty in that." She shook her head.

Emma smiled sadly. "There's no beauty in his death, Lina, you're right. Every person alive makes bad decisions with unknown consequences. All you can do is learn from them and move on, and continue to get better." She looked directly at Lina again. "Lina, you are amazing and resourceful, and you've shown me great kindness when you didn't have to. *That,* to me, is beauty. *That,* to me, is you choosing to be better. You can *always* choose to be better."

Tears fell from Lina's eyes, and she pointed at Dexter. "I can't make it better for *him*." She turned to Dexter. "I wish I could make it better, to go back... I wish it were me instead," Her body shook, and she fell to her knees with her head in her hands.

Dexter looked down at her and reached out his hand to softly tug at her shoulder. "Hey, you didn't pull the trigger."

Lina shrugged it off. "Yeah but I might as well have." She sniffled and wiped her face with the edge of her cloak while Dexter kneeled next to her and wrapped his arm around her. He looked up at Emma with knitted brows.

Emma rushed up to them and tightened her arms around them both. Despite everything, both her friends needed her now.

A rustling floated through the air. Maut screeched a warning.

"Move." Lina shot up and pushed Emma and Dexter aside as a blaster shot fired toward them. "I messaged the general when you arrived. There will be more. Go." She fired return shots.

Emma and Dexter ran behind the closest tree for cover. Craning her neck, Emma peered through the brush to locate the source of the blaster shots. At least twenty Scouts spread out among the trees, firing multiple shots. All directed at them. Shards of bark shot toward Emma. A small drop of blood trickled down her cheek. She brushed it away with her shoulder.

A shout called after her. "We need to get to the portal!" Dexter slid closer to Emma.

She nodded and grabbed her blaster. Four shots rang out at the Scouts. They took cover. Dexter grabbed the closest rock and chucked it passed the approaching Scouts.

The crash scattered two of the Scouts and forced them to fall back.

Crack. Crack. The tree above them wavered and tipped. *Crack.*

"Run!" Emma pushed Dexter out from behind the tree with one hand and fired shots with her other. She searched for the direction of the portal. Veribo ran up to them, shielding himself with a deflector field he placed at every step.

Snap! A broken tree trunk crashed toward them.

"Get down!" Veribo expanded the field around them, and they crouched down. The tree trunk shattered when it smashed into the deflector field right above their heads.

"Veribo! Do we know where the portal leads yet?" she shouted over the return shots from the Scouts. Maut flew to snatch another nearby Scout's blaster that was pointed at Lina's direction.

"No, and we don't have time to find out!" Veribo shouted, and Lina ran over to them. "Go, go, go, princess. We'll cover you." He disengaged the deflector field cylinder, handed it to Dexter and pointed at a nob at the edge of it. "Press here to engage." Dexter nodded.

Lina grabbed Emma by the arm and shoved her toward the portal. Blaster shots flew from Lina and Veribo. Emma and Dexter ran as fast as they could toward the portal. They ducked down to avoid shots fired at them. Dexter grabbed the deflector field cylinder, placed it in front of them, and triggered it.

Lina and Veribo slid behind it, continually firing shots at the Scouts surrounding them. A stray shot nicked the deflector field cylinder, and it powered down. Emma dashed to the portal and waved everyone over. "C'mon, let's go!"

Maut flew forward toward the Scouts surrounding them and grabbed the nearest blaster-held arm. A Scout dislodged a shot that just passed Emma's head. Dexter ran in front of her and pushed her toward the portal.

"You focus on going through the portal. We'll worry about things here." He nodded at the portal. "I'm right behind you."

Emma glanced at the portal then back to Dexter. She quickly ran up to him and placed her hand on the side of his face. "See you soon, Dex." She kissed him softly on the cheek.

"Get up there, E2. We'll be home soon." He gave her a reassuring smile.

Emma climbed on top of the portal and felt its familiar hum. "Wherever you are is home." The portal opened, turning the familiar red, and her body couldn't move.

A shot sliced through Dexter's side, and he yelped out in pain. His hand tugged his stomach, and he slumped over breathing fast, heavy breaths. Veribo ran over to him and pulled him up, while Lina stood shooting toward a mountain of Scouts piling in and around the portal. Emma tried to scream for them but soon they vanished into nothingness. She closed her eyes tight.

The humming stopped, and Emma felt the cool metal beneath her feet. She looked ahead, and her eyes were greeted with deep green geodes glistening in the small bit of light that surrounded her. She studied the masses of rock and features that were completely new to her. The walls looked like Verdite stone jutting up all around her. The silver portal cylinders stood as a tall contrast next to the deep green hues beyond them. She inhaled a slow breath of a floral scent that reminded her of dandelions mixed with lemon.

"This certainly isn't Kansas," she muttered to herself and hopped off the portal cylinder, looking around. She pressed her fingers into the hard cuts of stone on the walls. Behind her, the portal hummed, turning a dark red. The empty space between the portal cylinders soon filled with Lina, her blaster drawn.

"What's going on?" Emma asked, "Where are Veribo and Dexter?"

"The Scouts were moving in fast. They had a lot of fire power, and we could only make it one at a time. They pushed me up, I lost Maut and now I'm here. Where are we?"

The portal hummed again, and Emma's heart danced. Even in an unfamiliar place like this, she would soon feel at home again, as long as she had Dexter. The portal spouted its red hues, and the figure upon the metal was a prone and wounded Veribo.

"Veribo! Are you okay? Where is Dexter?" Emma cried out.

He coughed and sputtered a tiny drop of blood from his mouth. He had several blaster wounds and was barely moving. "They got him." He whispered through chokes and heaves of inconsistent breaths.

Emma's heart sank into her stomach. She had difficulty breathing, and she fell to a crawl on the ground. A tiny sob escaped her lips, and she hung her head. Sounds of feet surrounded the three of them and loud barks of noises enveloped the entirety of the portal area. Figures in cloaks approached them cautiously from a distance.

The area suddenly filled with a bright red light. Humming drifted from the portal and everyone stood up tensed. Lina pointed her blaster at the silver pad. Three shapes emerged from the glowing light. On the portal, August appeared with his arm held tight around Dexter while Maut screeched down at their feet.

"Dexter! August!" Emma screamed as she ran over and wrapped her arms around them. "You made it. How?"

"Maut!" Lina ran over to her tiny friend and grabbed him in a forehead nuzzle.

August scrunched his nose, "Good thing I came with the next wave of Scouts my mother sent to the portal. Fortunately, I got to Dexter before they got another shot at him. Hopefully the code I submitted into the portal before we left will jam it so we don't have any Kabiren guests. My mother is going to be maaad. Her fault though for letting me go," he shrugged. "Sorry, I had to give your position up when I was with her, otherwise she never would have trusted me to lead another set of Scouts to your location."

Emma reached up and squeezed his cheek. "Thanks, August." She wrapped her arms around Dexter. "Are you all right?"

He coughed. "My entire body hurts, but I think I'm okay." He reached his arm up to her face and winced but held her gaze. "I'm home." A smile crept across his face.

One hooded figure pulled forward from the crowd around them and bowed low.

"You got our message then?" Veribo spoke slowly in pain to the figure.

It lowered its hood to show an old woman with piercing blue eyes. She nodded. "It took some time, and the message had to go through a few galaxies. But we did." She turned her attention to Emma and smiled. "We've been waiting for you, Princess. Welcome to Featherstone."

Emma looked between the woman and Veribo and opened her mouth to speak. But she had no words. Featherstone, her mother's home planet. Then a thought buzzed in her head. The messages… She could send a message to her mother and let her parents, especially her dad, know she was okay. She exhaled a sigh.

"Tend to their wounds and find a place for them to rest," the old woman commanded. "My niece and I have a lot to discuss."

While chasing secrets—secrets of stolen technology, fighting peoples, and a world disappeared—led to their loss of their queen, it was those secrets that brought their Princess home.

The End.

Discussion Questions

1. In this novel, there are four main point of view characters, Emma, Dexter, Mylinah, and August. Which is your favorite, and why?

2. Emma has a hobby that she uses as an outlet when she is nervous. What hobby is it, and how does it affect your view of her?

3. While faster-than-light space travel is not a method of travel we use right now, Miguel Alcubierre is mentioned in this novel because he is credited for mathematically proving the possibility of warp travel. Where would you want to go if you were the first human to travel in a warp bubble?

4. Emma frequently talks about the stories her father would tell her about the Queen of Featherstone. Do you think that hearing these "secrets" helped or hurt her in the long run?

5. The Kabiren on Merah constantly talk about Emma being genetically cataloged, or DNA sequenced. When she finally agrees to it, do you think this was wise or not? Do you think she had a choice?

6. A big part of a Protector's job on Merah is to stop invasive plants and animals from making it through the portals. What does invasive mean, and how would it affect life on Merah if they were allowed through?

7. Dexter's idea for the DNA sequencer was fueled by the loss of his best friend, Emma. Do you think this drive was a good motivator or a bad one?

8. When the Kabiren and the general talk about their enemies, they use names that have negative roots. Mentiren being rooted in the Spanish word for lie or liar, and Nerezza, which is rooted in Italian, meaning darkness. Why do you think they would do that? Does it have a purpose?

9. On Merah, the Kabiren don't allow extracurricular activities outside of the work for technological advancement. What is the reason they give for doing this? Would you like to live in a world without hobbies and other extracurricular activities?

10. Merah is referred to as the most technologically advanced planet in the universe. Which piece of technology mentioned do you wish you could have in real life?

Acknowledgements

After years of wondering why authors have such a hard time writing acknowledgements, when it came time to write mine, I realized why it was so difficult. We may write whole worlds and characters out of thin air, but they don't hold a candle to the countless amazing people in our lives who support us and help us on our writer journey. There are no number of words that can fully convey just how much I appreciate them all, but I will do my best.

First and foremost, I would like to thank my editor Arielle Haughee at Orange Blossom Publishing for her belief in this novel and in me. Emma and the Queen of Featherstone would not be out in the world today without her. Arielle, I am forever grateful for all of your knowledge that you have shared throughout this whole process, and I am a better writer because of you. Thank you also, to Tamatha Cain for all of your wonderful insights to help this novel become the best version it could be. So many thanks for the absolutely stunning cover by designer Sanja Mosic. You are so incredibly talented, and I am so grateful to you for making the cover of my dreams. I cannot forget Autumn Skye for her book formatting skills, and Tonya

Spitler with all her behind-the-scenes work she does for Orange Blossom Publishing. I appreciate every single one of you, and thank you for the work you have done to bring about this book.

Emma and the Queen of Featherstone would never have been possible without my amazing husband and best friend, Ben. You tirelessly parented and worked at home while I was off writing this novel. You made so many sacrifices in order for me to have the brain space to be able to write a novel during a global pandemic, and I could never have done it without you at my side cheering me on and keeping me going.

To my parents, Mark and Joy, who not only brought me into this world and encouraged my love of reading, but also provided the quiet space where I could finish writing the ending of this book. I thank you so much for raising me to have the courage and drive to write about whole other worlds and fantastic adventures.

To the wonderful Writers Guild, my writing buddies and critique partners, Amber and Ryan. There would be no story without our group texts and the many times you said to keep going. Forever and always grateful for you both and I can't wait for your stories. Many thanks to Ivy, as a young reader, who graciously read and excitedly reviewed this novel in its early stages. Your rave review gave me the courage I needed to put this story out into the world.

Many thanks to my in-laws, Jim and Iris, who constantly offered to provide my family help and assistance whenever we needed it. This book would not have been possible without those free moments of time. Thank you to my brother and sister in-law, Jeremy and Joy, for simply being fantastically supportive human beings. I appreciate you all so much.

To my VBC friends, you all made me remember to enjoy reading just for me. I have loved talking about every single one of those books with you!

I, also, cannot forget the entire MGin23 crew! You are all amazing authors, and I am so privileged to be debuting with all of you. Your words of encouragement and support have given me so many happy tears, and I am grateful to be among you all. Thank you for being there for me throughout this debut experience; I don't know what I would have done without you.

Words in this acknowledgement section are not enough to thank my daughters, nieces, and nephew. They are the reason I write, and for whom I wrote this book. I hope they continue to grow and enjoy the endless possibilities of hope that can be found within written pages. And lastly, but surely not the least, I appreciate every single one of you readers. I am so excited and grateful that you chose this little book to entertain your bookish soul. Eternally and sincerely thankful for you always.

About the Author

Lindsay Fryc is the author of Emma and the Queen of Featherstone, a middle grade science fiction novel centered around an anxious STEAM-loving girl thrown into a technocratic world of unknowns. Lindsay is a nerd wife and the mother of two girls, one prima ballerina and one pure hurricane. She has been writing ever since she can remember, but now instead of penning words only for herself, she writes for her two girls, and maybe her rescue dog too (when he will listen). When she isn't lost in fictional worlds, you can find her gardening or planning a far-off adventure for her family to explore together. But no matter where the adventuring takes her, her heart is rooted home to those Michigan trees. For access to sneak peeks and updates from Lindsay, you can sign up on her website, www.lindsayfryc.com.

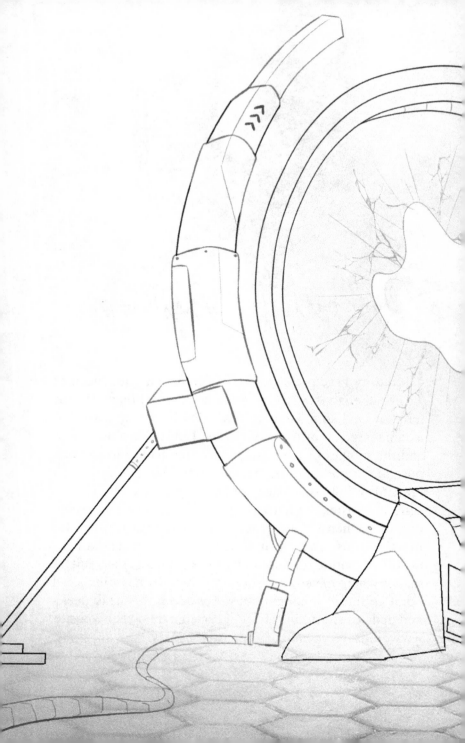

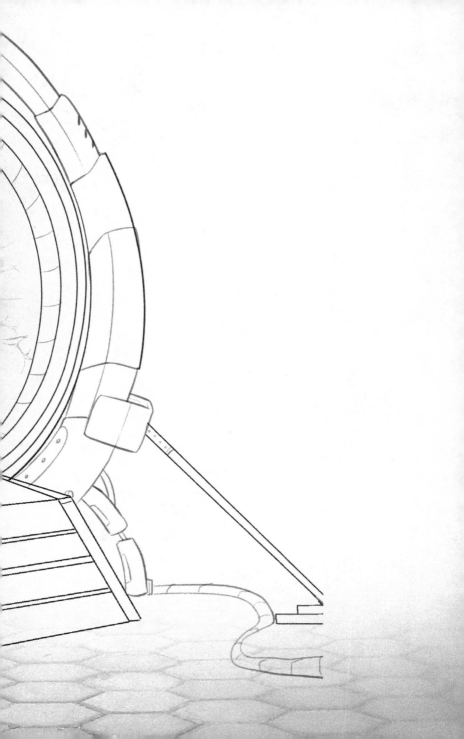

CPSIA information can be obtained
at www.ICGtesting.com
Printed in the USA
BVHW032013270223
659328BV00002B/53